Cave Canem
(Beware of the dog)
Petronius
Satyricon:
Cena Trimalchionis
Ist Century A.D.

Dog Day Dimp

PROLOGUE

David Ignatius Montgomery Parker is a one-armed dwarf from East Manchester. Some people call him Davey others call him Dimp for short. He lives with Zelda, an ageing prostitute, in sin – which was much the same as living in Kyrosjarvi, Finland, but without the accompanying angst.

Davey's life was (at the risk of drawing upon a couple of hoary old horticultural aphorisms) no bed of roses; but then, it was marginally better than pushing up daisies. He was unemployed and indeed, probably unemployable – unless, that is, one counted the time at the Openshaw Job Centre when a helpful claims clerk suggested there might be an opening for him at the Collyhurst Cleansing Department where they could tie a rope to his waist and use him as a drain pull-through.

Davey suspected that this was a case of sarcasm – but he didn't pursue the matter, he wasn't really looking for work, and anyway . . . he didn't like enclosed spaces.

There were a number of things that Davey didn't like. Like high bar counters and stools, enemas, shoelaces, and people who were not too particular about their level of crotch hygiene. These dislikes faded into mere insignificance however when placed alongside the one great dislike, nay, dread, that cast a mighty black shadow over his life:

dogs. Large dogs, small dogs; dogs that answered to the name of Butch, Tiger, Fang, Rambo, Pluto, Twinkle or Fluffykins; dogs in toilet roll commercials; dogs that wore deputy sheriff badges. ALL DOGS.

It wasn't really a phobia. Phobias are generally born of irrational fears, and built upon the rickety foundations of erroneous beliefs and/or insufficient or illogically compiled data. In Davey's case, Fate, not content with dealing him a deuce in the height stakes, had compounded the matter by restricting him to a single hand. As a six-year-old, a starving Alsatian had ripped his left arm off when he and some of the other neighbourhood kids had raided a car scrap yard in Ancoats in search of VW badges to flog as pendants.

Under any normal set of circumstances it would be very difficult for the injured party in such a situation when retrospectively viewing such an event to gain any degree of satisfaction from it. But Davey sometimes allowed himself a tight-lipped smile as he fingered the little fleshy stump where his left arm had been – and an image of the bastard noisily and painfully choking to death on its meal played across his mind.

For the benefit of those readers residing in Wilmslow, Chelmsford or Tunbridge Wells – and for Hiram P. Wankledorfer of Okmulgee, Oklahoma, there now follows an explanatory listing of words in common 'Mancspeak' usage:

ALECAN: An extremely non–abstemious person.

ALLUS: Always.

AMMERED: Exceedingly drunk or high on drugs.

ANALL: An old wood boring tool – or as in 'Anall the king's orses anall the king's men couldn't put Umpty togevver agen'.

ANGIN: A form of capital punishment, or extremely unattractive.

ARF: Fifty percent of a whole.

ARKID: An allusion to a sibling – as in 'Are you all right arkid?'

ATEES: (After Time) Consuming alcohol on licensed premises after official closing time.

A'YUP: Word of warning – as in 'A'yup there's a pianner about to fall on yer ed!'

BAFF: Where one keeps one's coal.

BAKKUL: A heated conflict between two or more protagonists.

BANG ON / BANGIN: Very good.

BARMPOT: An extremely non-Einsteinian person.

BAVE: To immerse oneself in water with a view to removing dirt or grime.

BANJO: An old stringed musical instrument, a shovel, or 'to banjo (hit, fump, kekkel, lamp, belt) someone'.

BEENEEF: Under.

BELT: A leather strap, or to hit, (etc).

BELTER: Something very good – nothing to do with chastising the missus.

BLADDERED: Inebriated, big time!

BINS: Refuse receptacles, or spectacles.

BOBBINS: Cotton reels, or rank bad.

BOKKEL: A thin-necked glass receptacle, or degree of intestinal fortitude.

BOVVER: worry, take care, or heated altercation.

BREEVE: Mark over short or unstressed vowel, musical note, or to inhale frew the nose or mouf.

BREFF: As in a breff of fresh air.

BUBBUL: Air or gas filled globule, or to inform on someone.

BUKSHEE: Free, for nothing.

CHUNNER: To rabbit on at length.

CLEMMED: Extremely hungry.

COB ON: To be very annoyed.

CUDDA: As in 'I cudda danced all night . . . done a fousand fings I've never done before . . .'

CUGGUL: A warm embrace.

CUT: To slice with a sharp implement, or a man-made watercourse.

DEF: Cessation of life, or unable to hear.

DIGGUL: To cheat or figgul someone.

DIMP: A small unsmoked remnant of a cigarette.

DUCKEGG: An extremely useless person.

EARWIG: A creepy-crawly insect, or to eavesdrop.

EEVER: As in 'I'm not bovvered, I'll take eever one.'

EYEVER: Ditto as above.

FANKS: Word of appreciation.

FARVER: A paternal parent, or a greater distance.

FEEF: A purloiner of money, goods or chattels.

FEFT: Act of purloining money, goods or chattels.

FEVVER: Appendage of a bird's skin.

FIGGUL: Nero played one while Rome burned – or see 'diggul'.

FIK: As in 'Do you want a fik ear?'

FIN: A dark triangular steering organ you definitely do not want to see arrowing towards you in the sea – or as in 'The fin red line'.

FINK: An American term for an untrustworthy person – or as in 'I fink Einstein's Feory of Relativity is fatally flawed.'

FIRST: The prime imperative, or a need to imbibe liquid.

FIRTY: Comes after twenty-nine.

FREW: As in 'Frew the keyhole.'

FROAN: Past tense of throw

FROAT: One sometimes finds a frog has taken up residence in one's.

FROKKEL: Vehicle accelerator, or to strangle someone by the froat.

FUMP: See 'banjo, lamp', etc.

GAVVER: To collect.

GAWP: To stare at, or a fik person.

GERREERNOW: As in 'Attend me post haste'.

GETT: A derogatory term.

GETTERFUKOUTERIT: An imprecation to go away – with alacrity.

GOBBUL: A goose's call, to bolt one's food, or fellatio.

H: Does not exist as an initial letter in Mancspeak.

INNIT: As in, 'Innit a luvly day'.

INT: Alternative to the above, as in 'Int it a bugger when yer wellies let in water?'

KAFFLIK: A member of the Church of Rome.

KAK: Very bad, as in Man City were kak on Satdee.

KAKKUL: A witch's laugh, or livestock animals.

KEKKUL: A receptacle for boiling water, or to seriously fump someone (with total disregard for split infinitives).

KEKS: Trousers or ladies' panties.

KEMIK: Alcohol.

KITE: A flying toy, or one's face.

LAMP: A device for shedding light, or to 'Kekkul, Fump', etc.

LEVVER: Tanned animal skin, or to kekkul, fump, etc.

LIKKUL: Opposite of large.

MADFRIT: Wanting something big time.

MANKY: Somewhat less than pristine.

MARD: A wimpy person.

MEGGUL: An award such as the Victoria Cross, or to interfere.

MEKKUL: Element such as gold, silver, etc.

MIGGUL: Something equidistant to each end.

MINGEE: Very mean.

MINT: A confectionery item, brand new, or dead good.

MIZZLED: Disappeared mysteriously.

MUGGUL: A state of disorder.

MUNF: It has firty days in September.

MUVVER: A maternal parent.

MYVER: To persistently annoy.

NAPPER: One's head.

NEEVER: As in 'Neever a borrower nor a lender be...'

NYVER: Ditto as above.

NESH: See 'Mard'.

NORF: 180 degrees to left or right of Souf.

NOWT: Nothing, zilch, zero, zip.

NOWTY: Personality trait opposite of pleasant.

NUFFIN: As in nowt, zilch, zero, zip.

OWT: Opposite of 'in' or 'anyfin'.

PEGGUL: A bicycle has two.

PEKKUL: Constituent part of a flower, or term of endearment.

PILLER: A supporting column, or a soft headrest.

RAKKUL: As in '. . . of a dying man' – or as in the non-business end of a North American desert snake.

RARVER: A preference.

RATARSED: See 'Kaylied', or 'Bladdered'.

RIGGUL: A conundrum, or to squirm.

SHUDDA: Something one should have done.

SHED: A rough wooden hut, or one's head.

SHUNT: To move railway rolling stock, or opposite of 'shud'.

SKENEYED: Cross-eyed – as in the immediate aftermath of a good banjoing.

SKRAM: Instruction to go away smartly, or item of food.

SKOFF: To denigrate, or to consume food.

SLUTCH(Y): Mud or muddy, or to enjoy outrageous

good luck.

SNIDE: Something that is not the real McCoy.

SOUF: 180 degrees to the left or right of Norf.

STRIDES: Large paces, or a pair of trousers.

SUMMUT: A mountain peak, a high level conference – or 'something'.

SUMFIN: As in 'summat', or the opposite of nuffin.

TARRAA: A verbal flourish, or goodbye, farewell, adieu.

TAKKUL: As in 'wedding . . .' or a defensive block.

TEK: As in 'Tek the ribbon from yer air, shake it loose an let it fall.'

THREPNEES: Threpnee bits – tits.

TORK: Twisting rotational force, or to articulate.

TROLLIES: Wheeled appliances, or mens' briefs.

TURKUL: A hard-shelled member of the reptile family, or a gay man.

UVVER: As in 'Pull the uvver one'.

WERF: Surname of an old comedian – or as in the value of something.

WINDERS: Spectacles – or as in: 'Tis said that the eyes are winders to the soul.'

WUNT: As in: 'She wunt do wot she wuz told.'

YERDOINME-EDIN! As in: 'You are annoying me to such a degree that I am developing a severe headache.'

YERWOT: As in 'I beg your pardon?'

1

Davey dropped the purse and scuttled for the door. He reached up, twisted the catch, and was almost through to safety – when the heavy brass ashtray thonked into the back of his head.

'Owww!'

Through a vapour trail of dirty grey falling ash Zelda's red-hot bark snapped at his heels.

'Gotcha; feevin likkul gett!' She was just a little bit annoyed.

The weight of the ashtray and the venom in her words propelled him through the open doorway and out onto the long communal landing, where his feet executed a smart ninety degree skidding left turn and pulled him towards and down the graffiti covered, stale urine reeking stairs.

At ground level he shot through the rough concrete stairwell and out into the weak mid-October sun; almost colliding as he did so with a hooded and scarf-swaddled youth on a mountain bike, who was doubtless in the process of delivering a range of non-proprietary stress-relieving products to an impatiently twitching local clientèle.

'Piss off freak!' the youth shot over his

shoulder, while pumping a third finger up and down as he wobbled on his way. Davey didn't pay much attention to the words or the gesture. Why? Probably because he was quite familiar with such scenarios – after all there is a marked difference between being clunked over the head a hundred times with a blunt instrument, and taking a single rapier thrust to the chest.

The pain is still there, admittedly, but because one is expecting it the degree of shock is nowhere near as intense. Instead, he took a long and careful look around him to check if there were any dogs in sight.

Fortunately, the only living creature on view was a thin black moggy, sniffing at a pancaked pigeon corpse that was plastered in the gutter at the side of the road.

'Good,' he muttered. Cats were not daft. If there were any dogs around this one would have been off like a shot. His safety ensured, at least in the short term, he blinked, lifted a short arm, and with stubby fingers gingerly felt the back of his head where, through the fair tight curls, a pigeon-egg sized lump had as if by magic sprouted.

'Owww!' he winced, before checking his fingers for any sign of seeping claret. 'Bloody bitch! Cudda cracked me bastid 'ead open that could!'

Satisfied that he was in no danger of bleeding to death, he screwed his eyes against the watery glow of the sinking sun and squinted up at the top half of the open doorway on the second floor landing. Seconds later Zelda's peroxide bleached head and wide bony shoulders – with all the slow majesty and terrible import of a monster rising from the deep – loomed into view over the chest-high parapet wall.

Davey swallowed and ran his tongue over his lips nervously as he saw the stony look on her hatchet-sharp face. *Uh-oh*, he thought, *she's goin ter give me grief*.

He wasn't really scared of her he often told himself. She'd never actually gone so far as to give him a really mega clip around the earhole like one would a ginger step-child.

No, it was just that she had a way of making him feel so much smaller than he actually was. A way of looking down her long thin nose at him; of sneering with her eyes and stabbing him with her tongue – and making him feel that perhaps it would be best if he did everyone a big favour by rolling up into a little ball and switching off.

He swallowed again, then decided it was time for a little bit of smokescreen spreading.

'I wasn't goin ter pinch anyfin, 'onest Zelda. I was just lookin fer a key . . . musta lost mine when we was shoppin in Asda this mornin.' Zelda shook her head and stabbed a nicotine-stained red-nailed forefinger downward in his direction.

'Lyin likkul gett! I'm warnin you now, you touch me purse agen an I'll 'ave yer guts fer knicker elastic, so 'elp me Mary!'

Davey sighed. She was in a fizzer of a mood all right so, with the smokescreen blown, he opted to play the pity card.

'Aw come on Zelda. I won't do it agen, 'onest. Let me back in eh?' he wheedled. 'It's cold out 'ere wivout me coat. I could catch me def; yuh wunt like that on yer conscience would yuh?' The blond-haired woman leaned forward and placed her forearms on the parapet wall; exposing as she did a zigzag of black hair roots.

Pointing to her mouth she said: 'Read me lips. PISS OFF!' Davey sighed again. It looked like he was going to have to do some extra special crawling this time.

'Aw come on Zelda, let me in, eh?'

'You erred me. Go on piss off, before I chuck a bucket of cold water on you!' Davey instinctively stepped back a pace; then, looking up, he smiled thinly. If angling for pity was a no-no then it was time for a spot of bribery.

'If you let me in I'll let you tie me to the bed . . . you know you like that . . .'

'Arrrggghhh! Shurrup you likkul bleeder!' Zelda hissed, looking sharply left and right along the fortunately neighbour-free walkway.

The little pleader appeared not to notice her annoyance.

'An you can put yer nurses uniform on an use that rotten emena fing if you want,' he shouted up at her through a tentative and hopefully, winning, smile. Her roughly rouged cheeks turned a few shades redder and her grey gimlet eyes, even from a two-storey height all but impaled him.

'ARRRGHHH! THE NEIGHBOURS! I'LL SWING FOR YOU, YOU . . . YOU . . . LIKKUL FREAK!' Davey's forehead creased into a frown.

'A'yup. That's not on Zelda,' he whined. 'Can't 'elp it if I'm likkul an only got one arm . . .' From her height she looked down on his even more truncated body and regarded him as one would a freshly trodden turd on the sole of one's best shoes.

'Yeah, one arm,' she said, 'an no bleedin brain. Now PISS OFF!'

Davey opened his mouth in a last ditch attempt at appeasement, but the words were chopped off as she shot him a searing Medusa look, spun on her heels, and slamming the landing door on the way, disappeared from sight.

As the hollow echo of the closing door bounced off the grimy dun brown concrete walls and pounded dully in his ears, Davey stood forlorn, alone and feeling very sorry for him self. It was another slap down to tag onto a long list stretching back into infinity. Would he ever really come out on top in a big barney with a normal sized person?

'That's it,' he sighed. 'Bitch'll keep me out 'ere fer yonks now jus ter show 'ow 'ard she is. Catch me def I will . . . bloody bitch.'

Defeated, he glanced up briefly at a heavy,

sullen grey sky that suddenly seemed to mirror his mood. A chunk of sky that, if it was suddenly blessed with the power of speech, would probably be muttering darkly to itself: 'What am I doing over this shit hole when I could be sunning myself above some glorious golden beach in Barbados?'

He sighed again and, rubbing the back of his head, turned and plodded off in the direction of the nearby Beswick Shopping Precinct.

2

In a politically correct world 30 year old David Ignatius Montgomery Parker would be referred to as 'vertically challenged', or a 'person of restricted growth'.

Those of a reasonably erudite nature might even have referred to him as a victim of achondroplasia.

However, while Political Correctness might very well be considered *de rigueur* in the more salubrious middle class areas of Manchester, in Beswick and nearby Openshaw, Ancoats and Clayton – an area designated in the early 90's as one of the most intense concentrations of deprivation in the country, where many residents were more concerned with finding a job or eking out their Giro's – the only PC's of general interest were of the uniformed variety, that had a disconcerting tendency to unexpectedly come knocking on the door in the middle of the night.

Consequently, most of those who didn't use his first name called him Shorty or DIMP. Some, like Zelda, made do with 'Short Arse', or 'Likkul Gett'. Some people – especially Zelda – said he was thick. This was not, strictly speaking, so.

Okay, for him the 24-hour clock was a mystery, as were the cut and thrust of debate and the intricacies of Keynesian economic policies. But ask him to work out the winnings on a 50p win three cross doubles and a treble at odds of 5 to 1, even money and 5 to 4 . . . no trouble.

True, he did possess a wide streak of naivety and he usually tended to take the spoken word at face value, and particularly so, if he was engaged in any sort of meaningful dialogue with 'big' people. For instance, if someone were to ask him 'how would you like a fik ear?' It was not unlikely he would have considered the question carefully before replying 'no fanks'. This would more than likely have been considered smartarsedness, and would probably have lead to just such an augmented aural accoutrement.

An example of his naive side was well illustrated when, at the age of 14, he had teamed up with Tommy Higginbottom – a six foot tall beanpole, with red hair and a speech impediment which turned 'esses' into 'ths' – to rob a corner shop in Ancoats.

'We'll wear Zorro masks,' said Davey.

'Yeth,' said Tommy.

And Davey was convinced it would have worked, if only Tommy hadn't demanded of the shopkeeper:

'Thtick em up an 'and over the bathtard cath!' To which the bemused man had replied: 'What?'

'I thed thtick em up, an give uth the fukin money!'

When this demand had also failed to produce results, Davey had taken charge and waved the Daisy air pistol in the general direction of the man's privates – and the penny had dropped at last. They got away with two pounds thirty, a jar of jelly babies and 12 months in Approved School.

'I shudda dun the torkin; then nobody'd of guessed it was us,' he had mused many times over the next 12 miserable months.

At 15 he left 'school' and signed on the Dole. He also refused Tommy's invitation to re-form 'the team'. Tommy, miffed, graduated to a Young Offenders Institution and from there to Strangeways prison, and eventually to a successful career with Social Services.

Davey graduated to ducking and diving; a spot of receiving here, a bit of contraband baccy and pirate cd's and dvd's there; which, when lumped together with his disability payments helped to put food on the table. Usually there was even a bit left over for the occasional pint, packet of fags and a little flutter on the gee-gees.

And so David Ignatius Montgomery Parker stuttered and spluttered down life's pock-marked highway, occasionally crunching into second gear – but by and large, having to make do with 'first' and the odd bit of 'freewheeling'. Then his mam went and died on him.

Ethel Parker was a large woman with a permanently florid face and beefy red hands. Hands that could knock him sken-eyed, then caress his singing earhole with a tenderness born of love – and guilt that her body had somehow been responsible for his 'shortcomings'.

She was a devout catholic and prayed on her knees every night, asking God to look after her little lad after she was gone. She also asked for forgiveness for living in sin as she had never quite gotten around to marrying Harry Posthlethwaite the father of her two sons.

Harry was a merchant seaman on Manchester Liner's Toronto run, who, soon after the birth of his youngest son, Davey, had decided that it was time to try his hand at being a free spirit – a decision which ultimately led him to Vancouver and the brawny arms of a Russian ex-shot-putter, who earned her living gutting tuna and in her spare time arm-wrestling all comers in the seedier dockside bars.

Davey was not aware of his father's fate and, even if he had been, it would not have concerned him – he had troubles of his own thank you very much. It wasn't enough that fate had weighed in by kicking him twice in the plums, now he had to contend with this.

'Skint an battered . . . an proberly 'omeless anall now,' he muttered, as he wandered onto the flagged – and depressingly flagging – precinct.

Eyes down, he trudged past a number of boarded up shop fronts – sad testaments to the odds-on futility of East Manchester conceived bright dreams that had mis-carried to produce smothered ambition – and on to the bookies. There, hand plunged deeply into an empty pocket, he paused for a few seconds to peer wistfully through the part frosted door. From inside, TV monitors winked seductively, flashing scenes of green turf and galloping horses, while the rough animated voices of punters provided a vibrant background to the race commentator's more cultured delivery.

Skint and proper pissed off, he turned away from the door and half-heartedly kicked out at a passing Beswick tumbleweed – an empty Carlsberg Special can – as, wind assisted, it clanked and rolled drunkenly on its meandering way. He missed.

'Figures,' he grumbled, as he made his way to a peeling green painted rotting bench and plonked himself down. Sighing heavily, he muttered 'Yeah skint an proberly 'omeless anall now . . .'

'What's that lad?'

Davey started, the sudden movement sending a bright pain stabbing up the back of his head.

'Oww! What?' he said, as he ran his fingers over the tender spot.

'I said what you goin on at?'

Through watering eyes Davey watched the small frail old woman, as on thin, unsteady legs sheathed in wrinkled dark brown stockings, she approached pulling a wonky-wheeled, faded tartan shopping trolley.

'Oh, allo missis Jones,' he mumbled, still fingering his newly emerged embryonic second head.

'I woz just finkin about that Zelda. Banjoed me she did . . . wiv a brass poker . . . an pinched all me money . . . an kicked me down the stairs . . .'

'She never!' The old woman tutted, pulled her worn coat tightly around her thin body and with a little groan of effort, lowered herself onto the bench by his side.

'Bloody did . . . bloody great brass poker . . . cudda took me bleedin 'ead off; 'ere, feel' The old woman raised a thin hand and gently touched the spot he indicated.

'Oh aye,' she said, 'belter that is. Just like a boil that's ripe fer poppin.'

'Yeah. Bloody 'urts it does.' The old woman

nodded in sympathy.

'You should get the Cruelty Man on 'er, doin that to a likkul lad like you.' Davey pursed his lips and briefly weighed up the pro's and con's of taking such drastic action.

'Don't know about that missis; wild woman is my Zelda when she's bin on't bokkel.'

'Ahh,' said the old woman sagely. 'The drink is it? I know all about that. My 'Enry used to be a drinker – till 'ee warked under a bus one night when cummin out of the *Church Inn* on the New Road. Aye, I know all about the demon drink all right,' she said, as her eyes took on a distant look, and her thin, pale, deep purple veined fingers began to tremble like startled fawns poised for flight. Davey nodded.

'Yeah. Allus batters me up when she's bladdered.'

The old woman's mind ambled back from the misty lanes of memory to the chilly bright here and now.

'What? Oh yeah,' she said crossing her arms tightly over scrawny breasts. 'Well you should do sumfin about it. Not right that, kekklin a likkul lad like you.' Davey nodded again.

'Yeah, you're right there missis. An I'm just the lad ter do it anall. One day she'll go too far an I'll fump 'er one, I swear I will!'

'Aye,' the old woman said. 'My 'Enry used t'say some wimmin need a good clout now an agen

22

ter keep 'em in their place. Yeah,' she murmured, ''ee was always quotin that writer bloke, Noel Coward. "Sum wimmin", 'ee would say, "need ter be struck reglar like gongs"'

'Yeah,' said Davey with enthusiasm.

'Mind you,' she continued, 'firty nine years wed, an 'ee never laid a finger on me did my 'Enry. Course if 'ee 'ad a done,' she added matter-of-factly, 'I'd a knifed the bastard in 'is sleep.'

'Yeah,' said Davey swinging his dirty size four trainers backwards and forwards, 'I might just go 'ome now, an when she opens the door an lets me in I'll say: Zelda, bend down 'ere a minit I want ter whisper summut; an when she does . . . Bam! I'll rakkul 'er bleedin earole good an proper!'

These were real fighting words designed to impress a sympathetic listener. Unfortunately that's all they were, because, even if she had given him a backhander first, Davey knew he wouldn't have been able to give her one back, as his mam had taught him that smacking a woman was only one step removed from robbing a church poor box.

'Course,' said the old woman with a degree of humility in her voice, 'there was times when 'ee cudda bin in order to chastise me . . . when I was younger, an 'ee was workin reglar nights at Johnson's Wireworks. Cupla dozen times when 'ee cudda bin in order then.'

She looked off into time and space. 'Just a likkul bit flighty I was in them days,' she murmured, more to herself than to him. Then more brightly: 'Mind you, you would be wunt you . . . young an 'ealthy an no man in yer bed? Course don't bovver wiv such fings now,' she added, 'ravver 'ave a cuppa cocoa . . .'

'Wunt she get a shock eh?' said Davey grimly.

'Who?'

'Zelda – if I lamped 'er one in't earole!'

'Oh. Aye.'

For a few moments they sat, each wrapped in their own private thoughts. His were coloured with the red of revenge, hers with rose-pink nostalgia . . . tinged with blue. The mood however was short lived, as suddenly the old woman was jerked back to reality by a low whimper at her elbow. Startled, she turned her head sharply in the direction of Davey's stricken stare.

It was a dog. A very large and very frisky dog of uncertain pedigree. A *vin ordinaire* dog, with a *soupcon* of rough cider and meths thrown in for good measure.

Davey eyed the dog. The dog eyed Davey. Davey thought *Oh fuk it's goin ter kill me!* The dog thought *Hiya. Do you want to play?* Davey scrambled up onto the bench. The dog thought *you do want to play!* and tongue lolling and breath steaming on the late autumn air, it scrabbled towards him. Its new playmate then entered into the spirit of things by screaming, and attempting to play hide and seek by dragging the old woman roughly in front of him by her coat collar.

'Urrrkk!' said the old woman as her breath was promptly curtailed.

'Nnnggghhh!' said Davey, as he held the living shield between himself and the devil beast intent on ripping him to shreds.

Bloody great this! the dog thought as it jumped up and thumped its muddy front paws into the old woman's lap, while its shaggy tail beat a frantic drum roll on the ground – the sheer vibrancy of which led to the demise of four ants, that were gamely struggling to extract a mangled portion of soggy chip from an interestingly-shaped large splatter of congealed vomit.

Flustered by the two-pronged attack, the old woman barked at one or the other, or both assailants, 'Gerrrofff yer barmy bleeder!' From behind, there was a slight easing of the pressure from fingers and knees. From the front there was a wheezing 'Woooff?' A woof that said 'make up your mind . . . do you want to play or not?' The answer came smartly from the old woman.

'Go on sod off! Bloody smelly fleabag!' The dog sighed, emitting a cloudy breath that hinted of rotting meat, stagnant water and mouldy cheese, and disappointed, thumped its paws back onto *terra firma* before trundling off with a single backward glance that translated as 'bloody humans!'

'Phew!' The old woman wafted a hand in

25

front of her face — a face which already well wrinkled, had taken on the appearance of a pickled walnut.

'Bloody 'ell! Last time I smelt anyfin like that was the mornin after my 'Enry 'ad six pints of draught Guinness an a chickin vindaloo at the Tibet curry 'ouse.' As she spoke a head appeared from behind her shoulder.

'Is it gone?' The old woman's wrinkled face softened and some of the deep crevasses eased themselves into mere shallow canyons.

'Aye it's gone. You can come out now.'

'You sure?'

'Aye. Anyway it wasn't goin to 'urt you. It was only playin.'

Davey slid out, and after a quick shufty to make sure it really was safe, he sat down again.

'Yeah, well,' he said quietly, 'dogs dunt like me. They allus want ter chase me.' The old woman smiled and looked down into his still worried face.

'They just want ter play, that's all . . . just play.' Davey shook his head.

'Yeah well, that bloody Benji in our flats dunt want to play. Allus chasin me it is.'

'What? Benji, that fat likkul dog wiv the likkul pink bow on is 'ead what lives wiv old Mrs Morris on your landin?'

'Yeah that's 'im, bleedin devil dog 'ee is.' The old woman snorted.

'Go on! 'Ee'd ave ter jump up to bite yer

ankles that one.' Davey was not to be deterred.

''Ee's vicious. Got teef like bleedin daggers 'ee 'as. If 'ee jumped up 'ee could rip yer froat out no messin.'

The old woman 'hmmmed'. Davey sensed she was not entirely convinced so he dusted off the well-used clincher.

'An anyway, what about that bloody great Alsatian then? That dint want ter play missis, I know that,' he muttered, fingering his empty sleeve. 'Slobberin gob an yeller teef. I remember that all right . . . that an the blood . . . an the crunchin an crackin bones . . .' The old woman's voice softened and she nodded.

'Yeah must a bin 'orrible that . . . 'orrible.'

'Yeah it was. Course if it 'ad 'appened nowadays,' he added lightly, 'they cudda got me arm back and stitched it back on wiv that micro surgery stuff they can do.' Glad of the change of tone the old woman agreed.

'Aye, yer right there lad. They can do some amazin fings now all right. I read once there was this bloke in China 'oo needed an 'ead transplant . . . only they couldn't find a youman 'ead that'd fit proper, so they used a goat's 'ead . . . an 'ee's fine now; cept 'ee only eats grass an when 'ee wants a pee 'ee as ter lift 'is leg.' Davey whistled.

'Go on!'

''Onest. Read it in one of our Wayne's old magazines so it mus be true. Aye . . . *Privit Eye* or summut, it were called.' Davey whistled again.

'Phew! Amazin, eh?' Then: 'Maybe if I went ter China they could give me an arm transplant . . . an maybe two leg transplants anall! Make me big! What you fink?' The old woman pursed her crepe lips and shook her head.

'Don't know about that lad; I fink they can only do 'eads.' Davey's face fell.

'Yeah . . . well . . . I fink I'll stick wiv this one, unless,' he added with what bordered on a hopeful edge to his voice, 'they cud give me one like that Olemar Sheriff bloke off the films; my Zelda finks 'ee's ace.'

The old woman's voice hardened and she turned to face him full on.

'Aye, well, you listen to me Davey Parker, your Zelda dunt know when she's well off. Nice flat . . . your disability allowance . . .' Her little companion nodded and sighed deeply.

'Yeah, an wiv all that, she as ter batter me up an . . . an pinch all me money . . .' The old woman shook her head.

'Scanderlus. Bloody scanderlus that is! An I fought she was a good kafflik anall!'

'Yeah. Well she does go ter mass most Sundees,' he conceded.

'Well then!' said the old woman indignantly, 'she should practice what she preaches . . .'

'What?'

'Do unto uvvers, that's what . . . do unto

28

uvvers as you would like 'em to do unto you.'

'Oh, right. Well not my Zelda missis, that's not 'er way. No, 'er way is to get in quick an do unto uvvers before they as a chance to do it to 'er.' The old woman sighed.

'Well it's a good parable that is anyway. Just like that other one about rich people.'

'Eh, what uvver one?'

'Like Farver James said at mass last Sundee,' she explained. "It is easier fer a rich man to pass frew the eye of a neagle than fer a camel ter get into 'eaven."'

'Oh yeah . . .'

They sat in silence for some seven long seconds reflecting on the wisdom of the good book, then, bored with introspection, Davey turned his attention to the old woman's anorexic looking shopping trolley.

'Goin shoppin are you?' he asked casually. The old woman shook her head.

'No. Bin. Just got some lamb chops fer our Wayne's tea. Likes 'is lamb chops does our Wayne.'

'Yeah. I like a bit of meat meself . . . but that Zelda won't do no cookin fer me.' The old woman nodded absently and muttered:

'Two-fifty fer free likkul chops! Scanderlus. . . bloody commun market. Decent folks can't afford meat no more!'

'Yeah. I like a bit of meat me . . . but that Zelda won't do no cookin fer me,' he repeated, with emphasis, 'only does me bread puddin an . . . an . . . corn flakes.'

'An look at the price of beer! Likes a pint does our Wayne. But 'ee as ter watch 'is pennies now 'ee's on't dole.' Davey nodded.

'Yeah. I like a beer anall . . . but that Zelda pinched all me money . . . before she battered me wiv that brass poker . . . an . . . an . . . frew me down't stairs.' He was well into martyr mode now. The old woman didn't appear to notice.

'I said to our Wayne; it's gettin so the workin class as ter live on fresh air an promises. An the air's not so fresh eever, wot wiv all them lorries an joggernauts chokin everyone wiv their rotten fumes.' Davey nodded in apparent earnest agreement.

'Yeah, an I'm chokin anall . . . me moufs like a dry stick . . . pinched me beer money, she did; before she nearly took me 'ead off wiv that brass poker . . . an . . . an . . . ' he added for dramatic effect, 'chucked me over the second floor parapit.'

It was now the old woman's turn to nod – but this time, absently. Then as though his words had taken time to seep through, she said brightly: 'Chokin, did you say?'

'Yeah . . . dry as a bone,' he rasped, tacking on a sad little cough for extra effect.

'Well then, 'ere lad . . .' The old woman unzipped her trolley and fished out a thin alopecia patterned purse. Davey grinned as she snapped open the catch, peered myopically inside, selected something and withdrew her hand.

"Ere lad,' she said kindly, 'just the job fer makin yer mouf water is these Opal Fruits.' She handed him a small dirty orange coloured paper wrapped square. Davey's grin died a quick death, as he looked at the offering nestling in his pudgy palm with about as much enthusiasm as one would look upon one's retreating hairline in the bathroom mirror.

'Fanks missis,' he muttered, coming as close to heavy sarcasm as he was ever likely to. 'Just the job that . . . just what I really need . . .' Pleased, the old woman smiled, and with a weary groan eased herself to her feet.

'Must be gettin on,' she said. 'Our Wayne'll be back from't pub soon an wantin is tea.'

'Yeah. Right,' he muttered to her retreating back as he gloomily fumbled with the paper of the tightly wrapped sweet.

After a few moments of total failure, his mouth began to work furiously in an effort to articulate his feelings. Air from his lungs rose and charged through the double-storey vocal tract of nose and mouth. Masses of brain-controlled muscle and tissue moulded and altered the shape of the tract walls, caused the soft palate to lift, shutting off air to the nose, prompting the tongue to change shape and position the lips to spread air; air that roared over his teeth and exploded from his mouth to provide the awesome wonder that was human speech.

'AWWW BOLLOCKS!' he yelled, and, with extreme prejudice, hurled the offending object at a foraging sparrow that had the bare-arsed temerity to be hopping around the place without an apparent care in the world.

3

Breathing heavily, Ernie lumbered onto the almost deserted precinct. In his black balaclava, heavy navy blue overcoat and fingerless mittens he was a little too warm for comfort, but it was October and his mam always said October was "only round the corner from the miggul of winter."

At six foot three and almost seventeen stone, 32 year-old Ernest Grimshaw was a big man – but a man in terms of years only. A psychological assessment that had taken place two years earlier when he had gotten into trouble when two young girls had said 'rude things' to him, had placed him in the five to six year mental age bracket.

As a child he had sometimes attended Grange Street Special, a school in Beswick for those with learning difficulties. Ernie's learning difficulties were nothing short of profound.

His mother, Edna, was a chronic alcoholic – a condition kick-started years earlier by the death of her husband, George, in a particularly messy accident at Johnson's Wire Works, when he had tripped and fell head first into a razor wire baling machine. While this tragedy had set her feet tentatively onto the slippery path to addiction, a year later when Marjorie, her 12 year-old daughter died under the wheels of a hit-and-run driver when crossing Ashton New Road, her until then aimless ramble towards alcoholism, turned into a full-blown lung-bursting sprint.

Left with only Ernie to look after she also developed a severe case of mother hen syndrome. She fussed and fretted over him. If he sneezed, she called the doctor. If he had trouble going to the toilet, she dosed him with syrup of figs. If he went to the toilet too often she dosed him with dia-calm pills. With the first hint of autumn she made him wear a balaclava, a heavy overcoat, fingerless woollen mittens and two vests – and Ernie being Ernie, accepted everything without complaint; she was his mam and she knew best.

In some respects he and Davey were kindred spirits – although Davey, if this had been suggested to him, would no doubt have hotly denied it.

Some of the less enlightened and politically non-pc of the local community referred to hulking Ernie as "Daft Ernie". Some also referred to Davey as "short arse".

To some people Ernie and Davey became invisible when they approached in the street, or they lowered their eyes, or found something particularly interesting going on over the road that warranted immediate close investigation.

Ernie was painfully shy and stuttered and stumbled over his words. Davey deferred to big people, and more often than not, accepted whatever they said as gospel. So yes, in some ways, as the fallout from life's capricious little games, they were two very alike if physically dissimilar, units of collateral damage.

Spotting Davey on the bench Ernie trundled over in that direction.

'Hiya D-Davey, wh-what yuh doin?' Davey — who had been staring moodily into space perhaps mentally nibbling at the edges of one of life's great imponderables, like: *Did the ball really cross the goal line in 1966? If Light is so bloody fast why, when it got where it was going, did it always find Dark sitting there waiting for it? Did Adam and Eve have belly buttons? What* did *Billy Joe McAllister throw off the Tallahatchie Bridge?* Or *where* does *earwax come from?* — looked up and groaned. He was in no mood for a dose of Ernie's sparkling conversational gambits.

'Wh-what yuh d-doin eh Davey?' Ernie repeated, as he loomed over the little seated figure. Davey craned his neck backwards and looked up into the black framed, heavy featured face.

'Waitin fer a bus,' he said sourly. Ernie frowned.

'They d-don't st-stop 'ere, th-they o-only stop on Grey Mare L-Lane,' he indicated, with a sideways nod towards the main road. Davey sighed.

'I'm not really waitin fer a bus; I was jus bein sarky.' Ernie frowned then beamed.

'Oh r-right y-you was j-jus k-kiddin! Then wh-what are yuh d-doin eh D-Davey?'

'I'm just 'avin a quiet sit down an a fink.'

'W-what you f-finkin about?' Davey sighed again. There was a danger that if left unchecked this could degenerate into an annoying little *tete a tete*.

'I'm finkin about 'ow long I would get in nick fer murderin someone.' Ernie's eyes opened wide and his jaw dropped in shock.

'Aw y-yuh c-can't do that D-Davey, it's n-not nice!'

'Yeah well, some people aren't nice eever.' Ernie considered this statement and then nodded.

'Yeah I-I know, b-but . . .'

'But what? There's plenty people tek the piss outer me an there's plenty 'oo call you Daft Ernie, an tek the piss outer you int there?' Ernie turned this over in his head for a few moments then decided on his answer.

'Y-yeah I know b-but it's still n-not nice.'

'No it's not,' Davey conceded, 'but nice is fer fairy tales. An anyway,' he continued, employing a diversionary tactic before the conversation got too complicated, 'what you doin 'ere? Does yer mam know yer out on yer own?'

'Y-yeah she s-sent me out fer a b-bokkel of tonic from Quick Save.'

'Figgers,' Davey muttered. Then: 'Well yuh better 'urry up or they might 'ave sold out if yuh stand 'ere gassin all day!' Ernie's smile disappeared quicker than a rat up a drainpipe.

'Oh r-right! I b-better go. Me m-mam gets u-upset if she dunt g-get 'er tonic!' Davey nodded as Ernie turned quickly and with an ungainly trotting run, made off towards the supermarket.

'Yeah tonic – a two-litre bokkel of Strongbow cider,' he said dryly to the broad retreating back. There was however just the faintest hint of the green-eyed in his voice – he could murder a pint now himself, and thanks to that rotten tight arse Zelda there was no chance of that.

'Yeah,' he muttered making and shaking a little fist in the general direction of the flats, 'tight arse bitch, she'll push me too far one day an I'll really get me mad up an give 'er a right levverin.'

Satisfied with the macho intent, he tucked thoughts of retribution to the back of his mind ready for dragging out again when the time was ripe.

Alone again he ran parts of the conversation with Ernie over in his head. Ernie really was thick he concluded. Couldn't he see that everyone took the piss out of him? Couldn't he see that people looked at him like he was a dumb animal? Like he wasn't able to think for himself.

'Okay, people tek the piss outer me, yeah; but I can fink fer meself all right,' he muttered to the empty precinct. 'I know when people are tekkin the piss. Yeah I know that all right.' He nodded to himself. But before his head had finished moving a little inner voice said: *Yeah but if Ernie dunt know then it dunt urt im does it?*

And there it was. There was the rub and the nub of it. Ernie didn't know. He was blessed with ignorance. And although ignorance was surely far from bliss, it was a bloody sight better than having to go through life being reminded in a hundred different ways every day how different you were from everyone else.

Unlike him Ernie could tie his own shoelaces (just). Ernie might not be able to tell the time but he could fasten a watchstrap. He could plonk himself down onto bar stools and easily see over bar counters and he could stand at the back of a crowd and not miss everything going on. If he ever decided to start smoking Ernie could roll a fag and he had the tools to unwrap a birthday present, deal a deck of cards and if he chose – to take up basketball, pole vaulting or swimming as a pastime.

Davey's mental processes were certainly not up to Mensa standards, but the little voice's barbed words were not lost on him – Ernie didn't know so it didn't hurt him. 'Yeah, I suppose not,' he admitted to the empty precinct, before adding: 'lucky bastard.'

4

Zelda unscrewed the top on the jar of cold cream, dipped two nicotine stained fingers in and scooped out a liberal dollop. She raised her hand towards her face then paused to study her reflection in the mirror. The face that stared back was not so much lived in as dossed in – by three tramps, four new age anti-road and runway protesters, and an unspecified number of first year university students.

Over-bleached dead dandelion hair framed a thin bloodless face and pale grey eyes; to the sides of which a murder of crows had performed a courtship dance, followed by an emu and an ostrich or two. The nose was long and pinched at the nostrils. The lips two pale parallel slashes that guarded nicotine stained teeth and a stiletto tongue razor honed by years of disillusion and collapsed dreams.

From either side of the nose and mouth deep grooves – lance corporal's stripes awarded for bravery in a thousand bedspread battles and car seat campaigns – gouged their way to a boney chin, before plunging over the edge to merge with a network of criss-crossing, interlacing trunk and B roads of a well mapped neck.

As she coldly studied the face that stared back with an equal lack of emotion, she murmured 'where's it all gone? All those years an all those dreams?' There was no response, only a slight shake of the other head that mirrored her abortive search for an answer. She took a heavy shuddering breath and, letting her mouth flap loosely said: 'A gokkel a geer.'

Once, she had been quite an attractive woman – a hundred thousand mouthfuls of milk of amnesia ago. Yet, even now, sometimes, memories clung like stubborn morning mist – a thin veil masking reality. Blurred images through a Vaseline-smeared camera lens, presenting a soft focus to mask the ravages of time on the face of an ageing movie queen. Ignored flaws for the sake of sweet nostalgia.

Cold-eyed reality blew away the clinging wisps of mist. Yes, she had been a pretty girl with innocence in her heart and a trusting nature that would always make allowances, always see the best in those who often exhibited the worst. *Was it my fault?* she thought. Her fault that her life had turned out the way it had. Had she been the architect of her own downfall or had she been a victim of Fate's cruel sense of humour?

She pursed her thin lips and shrugged her bony shoulders. *What does it matter who's fault it was*, she thought. *Ninety-nine percent of us get fuk all. One day you're sweet sixteen with the whole world opening in front of you like a flower and the next you're a wrinkled wreck dyin of old age.*

She had never considered herself to be the possessor of a philosophical nature. For her, life had always been a series of black and white choices with no room for the subtlety of greys, but here and now she nodded in agreement with the thought. 'I was once Aphrodite at the Water Hole,' she muttered. 'Now I'm Whistler's Bleedin Muvver.' (She had had a   short, but artistically educational dalliance with a successful London artist a few years back).

The only daughter of a Dutch trapeze artist from a circus and a one-time fairground booth boxer, Zelda Mary Magdalene O'Flerhity had been a good catholic girl for the first 17 years of her life. Mind you, any other options had initially been severely limited by the geographic bounds of a tiny County Mayo village and the Jesuit-like zeal of a father and three older brothers, all of whom were determined to keep coarse tongue-lolling lechers firmly at bay.

Zelda accepted their frequent intervention into her slowly developing social life. She was, after all very young, and the attention brought on by her budding teenage figure while secretly pleasing, was she knew, not something that a chaste young lady could openly encourage. That said though, there were many times when she suspected that the protection provided by her father and brothers was not so much born of a determination to maintain her moral welfare, but rather from a determination to retain the services of an unpaid housekeeper, cum cook, cum maid, cum general dogsbody.

When she was 15 her father, Patrick, by then a widower (her mother had taken a header from thirty feet into a sawdust circus ring five years earlier) had drowned on his way home from the pub late one night. It was said that he had mistaken a moonlit ribbon of river for a moonlit ribbon of road. At least that was the general consensus; although some – mainly coarse, tongue-lolling lechers – had remarked that the old man's saintliness had probably led him to believe that he could walk on water.

Whatever the reason for his premature demise – Patrick took his last drink and Zelda and the boys took themselves off to the bright lights of Manchester, where their paternal aunt, Kirvla, ran a boarding house in the Levenshulme district.

To say that Manchester was an eye-opener to Zelda was akin to saying that Armageddon, when it came, would be interesting. She was well and truly gobsmacked.

The place was full of godless English whose only interest it seemed was the pursuit of hedonistic pleasures. Worse though than this – for the English were a godless race anyhow – were her fellow countrymen and women, who were just as bad! Limerick or Cork, Dublin or Waterford, it seemed to make no difference. The common currency was a coarseness of spirit and tongue that combined to leave a semi-permanent blush of embarrassment on her cheeks.

The boys, without the heavy ham fist of their father's hand on their shoulders, were the first to succumb. Twins Noel and Liam formed a rock band, while Dominic, the eldest, took up with a Jamaican topless dancer from Raymond's Revue Bar and moved to Moss Side.

For over two years Zelda worked at her aunt's boarding house. She helped with the cooking, the cleaning and the washing, and with the passage of time the blush faded from her cheeks, as did the soft brogue from her lips. By her seventeenth birthday she had lost contact with the boys – and made contact with sex.

His name was Andreas, he was 21, half Italian, half Greek and drop dead gorgeous. His father had one of the first kebab shops in Manchester, on Stockport Road, and it was there that a blushing Zelda, while waiting for two donner all-ins fell head over heels – then two weeks later, heels over head in the back of his Ford Anglia. It didn't last long. In fact the two tiny dimples from her high heels in the Anglia's off-white plastic velour roof trim had barely faded before he dumped her for a Tesco shelf stacker called Tracy.

It was *Lesson 1* in the School of Hard Knocks. Men were devious untrustworthy bastards and a girl needed to develop a hard shell – much like the little round candy coated chocolate drops popular at the time, that could be handled without melting.

From now on, she had decided, she would do the dropping. And she did. Andreas was soon followed by Dermot, Billy, Ali – and Winston with the two-tone lime green and dark brown Vauxhall Cresta; the spongy black and gold spangled cloth covered roof trim of which left no tell tale dimples behind.

Winston was very upset when she told him she was giving him the elbow. He begged her not to do it. She refused. He cried. She smiled thinly. He asked for one last leg over for old time's sake. She told him to piss off. He offered her a fiver . . . and a seminal, defining moment twanged into being.

Winston got his leg over and Zelda received her first non-boarding house payday, or rather pay five minutes, as she was in a hurry to get to a nearby Dolcis shoe shop before they shut.

Six months and fourteen pairs of shoes later, she moved to Birmingham, where she opened herself up to vodka, gin, black bombers, uppers, downers, coke and a dose or two of the clap; before landing under the protection of a certain Maltese Tony, a pimp with a penchant for flick knives and obedient women.

Not being one of the latter soon brought her

into painful contact with the former, when, in a drunken rage, he carved his initials into her back (he wasn't so drunk that he risked marring any wobbly work-related bits). Three weeks later and high on coke, she slipped the same singing sharp sliver of steel from his pocket as he lay in a drugged stupor on the bed, unzipped his flies – and extracted her revenge by severing their relationship almost at the root.

A couple of days before a now more or less todgerless Tony was due to be released from hospital, Zelda took serious stock of her situation. The conclusion she arrived at was obvious: Birmingham was certainly too small and not a little unhealthy for a woman with balls.

'Look at it this way,' said her workmate Louise, 'London's full of sad bastards who'll pay us good to spank em hard.' So, with Louise in tow, London it was. And they did.

Zelda threw herself into her work and enjoyed it immensely.

In fact she entered into it with an almost evangelical zeal – which raised a welter of welts on many a maggot white flabby male posterior, and confirmed for her the fact that the male of the species was a contemptible waste of space useful only for its ability to assist in the procreation of daughters.

Customers were, in the main, middle-aged businessmen, plummy-voiced barristers, or

Conservative MP's. To them she was school marm, matron, miss whiplash or mummy. She chastised; they whimpered in pleasure or terror. And with every slap of the ruler or crack of the whip, the male perpetuated myth of hunter, warrior, mighty seducer, faded a little more; until dim, diminishing, diaphanous – it was gone.

Tempus, as is its wont, *Fugitted*. Zelda and Louise settled into a comfortable routine of Mondays: Black Leather and Studded Belts, Tuesdays: Plastic Sheeting, Snorkels and Flippers, Wednesdays: (half-day) Back To School, Thursdays: Whips, 12 volt car battery and Thumbscrews (not for thumbs), Fridays: Nuns and Dirty Habits, Saturdays: Elastic Bands, Paper Clips and Rolled-Up Copies of the Financial Times, Sundays: Off.

The routine was saved from becoming boring by the odd variation or re-arrangement brought about by late sittings in The House, or The Old Bailey, or the cut and thrust of High Finance.

Through the '80's boom and bust they prospered with busts and booms of cracking whips. Until, that is, Louise got greedy. He was a high ranking Met Officer (Handcuffs, Truncheon and Vaseline Jelly) who had taken over a Saturday slot vacated by a failed financier who had tried a one-off blow job on a twelve bore shotgun.

'Shaft me!' begged the Cop – and Louise, unbeknown to Zelda, did. She put the black on him. And he paid . . . at first. Zelda, in the dark, had assumed that he had moved on when he failed to turn up for his regular appointments.

'You win some, you lose some,' she had said philosophically to Louise, who had smiled thinly as if in agreement.

Handcuffs/Truncheon/Vaseline had almost fainted when he answered the phone at his Belgravia Town House and heard Louise's voice

'How . . . How . . .' he had stuttered in a sudden panic.

'Did I get your phone number?' He had nodded dumbly into the handset.

'I saw your warrant card when it accidentally fell out of your trouser pocket when you were . . . occupied. From there it was just, as in your profession you know very well, simply a case of lines of enquiry.'

HTV had blanched and, after shooting a quick agonised glance towards the kitchen – where Mrs HTV was knocking up a batch of fairy cakes for the Women's Institute, while belting out a rousing chorus of Onward Christian Soldiers in tune with Radio Five's Sunday Service – he had managed to mutter darkly: 'How much?'

As it transpired she wanted quite a lot. 'How much!' he had yelled, before clenching his teeth and shooting another agonised look towards the closed kitchen door.

He had paid the first thousand with a sinking feeling in the pit of his stomach. His professional experience told him that she would be back for more, but her demand for immediate payment had thrown him into a panic. He had too much to lose. There was a plump pension on the not too distant horizon. There was his high standing at the Masonic Lodge, and there was the gut-wrenching certainty of Mrs HTV's reaction – she would have his goolies on a porcelain china plate.

He needed time to think, to call in a favour or two from certain shadowy quarters. So he paid and waited. And sure enough a month later she was back. This time he was ready.

Louise had just closed the front door leading to their second floor Marylebone apartment and stepped out onto the pavement, when a large black saloon car with darkened windows slid stealthily alongside and a rear door swung open. She was pulled in and before she could utter a word the car had picked up speed and shot around a corner.

Inside, she had found herself sharing the back seat with a broken nosed thug, who upon a careful and very studied examination, could possibly pass for a member of the genus *homo sapiens*. This was enough to give even the most laid back individual cause for concern – but what had really freaked her out were the two plastic buckets and the large bag of quick drying cement at her feet.

She had become rather excited and then almost immediately very quiet, as a paw the size and consistency of a steel wrecking ball made intimate contact with her chin.

Back in the flat, Zelda was also excited. She had been casually glancing out the window as Louise had left to visit the nearby Victoria Wine outlet. She had seen the car pull up and watched with a little stab of alarm as Louise was bundled into the back. What should she do? Go out and see if she could find her workmate? Call the law? No, a little reassuring voice in her head muttered. It was probably just one of Louise's funny clients out for a variation on a theme. Into all sorts was Louise; or rather all sorts were into Louise. *Yes that's probably it*, she had thought, *just a kinky client*. Still . . . she had been acting a bit odd lately; as though she had a secret she was hiding.

And there had been the diamond earrings. Zelda had found them in a bedside drawer when she had been looking for a pack of three. Louise had seemed a little flustered when she had asked where they had come from.

'From HTV,' she had said, 'before he moved on. I'd forgotten all about them . . .' Zelda had shot her a quizzical look then said no more; for if you can't trust your work and flatmate who could you trust?

As soon as they had set up their little partnership they had entered into an agreement that any spare cash or trinkets gleaned from satisfied customers were to be placed in their safety deposit box. It was to be their retirement fund;

their little nest egg away from the prying eyes of the taxman. They had gone down to the bank the next day and deposited HTV's generous gift.

While Zelda was wrestling with her thoughts, unbeknown to her, back in the car, Louise had enough street savvy to open one eye very slowly as her head began to clear, and the realisation that she was in serious bother re-introduced itself to her brain.

From her position slumped half on the seat and half against the nearside door, she saw that the chrome door handle was a mere six inches from her left hand. She raised her head cautiously and noted with a flood of relief that the locking button was extended. She had to wait for the right moment.

Some minutes later the car began to lurch over uneven ground. They had left the main drag and were apparently travelling down a little used road. With senses heightened by her predicament, she thought she heard the sound of running water. That was all the impetus she needed. She shot out her left hand and jerked the door lever towards her, while at the same time throwing all her weight onto her left shoulder. The door yawned open and she was catapulted out onto the roadside and was up and running *a la* SAS Commandos before the car had a chance to scream to a halt.

Zelda had slept fitfully that night. By the next afternoon she had worked herself up into a fine lather and had almost made up her mind to call in the law – when the phone rang. It was Louise; who, with much prompting had told her the whole story.

Zelda was mortified – then terrified. What if they came for her thinking she was in cahoots with Louise! She would end up being tortured and find herself in deep water – just like her father. These thoughts were flashing through her mind at such a rate of knots that Louise's last words before she hung up didn't register for a moment or two. 'Sorry about the deposit box,' she had said.

Zelda had had to clutch the edge of the table to save her self from keeling over, as at the bank, she stared into the empty deposit box. Gone, all of it! Nearly fifty grand's worth of cash and jewellery, gone just like that. The fucking bitch! It was another of life's Lessons and one she had never expected: Men did not hold exclusive rights to bastardity!

As, later and still in a daze, she turned the final corner to the apartment block she was wrenched out of her bitter reverie by the sight of a large black saloon car parked twenty yards from the entrance to her block of flats. *Mother of God*! her mind had screamed. It's them. *They've come for me now!*

Five hours later she had stepped off the train at Leeds station with the clothes she stood up in and a hundred and eighteen quid in her purse. And now there was nothing for it, but to go back to common or garden whoring.

And she did. And she resented it mightily. She also resented the fact that pragmatic Yorkshire men didn't seem to want chastising at all. For them it was wham bam thank you lass and here's your tenner.

Leeds was followed by Nottingham and Leicester – which was about as near to Birmingham as she was prepared to go. Eventually, her tortuous journey through life brought her back to Manchester. A round trip fuelled at the outset by bright hope and optimism that had stuttered and finally stalled, as those twin cruel deceivers of youth had drained away with each passing year.

As her looks slowly faded so too did her number of clients – apart from one dotty old regular that got his jollies from playing doctors and nurses – until eventually she was reduced to offering fiver hand jobs to tanked-up punters mid-trek between pubs and Chinese chippies.

The inevitable downward spiral continued until, two years' ago, a casual arrangement had led to her moving in with Davey's mam Ethel. They had bumped into each other coming out of ten o'clock mass at Saint Bridgid's one chilly October morning, and a polite general conversation had suddenly blossomed into a more intimate chat as they walked along Grey Mare Lane.

In the space of two hundred yards Zelda had learned that Ethel had been abandoned by her partner; had two sons, one of whom had moved to

Canada and no longer kept in touch, while the other, Davey, was afflicted and was the worry of her life.

Perhaps recognising a fellow life sufferer, Zelda opened up to the large friendly woman. She admitted to her colourful past and was pleasantly surprised when Ethel smiled, patted her on the arm and said: 'Your namesake was a sinner too and she was forgiven – just like you will be.'

They had met again the following Sunday and Ethel had invited her home for a warming cuppa. As they sat in the neat little kitchen drinking tea out of delicate china cups and nibbling on chocolate digestives, Zelda had casually mentioned that she was having landlord problems at her bed-sit. Ethel, ever the helpful Samaritan, suggested that she might like to move in to her flat on a temporary basis. It wouldn't be a problem she said, there was a spare bedroom that had been her eldest son's and a little extra money would come in handy.

'Just one thing though,' Ethel had said firmly, yet kindly: 'I won't have you doin any business if you catch my drift.' As business was, apart from her dotty regular punter, Mr Smith, practically non-existent, Zelda had agreed.

The business block was no great problem. She would just have to put herself out a bit by entertaining him over at his place in Didsbury. Yes, the arrangement suited her well. She had a part time job behind the bar at a local nightclub – the

Blue Cockatoo – and this, coupled with a bit of social security money, was enough to keep her in fags and the little luxuries in life, like a weekly bottle or two of gin and the occasional pair of new shoes.

Two months later, just before Christmas, the temporary arrangement became a permanent one when Ethel's tired old ticker gave up the ghost and she passed on, prising from Zelda before she did a promise to: 'look after my poor Davey.'

While Ethel was alive Zelda had not needed to enter into any meaningful level of social intercourse with Davey – in fact as the flat was quite large for the three of them to rattle around in she had pretty much been able to ignore him. As soon as Ethel passed on though, she realised that things would obviously have to change. While she resented this latest twist of fate that had conspired to leave her in a position where she was reduced to being a nursemaid to one of God's less fortunate creations, she recognised that in order to turn the situation to her advantage, her status in the flat needed sorting.

What was required was the application of a little bit of feminine subterfuge. Accordingly, she got him blind drunk one night and tumbled him into her bed. The next day he was so embarrassed and red faced at the disgusting and perverted things that (she insisted) he'd done, that he didn't raise any objection when she asked for her name to join his on the rent book.

'It's the only way I can protect myself from being a male plaything, abused, used and discarded at any time it suits you,' she had said tearfully.

It was odd though, he often thought over the following weeks, that he should even consider – let alone engage in such actions. He didn't have a perverted bone in his body, and if he was so pissed that he couldn't even remember anything about the events, how could he, a little person, have had the ability to force himself on a big person? Still, he reasoned, she said it had happened so it must have, for what reason could she possibly have to make up such a thing?

Davey, Zelda had discovered soon after moving in with Ethel, slotted neatly into one of the categories that she had placed men in. Where others over the years had been pigeonholed as Peacocks, Perverts, Bastards, Sadists or Masochists, he was a Mummy's Boy. He had never known his father and had never as far as she knew, even had a girlfriend. Ethel had mollycoddled and bullied him in more or less equal measure and he had accepted both without question.

With Ethel gone she took her place – except when it came to the mollycoddling and the very occasional bout of physical intimacy. In terms of the latter, he had been quite taken aback when she informed him that she had moved them both into Ethel's bedroom, and by association, her large double bed. 'Bit late for you to go all bashful . . .

after what you did to me before,' she had added meekly, making him blush.

'Anyway,' she had pointed out in a more this is not up for debate voice, 'it'll save on the gas bills cos we can turn the radiators off in the other bedrooms.' As there was not a lot of money coming into the flat this statement made sense; but her main reason was to cement her position by imposing her presence on him.

That was something she had been accustomed to doing over the years, imposing her will on men, be they young men, old men, rich men, poor men, beggar men or thieves. Age and life station had never mattered, she was the boss.

Even when she was finally reduced to dispensing fiver hand jobs she was still the boss. Why? Because even in *extremis*, apart from holding a male member she held the power to dispense pleasure, or alternatively, should the whim take her, intense pain, in the palm of her right hand.

Davey had accepted the news without complaint. She was after all much bigger and older than he was and therefore by his definition she was almost certainly much cleverer.

The new arrangement had bedded in quite well after an initial bit of obedience training, when a couple of quick clips around the head had resulted in the desired effect of putting a stop to his annoying habit of attempting to cuddle up in the dead of night.

Now, she raised her fingers to her face and dabbed each cheek before roughly rubbing the cold cream into her skin. That done, she painted on two thick bows of lipstick, patted her wispy hair into place, plonked her fists on the dressing room table, and with knuckles white and cracking, heaved herself to her feet – all the time maintaining dead eyed contact with the granite hard face that looked back at her in the mirror.

'Right, that'll 'ave to do,' she said, as she opened the double wardrobe door and surveyed the three long ranks of shoes arranged by heel height; four inch at the back, three inch in the middle and the rest at the front.

The mortality/age confirming little session in front of the mirror had left her on a downer. She needed a bit of a lift. She ran her eyes over the serried ranks of reds, blues, pinks, blacks and two-tones. Something bright she thought, something that will raise me above shit street level. So she picked out a pair of cerise four-inch, open-toed, sling backs with cute little yellow and blue bows.

She slipped them on then sat on the edge of the bed and held her feet out in front of her for inspection. Her mood lightened a fraction. She nodded, stood up and reached back into the wardrobe for her imitation leopard skin coat, slipped that on, made her way to the front door, down the stairwell and out into the nippy early evening air.

As she crossed the square on her way to Choudrey's Newsagents/Off-Licence – where a bottle of gin had her name on it – she casually glanced left and right to see if she could spot a skulking little figure in the gloom. No, the little pain was nowhere in sight. 'Okay,' she mouthed quietly to herself 'but don't think that this is the end of it, I'll sort you out later you likkul shit.'

5

The sun went down like Zelda's head on a client – cold, distant and divorced from matters earthly or earthy. As it sank, black fingers of shadow crept from their secret hiding places, probed the barely warm flagstones and emboldened, extended arms and then grotesque bodies, dark menacing distortions of the sand brown, squat featureless structures that lined three sides of the silent precinct.

Windows on the unboarded shops, which earlier had glowed with the pale golden hue of autumn sunlight darkened like dying eyes – reflecting nothing, absorbing less.

As the shadows grew, lengthened and slid across the ground, their passing seemed to raise a chill breeze that seized upon and stirred a thin scattering of shrivelled fallen leaves and grease stained white chip papers; whirling them together in a sad little slow motion gavotte. The dead dancing with the discarded; the discarded dancing with the dead.

Somewhere, far off, a dog howled. Davey shivered with the cold, and the ever-lurking unease that was forever creeping back like a thief in the night to rob him of his peace of mind. And with the howl images of pouncing Alsatians and berserker Maltese terriers ripping flesh and crunching bone, replayed in glorious technicolour on the looped tape that was embedded for life in his brain.

Had he possessed a whimsical streak he might have thought it wryly amusing how the fabric of one's life could be so indelibly dyed by a surging spurt of scarlet. He didn't – so he didn't. No. Instead, with a little bit of mental application he thought: *I wonder if we'll keep a clean sheet against them rotten Liverpool sods this Satdee?*

A casual observer granted sudden access to the workings of the mind of David Ignatius Montgomery Parker would, no doubt, have been somewhat confused by the conjunction of neural links which threw forth such a thought at such a time, in such a place, in such a situation. But this was Davey and Davey is as Davey duz.

Actually, the thought was not so much of a rogue as might at first appear – for two reasons:

Davey was a Manchester United fanatic and he took a deep professional interest in the art of goalkeeping,. being a member of that nutters' union himself. That said the term fanatic was perhaps a little on the strong side bearing in mind the fact that fanatics spend virtually every waking moment engrossed in the subject of their fanaticism.

In Davey's case he only thought about football and United once a day . . . even though that was every day . . . and almost all day long.

At the age of six, several months after the event, his big brother Arthur had written to United explaining the details of the accident and asking if it would be possible that Davey could be a mascot for the day. The club had agreed – and young Davey had found himself leading out the team in front of 55,000 roaring fans.

The match itself did not live long in his young mind; but what did, and indelibly so, was the memory of a blond giant in a green jersey who had bent low to shake his hand and to ask in a South African accent, his name. 'David Ignatius Montgomery Parker,' he had mumbled awe-struck, and looking up into the smiling face.

For years after that wondrous day he dreamt of playing in goal for Manchester United, where he would be the world's first one-armed, four-foot tall goalie (he had seriously over-estimated his final height).

As he grew older he realised his dream was

destined to remain just that, a dream. So, instead, he made do with playing in goals during kickabouts with other local kids on spare ground opposite Barmouth Street swimming baths; displaying as he did an almost uncanny knack of attracting the ball to his face as he threw himself valiantly into the line of fire. He also became a super fan.

He and Arthur, along with four or five other local lads, travelled by bus or coach home and away, rain, hail or shine. They were Beswick Reds. And as one of their number, Tommy Higginbottom, would say: 'You don't meth wiv Bethick Redths!'

They tied their scarves around their wrists, wore bovver boots and swore a lot. Nobody seemed to pay much attention, as this was pretty much the order of the day.

The seasons came and the seasons went, as did Arthur, who got married and buggered off to Canada, leaving Davey with their mam Ethel. This desertion annoyed the young Davey very much. Arthur was one of the founder members of the Beswick Reds and you don't bugger off and leave your mates just because some bint gets inside your trollies and raises your expectations.

'Bloody stuck up cow,' he often mused, 'Manchister's not good enough for 'er. Oh no, she as ter want ter go ter bloody Canerda where they don't even play football . . . not proper football anyway.'

Still, he had got a little bit of satisfaction from

wrapping a dead rat in a pair of her fancy silk knickers as she packed her suitcases ready for the off.

'She'll remember me all right,' he told the Beswick Reds, 'every time she pulls on a pair of keks.' A statement which, when you think about it, would constitute an *aide mémoire* to bring a smile to the face of any red blooded sexually active young male.

Back in the precinct Davey shivered again as the wind picked up and plucked at the empty shirt sleeve pinned neatly across his chest, causing it to lift and flutter as if from the movement of a phantom arm. He looked around at the silent square, empty now even of the foraging sparrow so recently a target for his frustration. 'Might as well piss off,' he mumbled. 'Nuffin 'ere to keep me . . .'

As he slid down from the bench a sudden gust of wind blew in and whipped up a mini dust storm, driving grains of grit and tattered scraps of paper in his direction. Instinctively he lowered his head and slitted his eyes as the tiny particles stung his cheeks. A thousand rebukes for simply being. Then, as suddenly as it had begun, the wind died away. Still looking down, he opened his eyes . . . and his heart skipped a beat. There was a tenner plastered against his left shin.

'Yeeaahhh!' he crowed, bending and snatching the flimsy paper to his chest. 'Bloody yeeaahhh!' He punched the darkening air in triumph and performed a little jig of celebration.

If anybody had been around to see his animated reaction they would probably have mentally stamped OTT across it in 72 point bold letters; but the fact was that in his case – as in the case of many East Manchester residents – the difference between having 10 pee and 10 pound in the pocket was not simply £9.90 it was more like bloody UNDREDS!

He slipped the note into his pocket then tamped it down firmly, and with a little skipping first step, set off towards the *Derby Arms* and a pint or four of Boddies.

On his way up Grey Mare Lane he passed the boarded up *Queen Victoria* which was the Beswick Reds' usual base but was in between landlords after the last incumbent had been carted off to Strangeways due to a spot of bother with the Drug Squad.

As he drew level with *The Manchester* – where he was not welcome due to a regrettable ball biting incident a couple of months ago – he crossed the road towards *Mary D's* (which he refused on principle to frequent since it had painted its exterior in 'City' sky blue).

There he paused briefly at the top of Grey Mare Lane to glare across Ashton New Road at that club's stadium. The aesthetic beauty of the imposing edifice cut no ice with him. He did not appreciate the silky curves of the suspended roof or the towering sweep of the stands.

He thought nothing of the dozen enormous angled, roof tensioning poles with their thick steel hawsers and their triangular harpoon tips thrusting up to prick the blue-black, bruised sky. Instead, he thought: 'Bloody City!' and, noisily hawking up a green one, he gobbed with venom in the direction of the enemy's fortress. Suddenly, and as if in sharp retaliation, the sky gobbed back.

'Bloody Rainy City,' he mouthed as heavy drops spattered into his upturned face and blurred his vision. 'Just when I've not got me coat . . . figgers . . . bleedin figgers.'

His obvious *chagrin* at being caught some two hundred yards from any real cover without a coat was perhaps understandable. Having said that however, directing the blame onto his mother city was possibly a little unfair as there are certainly a number of much damper places than Manchester.

For instance: there's the beds of several canals and rivers, the inside of plenty of goldfish bowls and the knicker gussets of thousands of screaming teenage girls at any boy band concert.

As the rain drummed and pattered onto the pavement like falling globules of mercury, he pressed himself tightly against the wall of a closed and shuttered office supplies shop and glumly waited for an easing off. After several minutes, and two 'bastard!' three 'shit!' and one heartfelt 'fuk!', the heavens relented and the deluge wound down to light drizzle.

'Right,' he muttered. 'That'll do it.' He pushed himself off the wall, turned, and legged it up Ashton New Road. He passed the site of the once towering 184 foot high rust brown, steel star burst that was supposed to represent the *'B' of the Bang'* of a starting pistol, but, before it had been dismantled due to bits falling off in a slight wind had looked more like hedgehog road kill – and jogged over the road bridge that spanned the canal and on towards the dry and thirst-quenching oasis that was the *Derby Arms*.

6

'**B**it of a dead 'ole this int it?' said Hilda, casting her eye around the room with its dark dreary wallpaper and 40 watt fuelled imitation Victorian hanging light fittings. In one corner a gnarled old man in a flat cap, was, like a crystal ball gazer, staring into the dregs at the bottom of a pint pot. The arthritic fingers of one hand were wrapped around the glass as if to keep it from slipping away before he could read its message of a future.

A bleak set in stone future that lay in wait for all cast iron old men who tried to read beer dregs in 21st Century plastic pubs.

In another corner that backed onto Ashton

New Road, two teenage girls whispered and giggled as the muted sounds of passing traffic added to their air of youthful intrigue.

'Yeah, well,' said Mavis glancing out the window, 'we'll just 'ave the one, then when it stops rainin we'll shoot down to the *Manchister* if you want.' Hilda nodded and took a seat at a table near the door while her companion crossed over to the bar to order drinks.

As she passed the street door on the way back with two pints of bitter in her hands it shot open and a small blur almost cannoned into her.

'What the bleedin . . . watch where yer goin will you!' she yelled, performing a little shimmy of evasion.

'Sorry missis . . . dint see you there,' Davey offered to the stout, black haired, heavily made up middle-aged bargoyle.

'Not bloody surprised, bloody rate yer goin at. Nuvver five 'ours to closin time you know.'

'Yeah. Sorry, I was runnin ter get away from the rain.'

'Right then,' she threw over her shoulder as she made her way to her seat.

'See that,' she said, as she carefully placed the two pints on the table. 'Likkul bleeder nearly 'ad me arse over tit on't floor.' The slightly younger, mousey-haired, and much thinner woman smiled, exposing large crooked, and nicotine stained teeth.

'Wunt be the first time would it . . . you on't

floor wiv a bloke on top of you?'

'Bloke yeah, but look at 'im, 'ee's only free foot tall.' Hilda tilted her head back slightly, and with a sunbed ravaged wrinkled face that could've been twinned with a badger's ball bag, studied the little figure critically.

'Naw,' she said, 'bit more than that I'd say . . . closer to four foot, more like.'

Back at the bar somebody said: 'A pint a Boddies please mate.' The barman looked round, puzzled.

'A pint a Boddies please mate . . .' Startled, the barman leaned forward and peered over the edge of the tall counter and frowned.

'Oh it's you. Well I told you before; no bloody tick... so on yer bike!'

'Don't need it mate,' smirked Davey, flourishing the note. 'Just backed a ten ter one winner at York.'

On his way back from the bar and carrying his beer as carefully as one would a pint of nitro glycerine, Davey drew level with the seated women.

'All right then tiger?' Davey stopped and turned to face the black haired woman.

'What?' The woman nodded towards him.

'I said are you all right . . . tiger?' Hilda laughed.

'Aw look Mavis; 'ee's shy. 'Is likkul cheeks is goin all red.'

'Shy are you then tiger?' said Mavis sweetly.

'No.'

'What's yer name then?' she cooed.

'David Ignatius Montgomery Parker.' Mavis glanced sideways and with a little smile that read: We've got a right one 'ere 'ilda, she winked, then turned back to face the little man.

'Wow, Ignatius Montgomery, where'd you get that lot from then?'

'Me mam was a big kafflic and me dad was a war nut.' Mavis glanced sideways and winked again.

'Yer dad was a wall nut?' she asked innocently. Davey snorted.

'A war nut not a wall nut! 'Ee was into the war and tank bakkles . . . an fings . . .'

'Oh, right.' Then: 'Live round 'ere then do you, David Ignatius Montgomery Parker?'

'You can call me Davey.'

'Oh, right. Well?'

'Yeah. Ant seen you before though . . .'

'No,' piped Hilda, 'we just moved in last week from Salford. Got a nice likkul flat over on Varley street, ant we Mavis?' With her eyes still on Davey, Mavis grinned.

'Yeah. Nice an cosy it is . . . get up to anyfin there we can . . . an no one the wiser . . .'

'Oh,' said Davey. Mavis giggled.

''Ee's a cool one int 'ee Ilda?' Hilda narrowed her eyes and smiled.

'What 'appened to yer arm then tiger?' she said nodding towards his empty sleeve.

'Bear bit it off in Canerda.' Hilda started.

'Ewww! That's 'orrible that is!'

'Yeah it was.'

'Dint rip anyfin else off did it?' said Mavis laughing.

'No. Just me arm . . .'

'That's good int it 'ilda?' Then turning back to face Davey, said:

'Everyfin else in good workin order is it?'

'Yeah,' said Davey, slightly puzzled.

'Int 'ee a cheeky likkul fing Mavis! Crackin on all innercent.' Mavis smiled and patted an empty stool by her side. 'Come an sit wiv us tiger,' she invited. 'We can 'ave a nice likkul chat.'

Davey gently placed his pot on the table, hitched himself up onto the stool, carefully hoisted the pint and took a long swallow.

'Needed that did you?' said Mavis. Davey nodded and wiped away a moustache of froth.

'Live on yer own then do you?' Hilda said.

'No. Live wiv my Zelda.' The two women exchanged quick glances.

'What, Zelda O'Flerhity?' said Mavis.

'Yeah. She looks after me . . . sometimes, 'cept not right now, banjoed me she did wiv a bloody great brass poker an frew me down't stairs.'

'Well fancy that!' said Mavis.

'No, I din't fancy it missis, bloody 'urt it did.'

'I din't mean did you fancy bein twatted tiger, I meant fancy that, your Zelda bein Zelda

O'Flerhity.'

'Oh.'

'Still on't game is she? Still turnin tricks?'

'Sometimes . . . when she wants a new pair of shoes or summut . . .' Hilda laughed.

'Yeah allus was a shoe freak was Zelda. Shudda bin called Imelda, not Zelda.'

Both women laughed. Davey, puzzled, looked from one to the other. He shrugged, and took another mouthful of beer then placed his glass down gently on the table.

'You know 'er then, my Zelda?' he said, wiping his mouth again.

'Oh aye,' said Mavis, 'we boaf worked wiv 'er in the old days.'

'Yeah,' Hilda confirmed, 'rum girl is old Zelda. Still inter whips an fings is she?' Davey shook his head.

'Naw. She just does doctors an nurses fings wiv mister Smiff an a rotten emena fing . . . don't like it me . . . rotten emena . . .' He pulled a sour face, reached for his glass and took another gulp of his beer.

'An 'ow about you tiger – you keep 'er 'appy do you?' Hilda asked, making a piston movement with clenched fist and forearm.

'Eh?'

'Give 'er plenty do you?'

'Naw,' said Davey, 'Can't work me, wiv one arm.' The women exchanged glances.

'You know what Mavis; I reckon 'ee's tekkin the piss. What you fink?'

'Aye. Likkul tiger!' Davey frowned.

'What you keep callin me tiger for; me names Davey.' Hilda laughed throatily.

'Tigers is all 'ot an sexy,' she said. 'Does it fifty times a night does tigers, don't they Mave?' Mavis winked and leered.

''Ow about it then tiger. 'Andle a cupla bitches on 'eat could you?'

'Don't like dogs.'

'Ayup 'ilda 'ee's at it agen . . . cheeky likkul bugger callin us dogs!'

'What you on about?'

'The uvver, that's what . . . the uvver!'

'The uvver what?'

'I'll say this fer 'im,' said Mavis, 'likkul tiger knows 'ow ter get a woman on't boil!' She reached forward and tweaked his cheek.

'Oww! 'Urt that!'

'A'yup Mave! You got 'im goin now. Anyfin could 'appen. Might ravish us boaf right 'ere on't pub floor!' Mavis chuckled throatily.

'Ooo I do 'ope so . . . never bin ravished onna pub floor . . . don't fink.'

Davey looked from one to the other and shook his head slowly. *Wimmin*, he thought, *why can't they tork proper, stead of in bleedin riggles.*

Some two hours later and thanks in no small part to a decision somewhere along the way to order whiskey chasers with the beer, they were all well on the way to becoming *non-compos mentis*.

'Why,' slurred Davey to Mavis, 'why does . . . does, she keep lookin at me all funny like?'

'What like?' said Mavis.

'All, all, funny like . . .' said Davey screwing up an eye and tilting his face slightly sideways.

'Oh that. Eh 'ilda . . . 'ilda . . .'

'What?'

'Show im yer trick . . . wiv yer eye.' Hilda grinned, raised her glass, and then lifted her other hand towards her left eye.

'What kind a cocktail does this remind you of?' She twisted her left hand and there was a soft 'plink' as something dropped into her drink.

'Tarrraa!' she crowed, holding the glass in front of Davey's suddenly drained face. 'It's an 'ighball, geddit? an eye-ball!' Davey looked at the eye. The eye from the bottom of the glass, stared blankly back.

'I fink,' he said very quietly, 'I've 'ad enuff fer terday . . .'

Hilda tilted the pot and fished her eye out then she raised the glass to her mouth and drained it in one long noisy swallow.

'Naw,' she said, licking the eye, prising up her eyelid with one hand and popping the eye back into its raw, red veined socket with the other, 'we just got started. Ring us a taxi tiger, yer cummin over to our place.' Davey pulled a face.

'Don't fink so. I fink I better get back 'ome,' he said draining his pot. 'I'm in enough shit now wivout stayin out all night.' Mavis heaved herself to her feet, reached forward and hooked a thick hand into the back of Davey's shirt collar.

'We got a good bokkel of Japanese scotch just beggin to get drunk,' she said pulling him to his feet, 'an yer goin to 'elp us drink it.'

'An then,' Hilda added, 'we might just 'ave ourselves a likkul private party.'

The lift juddered to a stop and spewed them out on the ninth floor. They elbowed their way through a pair of battered swing doors and staggered down a dimly lit small corridor that carried the lingering odours of boiled cabbage, damp washing and the flat musty aura of resignation. The women pulled up suddenly outside a roughly painted green door, the face of which was studded with a dozen round ball hammer sized, indentations. Davey's legs kept going and carried him into the rear of Hilda, who giggled.

"Ome sweet 'ome,' Mavis slurred, managing to push the key into the lock at the third attempt. 'C'mon,' she said with her back to Hilda and Davey, 'C'mon in.' She made a wagon's ho gesture, stumbled into the darkened flat and groped for the light switch.

'Kin fing! Where the fuk is it! It's 'ere somewhere . . . Ah, there it is . . .'

There was a click and the room was flooded with the light from a bare sixty-watt bulb hanging from a flex pendant. Davey tripped in after Hilda, who turned and closed the door after him.

'I'll fetch us a drink. You . . . you mek yerself comf . . .ee.'

Mavis waved an arm in the general direction of a black vinyl moquette two-seater settee that shared the room with two matching spindly-legged arm chairs, a small square of muddy red threadbare carpet over equally tatty red and yellow patterned lino, a battered television resting on a rickety corner table, a coffee table bearing a Lakeland scene and a tall thin standard lamp that leaned drunkenly to one side.

As she disappeared into the kitchen, Davey hitched himself up onto the settee and took a slow look around. Hilda sat beside him.

'Snot much,' said Hilda, sweeping her arm loosely around the room; 'but it's a roof over us 'eads.' Davey nodded.

'Yeah. More'n I got ternight I fink. Bloody Zelda. Did . . . did I tell you . . . twatted me wiv a lump 'ammer an frew me over the second floor para . . . para . . . landin . . .' Hilda's head bobbed slowly up and down in sympathy, like a nodding dog in the back window of a flat out Lada.

'I can ble . . . ble . . . bleeve that all right. Allus was a 'ard woman was Zelda. Could tell you sum fings bout 'er what would mek yer teef curl. There was this pimp in Ber . . . Berm . . . ing . . . am once . . .'

"Ere you are,' Mavis interrupted, as she staggered back into the room carrying a small round tin tray with three half pint glasses and an almost full bottle of genuine Japanese scotch on it.

She placed the tray down heavily on the coffee table, unscrewed the cap off the bottle and sloshed out four fingers (four of theirs and six of Davey's) into the glasses.

"Ere you are then tiger . . . get yer laffin tackle round that.' Davey took the glass gingerly and tried a tiny sip.

'Huuuhhh!' he gasped, as the fiery liquid savaged his windpipe.

'Good eh?' said Mavis, handing a glass to Hilda and taking up her own.

'Yeah,' said Davey with watering eyes, 'jus the job that . . . fer tekkin paint off walls.' Mavis giggled as she lowered herself into a chair, exposing as she did, a great blue-veined wobbly slab of thigh.

'A'yup Mavis, you'll be gettin im goin showin all that!' Hilda nodded in the direction of the meat mountain.

'Oh I do 'ope so,' cooed Mavis, sliding her skirt up another couple of inches and undoing the top two buttons of her somewhat less than pristine white blouse.

'Is it me or is it 'ot in 'ere?' she asked innocently.

'Oh it's 'ot all right,' laughed Hilda, unbuttoning her own blouse; 'an it's goin ter get a lot 'otter anall in a minute . . .'

Davey looked from one to the other – and took another mouthful of whisky.

'Yeah, it is 'ot,' he gasped, 'must be this bloody whiskey.'

'Why don't you then,' said Hilda – leaning over and exposing ample portions of flesh as her blouse fell open – 'loosen yer shirt a bit tiger . . .'

'Yeah, an yer pants anall,' added Mavis, grinning drunkenly. Hilda nodded and, leaning forward, she undid Davey's belt and slid it through the loops with practiced ease.

'There that's much better innit,' she cooed, introducing her heavy breasts to Davey's ears.

'Mmpphh,' said Davey.

'Har Har!' said Mavis, as she heaved herself out of her chair and sidling over lifted Hilda's blouse and unhooked her bra from behind. Freed of their uplift and restriction, Hilda's pendulous breasts shot forward then collapsed onto Davey's shoulders.

'Mmpphh,' said Davey.

'Har Har!' said Mavis.

'Ooohhh!' said Hilda, taking a mammary in each hand and rubbing it into Davey's flushed face.

'Like that do you tiger?'

'Mmpphhh!'

'A'yup, give 'im sum air 'ilda . . . poor likkul bleeder's goin all blue,' Mavis observed casually.

Hilda, her face and throat brightly flushed, laughed and leaned back.

'Now yer really are 'ot aren't yer,' giggled Mavis. 'Ere,' she continued, 'let me 'elp you out of that.' She took hold of Hilda's blouse collar and slid the garment over her shoulders, down her arms and dropped it, with the loose bra, by the side of the settee.

'Let me 'elp you out of that anall.' She reached around Hilda's waist and unbuttoned her skirt. Hilda giggled and raised her buttocks off the settee as Mavis slid the garment and then the panties off, and deposited them with the other clothes.

Davey looked blearily at the naked Hilda, who, now even more flushed, leaned over and began to unzip his pants.

'Four foot of dynamite,' she husked.

'Yeah, an let's 'ope 'ee ant got a free inch fuse, or a tool like a bookie's pencil,' said Mavis.

Davey, well oiled, didn't try to stop them as they roughly dragged off his pants then underpants.

'Bloody 'ell!' gasped Hilda. 'No fear of that!'

'So that's where is uvver arm went!' said Mavis admiringly. Davey blushed.

'Ayup, did yer mam only 'ave one arm anall?' Hilda asked, with her eyes glued to his semi erect member.

'No, she 'ad two arms,' said Davey.

'Oh I fought mebee she only 'ad one an she

76

usedta lift you outa the baff . . . wiv that!' she pointed.

'No, she ad two arms all right.'

'Yer a dry likkul bleeder all right,' said Mavis, as she slipped out of her own clothes and stood leering down at them.

'Go on then girl. Get a grip on it then!' Hilda grinned wickedly and grasped Davey's penis.

'Ahhhhh,' he sighed as the blood began to flow into his organ. Then: 'Ooohhh,' as his eyes suddenly glazed and he slumped, apparently lifeless.

'Bleedin 'ell!' Mavis exploded. ''Ee ant gone an froan a wobbler as 'ee?' Hilda released Davey's penis quickly and peered into his face.

'Don't fink so. Is face int all twisted or nuffink.'

As Davey's erect member began to subside he gave a little groan and fluttered his eyelids.

'Bleedin 'ell! Ee's fainted,' said Mavis. 'It mus be all that blood rushin into is tool what did it . . . made 'im all light 'eaded, like.'

'Oh great!' Hilda exclaimed. 'Ow the fuk we gunna use 'im then, if the likkul bleeder keeps keelin over every time is prick raises its ed?'

'Fuked if I know.' Mavis scratched her head in confusion.

Then: 'Wait a minute! I know!' Hilda looked on puzzled as Mavis tottered into the kitchen. There was the sound of a cupboard door opening, followed by the sound of a tap being turned on then off again; then Mavis staggered back into the room carrying a dripping wet window leather.

'When 'ee wakes up agen an gets anuvver 'ard on you pull 'im inter you quick like an start the business . . . then when 'ee keels over I'll whip 'is arse wiv this . . . that way 'ee should keep cummin an goin all night . . . wivout cummin!'

Davey groaned and opened his eyes – to find Hilda's head bobbing up and down between his legs.

'It's cummin up!' she mouthed indistinctly.

'Quick pass 'im 'ere!' said Hilda as she threw herself back onto the sofa and spread her legs. Mavis grasped the semi-inert Davey under the armpits and heaved him on top of her workmate.

'Yeesss!' moaned Hilda, thrusting upwards, while at the same time dragging his little buttocks onto her.

'Aaagghhh,' Davey sighed. Then thirty seconds later, 'Oooohhhh . . .'

'Quick!' Yelled Hilda, 'The winder levver!' Mavis jumped forward and the wet leather whooshed down to explode with a shower of cold spray onto Davey's bare posterior.

''Ee's cummin round agen!' Mavis crowed triumphantly.

'Yeah . . . an it's cummin up agen!' gasped Hilda, pumping away wildly for half a minute, before a drawn out:

'Oooohhh . . .'

'Winder lever . . . QUICK!'

An hour and several female orgasms later, Mavis muttered: 'Right my turn; pass 'im over . . .'

7

Dawn's rosy fingers were caressing the lightening sky as a well shagged, naked and ashen-faced Mavis leaned on the little balcony rail gasping for breath.

From inside there came the intense moans and groans of a woman on the verge. The cries reached a climax and, unheard by Mavis, were followed immediately by a small popping noise and the sound of something, like a glass marble, rolling along a floor.

'Bleedin 'ell!' gasped Hilda, as on shaking legs she tottered towards the open balcony door. 'That was some fu....KINNNELLL!' she yelled as she stepped on something hard and round and her feet flew forward.

'Whoooaaa!' she screamed as she barrelled towards the open balcony door and a startled Mavis, who had spun around at the sudden shout.

'Nooo!' yelled Mavis as Hilda thudded into her, and the two of them were catapulted over the low balcony rail; their naked bodies executing two excellently synchronised somersaults; the aesthetic beauty of which were marred somewhat by a slightly out of sync Whump! Whump! as they planted themselves head first in a grass verge nine floors below.

Back on the balcony, a small round glass object ceased spinning, and gazed up into a bright new, faintly star spangled dawn; while in an untidy living room a small trouserless man moaned gently in a stupor as his semi-erect penis raised its head and like a spitting cobra with a post-dental numb lip, went 'pfftt', once before subsiding into quiescent non-tumescence.

Davey opened his eyes and groaned. Five clog-shod little men were performing a Riverdance in his head, two were jabbing the back of his eyeballs with blunt needles, while another was busy stirring the contents of his stomach with a bloody great spoon.

'Oohh, me bleedin 'ead! Someone get me a drink a water!' Nobody answered. He sighed deeply and dragged himself slowly off the settee.

'Musta gone out,' he muttered, shivering slightly as he passed the open balcony door and staggered into the grubby little kitchen to fill one of the used whisky glasses with water.

Three glasses later he returned to the living room and after a jaundiced look around, struggled into his clothes and trainers.

'Might as well slope off,' he muttered, 'affore them sex mad wimmin come back wantin more.'

As he passed through the ground floor stairwell and stepped out into an alcohol induced eye-stabingly bright morning, he noticed a little knot of people and two policemen on the grass verge that skirted the tower block.

They seemed to be looking down at something, but he was in no condition to take much notice. His head was clanging and he was worrying about what he was going to say to Zelda; or more to the point – what she was going to say to him.

He was so wrapped up in little cameo visions of acid words and clipped ear holes that he didn't hear the man say to one of the officers:

'I was jus warkin me dog, an there they was, strip bollik naked, buried 'ead first up to their waists. I run over an pulled 'em out. Orrible it was. One of 'em even 'ad er eye out!'

8

Right you likkul shit, where you bin till now?' Zelda was not best pleased.

'Er . . .'

'Arf the bleedin night I bin awake waitin for

you ter knock me up. Arf the bleedin night tossin an turnin. No bleedin consideration at all!'

'Er . . .'

'Well then?'

'You chucked me out . . .'

'I chucked you out? I . . . Chucked . . . You . . . Out?'

'Yeah yuh did.'

'Well next time I chuck you out you better come back at a decent hour . . . costin me me beauty sleep.'

'Bit late fer . . .'

'What?'

'Nuffin.'

'Well then?'

'What?' Zelda sighed.

'One . . . two . . . three . . .

'What you doin?

'I'm countin ter ten. Four . . . five . . . six . . .'

'What for?'

'What for? Cause torkin to you is like . . . like tryin to shovel shit back into a donkey while bleedin tap dancin on quicksand, that's why . . . seven, eight, nine . . . ten.'

She took another deep breath and allowed the corners of her mouth to crease into a tight little smile.

'Now then,' she said sweetly, 'shall we try agen? WHERE YOU BIN!' Davey jumped.

'Er . . . I kipped at Ernie's . . . 'is mam was . . .

was goin ter late night bingo an . . . an she wanted me ter look after 'im.' Zelda's eyes narrowed into twin slits of suspicion.

'That so?'

'Er, yeah 'onest.' Hands on hips she looked down at him.

Davey, hand in pocket, looked down at the floor. She knew he was telling porkies . . . she always knew.

'Right then,' she said abruptly, 'we'll leave it at that . . . fer now.' Davey, a little look of relief playing across his face, glanced up. It was soon replaced by a little obstinate pout, as Zelda added:

'Mr Smiff will be 'ere soon. You gotta get undressed. '

'No,' he said.

Sometimes, when she forgot to concentrate and allowed the steel trap of her mind to ratchet down a notch or two, she felt almost . . . sorry for him. He wasn't bad. She'd had Bad. He was thick . . . one-dimensional . . . yes. But he wasn't bad. He made no real demands of her other than requests for beer and fag money.

He was happy enough for her to be the boss, to make any decisions that would in the past have been his mother's to make. He didn't even pester her for sex – and on the very rare occasion when she was in the mood for it herself, his problem allowed her, with her well trained pelvic muscles, to get on with it more or less on her own.

Sometimes, when she looked down at him without him being aware, as well as the inherited penance for a selfish and sinful life, she saw the child she'd never had; the little pudgy fingers, the wide blue eyes, the tight blondish curls, the open face that masked no real deceit; no dark secrets, no important hidden agendas – and she felt a strange and very alien gentle ache in her chest.

At her age her biological clock had slowed to a quiet and very infrequent tick. Yes; there was a time a few years ago when she had briefly toyed with the notion of motherhood; but the absence of a suitable partner and the demands of her 'profession' had soon knocked such barmy sentimental nonsense out of her noggin.

Now if she was out and about and she saw a group of kids laughing, fizzing, sparkling with the sheer exhilaration of being, she allowed herself a sour smile that said: Yes go on enjoy it – before the shit encrusted blanket of life smothers that silly childish innocence out of you.

She knew that he adored kids, or rather babies and toddlers. She had watched him once awkwardly hold Curtley's little Millie on his knee and look lovingly into her big brown eyes, and make silly little cooing noises until she giggled, chuckled and chinked like a drain. It was only babies and toddlers though that caused such a reaction in him.

This was probably because their innocence stopped them from sticking a label on him. A label that read 'likkul gett', or 'short arse'. These appellations she knew would come later as they reached the age of four or five and began their indoctrination into the brutal world of adults. A world where an innocent question like: 'why is that man so small?' would likely bring the response: "Ee's so likkul cos 'ee's a dwarf. And the word 'dwarf' would come out sounding like 'freak' or 'bogeyman'.

Yes, like babies and toddlers, he too was something of an innocent and it was probably this innocence that she saw in him, that caused her to treat him like she often did. He had no right to it. He was over 30 for Mary's sake! It should have been well smothered out of him by now.

She resented him . . . and yet . . . sometimes, in the dead of night with the clock well east of midnight, when woken by footsteps echoing down the long landing outside their bedroom window – sounds that perversely stirred feelings of isolation – she would reach out in the dark and gain comfort from the fiery curve of his little dreaming thigh. Sometimes, his whimpering – probably caused by nightmare flashbacks featuring snarling Alsatians – would wake her and she would put her hand on his shoulder and gently 'shush' him back to a dreamless sleep.

That was sometimes. Now was different, very definitely different. The little shit was being awkward.

Zelda glowered.

'Yes you will.'

'Won't. Bloody rotten emena fing!'

'No em . . . no enema . . . no beer money . . .'

'A tenner,' he demanded.

'Five,' she said.

'Seven,' he countered.

'Four,' she spat.

'Four-fifty an that's it,' he replied.

'Okay, four-fifty,' she conceded.

He frowned then sighed. She'd had him over again. *Still*, he thought, *I held out for fifty pee more than last time.*

Milk bottle bottom spectacles apart, Arnold Smith was spectacularly non-descript. He was of average height, average weight and build. He had no heroic chin, no piercing blue eyes, no regal bearing to mark him out as a little bit special. One could not however relegate him to the other end of the social classification scale as he lacked a slovenly slouch, ferret sharp features or a tendency to regard everyone else as a pocket ripe for picking.

His thin, mousey brown hair was receding like the Blackpool tide, swiftly and in a line. Not for him the rakishness of a widow's peak. He was also far from being in any way unique. There are Arnold Smith train and plane spotters. Arnold Smith antique teapot collectors. Arnold Smith philatelists, numismologists and ordnance survey map buffs.

Although they inhabited the real world where they lived, breathed, ate, drank and evacuated their bladders and bowels, Arnold Smiths' existences were on the periphery of vision, where they flitted through life generally creating about as much impact upon the world in general as a grey moth's sigh.

Our Arnold Smith had wanted to be a doctor for almost as long as he could remember. This desire had originally been kindled when as a 12 year old he had indulged in a game of doctors and nurses with Betty Taylor, a very forward girl of the same age. Betty had long black hair, big blue eyes and two enchanting little lumps on her chest.

'You'll have to examine them,' she had said hiking up her blouse, 'in case they need some ointment or something.' Near sighted Arnold had screwed up his eyes in amazement, blushed and stammered: 'I can't. What if my mother finds out!' Betty had shrugged and smiled slyly.

'I'm not going to tell, are you?'

'No way! She'd only tell my dad and I'd end up in big trouble!'

'Well then?' she had said, thrusting her chest out. Arnold had taken another close look, pushed his glasses firmly up onto the bridge of his nose – and dived in. It was a great game and he entered into it with snowballing enthusiasm.

Unfortunately the game didn't have time to

develop much further, as during a later examination in Betty's father's tool shed, a sudden appearance by the latter had put paid to a blossoming medical partnership.

Deprived of a hands-on approach, Arnold took to scouring newspapers and magazines for anything relating to health and hygiene. He also – much to his father's annoyance – became addicted to sitting with his mother to watch every episode of Emergency Ward Ten, a popular medical television soap drama of the day.

As he grew older Arnold's desire to be a medic was gradually submerged by the pressures brought on by puberty and by the persistent prodding of an acerbic father hell bent on kicking him up into 'C' grade student status.

Eventually, accepting failure in his pursuit of a hopeless cause, his father desisted from banging his head against a particularly dense wall and retreated to the cerebral comfort of the *Times* and *Guardian* crosswords.

Although submerged Arnold's desire was not entirely sunk. It could still, on occasion, be detected just below the surface, like a little black tiddler sometimes glimpsed, sometimes hidden against a shimmering background of pebbles and moss. And then, one day: 'I want to be a doctor.' His father, startled, had put down his *Guardian* and said: 'What was that?'

'I want to be a doctor,' Arnold repeated.

Roger Smith, a partner in the accountancy firm of Cadwalader, Plantaganet and Smith had reluctantly come to the conclusion that his only child would never follow him into the firm. The boy was, not to put too fine a point on it – thick. He had, with costly private tuition, scraped a few poor O' Level grades and was currently in between casual jobs.

Although he had heard his son express the wish to become a doctor before, he had never taken it as anything other than a passing fancy, like being a pop star, a fireman or a bus driver.

'He wants to be a doctor,' Roger had said to his wife. 'Do you think it's possible – bearing in mind he's thick as pig shit?'

'He's not as thick as . . . as what you said! He's just sensitive,' she had replied indignantly. So Roger had capitulated and Arnold; with some judicious string pulling was shoehorned into a trainee nurse position at the local hospital.

'It won't last,' Roger had mused to him self. 'But at least the thickey and his mother can't say I didn't do my bit.'

And he was right. Within six months his mother's darling had been politely asked to bugger off due to incompetence, rapidly failing eyesight and a tendency to pester student nurses to strip off for examinations.

As the years (and his parents) passed, Arnold, now relatively comfortably well off, still harboured his cherished dream. He bought a stethoscope, a white coat, a medical skeleton (Hubert) and a doctor's bag that he stuffed with bandages, plasters and an amazing variety, shape and colour of pills and capsules.

He took to roaming the streets in the hope of chancing upon a major disaster, a car crash, or someone not feeling too well. Eventually, frustrated, he fell into depression; which, considering his particular calling was not such a bad thing, as he was then able to prescribe himself a bumper assortment of pills from a stock that he had built up over time.

Unfortunately this mega dosage, and its affect on an already dodgy persona, soon resulted in an appearance at a magistrate's court where he was charged with lewd and lascivious behaviour for asking a checkout girl in Asda to get her tits out so he could give them the once over.

'I'm a doctor!' He had screamed as they took him away.

It was while he was at court that he bumped (literally) into Zelda. She had just been fined £25 for soliciting outside Fong's chippy, and as she left the courtroom he cannoned into her on his way in. He had doffed his trilby and apologised profusely and something in his middle class manner had prompted her to make her way back to sit in the public gallery.

Arnold's actions at the Asda supermarket had resulted in a £50 fine and in a firm direction from the chief magistrate that he seek psychiatric help to address his problem.

'Ah,' Zelda had muttered from her seat in the public gallery, as the soft delicious crinkle of folding money rustled in the air above her head.

As he left the courtroom Zelda had donned a sympathetic look and buttonholed him.

'I'm SISTER Zelda O'Flerhity.' she had said, 'and I can't believe how awful they were in there to you.' He was delighted with her support.

'DOCTOR Arnold Smith at your service sister,' he had replied doffing his trilby for the second time that day. Zelda had inclined her head demurely.

'My,' she had cooed, 'how very nice to see that there are still some gentlemen left in the world.' Doctor Smith had performed a little bow and gallantly said: 'Perhaps, Sister, you would do me the honour of sharing a pot of tea and a cream bun?' With his poor eyesight her shark like smile had failed to register beyond the surface level of good manners as she accepted his offer of refreshments.

Nine months and sixteen sessions of doctors and Nurses later, his libido had risen in inverse proportion to his bank balance.

'Still,' he often mused to Hubert of an evening as they sat around the dining table, 'you can't take it with you can you? And when all's said and done it is going towards a good cause – the easing of pain and suffering.' Although Hubert was never very forthcoming with a response, his demeanour at least never gave Arnold any reason to believe that his companion did not hold with his view.

As he paid off the taxi driver outside Fort Beswick flats he glanced up at the second storey.

'Oh yes, it's worth every penny,' he said brightly as he made his way cautiously over the road towards the stairwell entrance.

On his way he passed a bright yellow *Manchester Evening News* placard outside a Newsagents/Off-Licence that proclaimed in large bold black letters: **Lesbian Lovers Naked Death Leap**. He couldn't make out the wording, so he did not stop to try and read it.

He now used a white walking stick, although he wasn't blind – not quite. Granted, he did, on occasion, stop to ask directions of the odd lamppost – and he had been known to doff his trilby to a shop dummy or two; but he still knew a pretty face when he peered into one, and Zelda, he knew, was a peach. She had lovely blond hair, limpid grey-blue eyes, creamy skin and a figure to stop a charging rhino in its tracks. And she was the best (and to be honest the only) theatre sister he'd ever had . . . in any/every sense of the word.

His heart began to beat faster as he fumbled his way up the dingy stairs to the second floor landing and tap tapped his way to the third door on the right. There, through his bottle bottomed

glasses he peered up and with a slightly

trembling finger, traced the white plastic numbers 2...0...3. He smiled and knocked.

'Doctor! Right on time as usual,' said blue-clad Sister Zelda. 'Do come in.' Mr Smith smiled broadly as he entered.

'Thank you sister, you're very kind. And may I compliment you on your usual immaculate turnout,' he said to the coat stand in the corner. Zelda inclined her head modestly and ushered him along the hall and towards a door that had a white card with the words Operating Theatre in red biro tacked to it by a rusty drawing pin.

'This way doctor.' She opened the door and standing slightly to one side, stuck out her scrawny chest as he squeezed past.

'If you'd like to check the instruments doctor, I'll go and see if the patient is ready.' She indicated a small white tea-towell covered table.

Mr Smith smiled and ran his hands lovingly over the 'instruments': a thermometer, two stainless steel balti dishes – one containing a weak solution of water and Domestos – the other water and Fairy liquid, a quantity of vari-coloured pills (Smarties) on a saucer, a wooden spatula, a folded face cloth, a small hand towel, a steak knife (and fork), a pair of canary yellow Marrigold gloves – and a sinister looking orange rubber tube with large attached bulb.

Satisfied, he nodded and unbuttoned and removed his raincoat, revealing a crumpled white medical jacket with a well-worn stethoscope sprouting from its top pocket.

Squeak, squeak, went the wine trolley as Sister Zelda pushed it towards the operating room door.

'Shit, shit,' muttered Davey under the bath towel.

'He's ready for you doctor,' Sister Zelda sang.

'Like fuk,' Davey Muttered.

'Shurrup!'

'Right Sister, wheel him in if you will.'

Zelda rammed the door open with Davey's head and pushed the trolley into the centre of the room.

'Right,' said Mr Smith rubbing his hands together, 'what have we here then sister?'

'Bad car crash doctor . . . lost 'is arm, you treated 'im last time you were 'ere.'

'Did I?'

'Yes indeed doctor.' Arnold's face lit up.

'Ah! complications!' He savoured the word as one would a glass of vintage port wine. Zelda nodded.

'Fraid so doctor. Looks like you must work your magic again!'

'Not magic sister – just pure skill and application,' said Mr Smith pulling on his Marrigolds with a dramatic flourish.

'So modest . . .' Zelda simpered.

'Yuk!' Davey mouthed from under the towel.

'Ah! He's awake is he?'

'Yes doctor, I thought it best not to sedate 'im in case you wanted to ask 'im any questions.'

'Quite right sister . . . quite right – let's have a look at him then.' Zelda whipped the bath towel off, to reveal a naked Davey.

'Hmmm. Arm seems to be doing quite nicely . . . penis seems rather swollen though . . .'

'Yes. But that's not really the problem doctor.' Mr Smith frowned lightly and leaned closer to peer into the face of his patient.

'No? What is then?'

'Constipation doctor. Con-sti-pation,' she repeated slowly, looking down with a tight smile into Davey's anxiety filled eyes. He groaned and the doctor's face lit up with anticipation. Here was a poor soul in desperate need of his ministrations.

'Ah yes!' said the doctor, 'I can see it's giving him some pain.'

'Yes doctor, a right pain in the ar . . . posterior.'

'Well then,' said Mr Smith rubbing his rubber-clad hands together, 'we'll soon sort that out – but first let's check his arm again shall we . . .' Zelda simpered: 'You know best doctor.'

'Right then young man,' said the doctor, slopping the face cloth into the dish of disinfectant. 'Let's kill those nasty germs first.' Davey sighed and proffered his stump, which was duly soaked, dried, patted and prodded – to the accompaniment of several professional 'hhmmms' and knowing nods.

'Right then, seems to be healing quite nicely,' said the doctor, pushing his glasses firmly up onto the bridge of his nose.

'Should be,' Davey muttered. 'Twenty odd bleedin years to 'eal.' Zelda jabbed a spear-tipped finger into his ribs.

'Oww! That 'urt that!'

'What did!' said Mr Smith eagerly.

'Nuffin! Nuffin! It was jus a likkul twinge. Must be me gettin old or sumfin,' Davey said quickly.

'Ahh. Yes indeed, the relentless march of Old Father Time. Comes to us all sooner or later I'm afraid. Still,' he added, 'I can help you there. These tablets will do the trick. Take two red, two green and three orange, four times a day,' he said, struggling to pick up the saucer with his gloved hand.

''Ere, let me 'elp you doctor,' cooed Zelda, picking up the saucer and tipping the assorted pills into her nurses uniform pocket.

'I'll see 'ee takes them later – as prescribed.'

'Good. Good. Now then,' he said clipping the stethoscope to his ears, 'heart first then lungs.'

After much 'hmming' and nodding, he declared himself reasonably satisfied with his examination.

'Little bit chesty though. Does the patient smoke sister?'

'Yes doctor; always nickin me fags the minute me back is turned.'

'Ahhh. Better check his throat while we're at it then. Say Ahhh,' he demanded, picking up the wide bladed spatula and advancing with intent. Davey clamped his teeth together.

'Nnngghh.'

'No. Ahhh.'

'Nnnnggh.'

'Allow me doctor,' said Zelda reaching for Davey's testicles.

'AAAHHH!' then 'UUURRKK!'

'That's better,' said the doctor as he rammed the spatula between Davey's teeth and levered his jaw down.

'Such a fuss my lad; for your own good you know,' he said pleasantly, peering myopically into the dark cavern.

'Hhmmm. Wiggly thing . . .'

'Epiglottis,' said Zelda.

'That's it. Looks a bit inflamed. Better give him an ice lolly – twice a day for three days.'

'Ice lolly; right you are doctor, twice a day for three days.'

'Well then, that's about it I think . . .' Zelda's thin lips creased slowly upwards.

'Not quite doctor. There's still the con-sti-pation.

Her smile widened as Davey's brow creased.

'Oh yes! Of course! Silly me!' said the good

doctor. 'What would I do without you sister!'

'Just doin me job doctor,' she replied, picking up the length of rubber tubing and slapping it firmly into his gloved hand. Davey groaned.

'Don't worry young man,' said Mr Smith picking up on his patient's obvious discomfort as he squeezed the bulb and inserted the tube into the dish of soapy water. 'We'll soon have you up and going. Right sister, onto his side . . . and knees drawn up . . . thank you that's fine.' Squeeze. Groan. Squeeze. Groan.

'All done. Now that didn't hurt did it?'

'Excuse me doctor . . .' (Wolfish grin).

'Yes sister?'

'The patient has very large bowels I'm afraid. I've got a bucketful out back. Won't be a tick . . .'

'My word!' Mr Smith marveled as the bucket emptied. 'He has got large bowels hasn't he!'

Zelda thrust out her breasts, and – to a protest of squeaking wheels and gurgling innards – she batted the wine trolley out of the way and sashayed over to his side.

'You know doctor,' she simpered, 'every time I see you operate I get all 'ot an bothered. I could put myself entirely in your 'ands . . . if you know what I mean . . .'

'Oh sister!' said the doctor, then: 'Honk Honk' as he gave her sagging breasts a double squeeze.

'Oh doctor!' Zelda gasped in pre-orgasmic

heaven, 'Take me now!'

'Yes! Yes!' said Doctor Smith through suddenly steamed up glasses, 'but what about the patient!'

'I'll take 'im to Recovery,' she said in a matter-of-fact voice.

In the loo that on Doctor Smith's visits doubled as Recovery, the patient sat on the pan and for some ten minutes and sourly popped the bubbles that floated up from between his legs with every watery fart.

'Bloody emena!' he moaned to the background accompaniment of a selection of personal gurgling noises and the muted sounds of carnal carryings-on.

'Must 'ave the cleanest guts in Manchister by now,' he muttered through clenched teeth.

As he waited for the sounds of fornication to die off, Davey, being Davey, allowed his thoughts to turn to a topic of intense personal interest – the night's big match.

'I'll want at least an extra two quid towards a meat pie an a Bovril fer this,' he muttered rebelliously, as he reached for the toilet paper, gingerly wiped his nether region, slid down from the throne, and gave the flushing lever a savage twist.

9

At the 'Theatre of Dreams' the chill early evening air throbbed with expectancy as 75,227 thumping hearts pumped blood to the Creature's 300,908 (almost) cold limbs. 75,227 heads bobbed and dipped. 75,227 mouths exhaled clouds of white mist, some of which (contrary to current no smoking regulations) was tinged blue-grey.

Although the Creature had separate parts of vastly differing ages, in its composite form it was as old as human history. It knew no death, no permanent home; but roamed the world on wings of fire, claiming all those who were receptive to its earthy but oh so exciting tongue.

Tonight it was Manchester. Tomorrow it might be Milan, Rome, Rio, Athens or Ankara. One thing though was constant; wherever it alit it held all, willing captives, until like some giant vampire gorged on the primal life force, it moved on to seek fresh meat leaving the separate parts of the creature to disperse into the night – tiny pinpricks of elation, despair, hope, dejection . . . simply human again.

One of those erstwhile pinpricks was becoming well and truly pissed off.

'Eh Ironside!' Davey shouted to the visiting wheelchair fan that blocked his view on the front row of the East Stand. 'Shift outter the way!' The fan – who appeared to be around Davey's age – without turning his attention from the match, stuck a rigid third digit in the air and slowly pumped it up and down twice.

'Bastard!' Davey shouted. 'I know what that means scouse gett!' Further protest was drowned out by a roar, followed by a groan, as a United breakaway brought a flying save out of the Liverpool keeper.

'Wot was it?' Davey yelled.

'Brill shot an a jammy save.' said Tommy. 'Nearly thtuffed one right up 'em!'

After the excitement, a quiet spell of midfield fencing, parry and riposte brought on the tribal songs of encouragement which ranged from the pugilistically primitive 'Build a bonfire, build a bonfire, build a bonfire on the Kop – put the City in the middle and the Scousers on the top', to the positively poetic ode to Monsieur Cantona: *'My eyes have seen the glory of the coming of The Gaul. My eyes have seen the glory of the passing of The Gaul. My eyes have seen the glory and the passing of The Gaul . . . but the Reds go marching ON . . . ON . . . ON!'* To which one increasingly irate voice added: 'My eyes can't see the passin of fuk all!' (Three pints of bitter topped up with 13 percent proof Gold Label barley wine – their usual tipple on the way to the match –often brought out the flippant or acerbic in him. Today it was very much the acerbic).

After several more partially obscured attacks and counters, DIMP was well alight.

'Right, that's it! He yelled to no one in particular.

'That's it I can't tek no more! I'm goin over the top!' The fact that he ducked under the railings and onto the running track was irrelevant – the spirit of the statement held good.

'Right you!' he shouted in the ear of the wheel chair fan, who, startled, turned to be confronted by a puce-faced little apparition.

'Are yuh goin ter move, or am I goin ter 'ave ter move you meself?' Regaining his composure, the visitor sneered:

'You'll need to get yer six brothers first . . . shortarse!' Davey bridled.

'Wot six bruvvers. I ant got six bruvvers . . . scouse gett!'

'Then go an fetch yer sister, Snow White!'

'An I ant got no sisters eever. Don't need no 'elp ter sort you out shit face!' Davey yelled, jumping up and down with rage.

'Go on piss off, before I give you a slap,' said the other, extending a muscular forearm in Davey's general direction.

'Right. That's it!' Davey screamed, as he lunged forward and landed a flying kick on the chair's wheel.

'Ehhh!' yelled the scouser, as he was tipped

over and dumped, tangled in his thick blanket, onto the running track.

'You Manchester bastard! I'm goin ter rip your bleedin 'ead off!'

'Yeah?' said Davey, looking down at the sprawled and legless (in the literal sense) figure. 'You'll 'ave ter get some legs first ter catch me!'

The Liverpool fan groped for his chair, tugged it upright and dragged him self back into the seat – just as Davey launched himself forward and attacked the chair by clamping his teeth onto a tyre.

'Gnnnrrr!' roared Davey as he savaged the rubber. Bang! went the tyre. 'Buuufft' went Davey's cheeks as his mouth was filled with stale air and the taste of rubber. 'Aarrgghh!' went the scouser as he wrapped a brawny arm around Davey's neck. 'Whooaa!' went the linesman, as, following the ball out of play, his feet became entangled in the woollen blanket and he pitched head first onto the cinder track and under the wheels of the chair.

Suddenly; in that vast cauldron of noise, a relative silence descended, as 75,227 pairs of eyes battened onto a bizarre tableau that was made up of a sprawling, unconscious linesman entangled in the wheels of an invalid chair, while the chair's owner, a double lower limb amputee, was apparently in the process of throttling a purple-faced one-armed dwarf.

A number of police and players, due to their relative closeness to the scene, were the first to react. A fiery Irish midfielder in the red of United raced across, closely followed by a beefy Liverpool defender. The two of them had just spent the last fifteen minutes kicking lumps out of each other and were nicely wound up to start with.

The crowd murmured in confusion; then roared as they smelt blood. 69,067 saw a brawny Liverpool scarfed supporter throttling the life out of a tiny United fan. 6,160 saw a poor wheelchair-bound cripple bravely fighting off a berserk attack from a rabid Man.United supporter.

The red clad Irishman, to 69,067 roars of approval and 6,160 boos, wrapped a thick forearm around the wheelchair fans neck.

'Drop him you scouse bastard!' he snarled. The scouse bastard dropped him – directly in the path of the charging white-clad defender who, not exactly renowned for his balletic poise or twinkle-toed dexterity, proceeded to leave muddy sized twelve boot marks all over the small figure's back in his single-minded determination to rescue the poor pool fan.

'Gerroff im you thick bark!' he roared.

'Twat!' shouted the Irishman, as a looping right- hander bounced off his closely shaved skull and his own straight left grazed a stubbled chin.

Phweeet! Phweeet! Phweeet! went the referee's whistle as, hand in shirt pocket, he raced over to administer instant red card justice.

Unfortunately for him, his approach was from

the rear of the Irishman who chose that instant to draw back his right for an exocet blinder.

Pheeet! Pheee– 'Awwk!' went the referee as a pebbly elbow smashed into his mouth, and the whistle – closely followed by two front teeth – was introduced to the back of his throat.

'Hel-pheee, Hel-pheee,' begged the suddenly horizontal referee to the darkening evening sky, as he blew his own personal full time on the match.

Davey, from his own position on the deck amid a forest of trampling feet, decided it was time to get out of it – *toot sweet*. He wormed his way through a minefield of legs and exploding oaths and with a little sigh of relief, slipped over the low concrete wall and into the crowd. He would have gotten away with it too, but for the fact that his disoriented escape had landed him slap bang in the middle of enemy territory.

'Oh shittt!' he yelled, as a forest of angry faces closed around him. He winced and squeezed his eyes shut as a heavy hand thumped down on his shoulder, only to be followed by the welcoming words:

'Right me lad . . . yer nicked.'

'All rise,' boomed the Clerk of the Court, as the three magistrates entered and took their seats on the raised dais.

The Chief Magistrate, a tall thin, grey-haired and pinched-faced man, looked over the top of his rimless glasses and regarded the two heads that barely poked over the lip of the Dock – then turned his attention to a sheaf of paper in front of him.

After a long minute's silence, broken only by the soft rustle of turning sheets, he looked up again, set his features sternly and addressed the two heads.

'You are charged,' he intoned, 'with causing an affray that contributed to several after-match examples of public disorder and a number of physical injuries. Included among which were an emergency operation to remove a metal whistle from the gullet of a match official.' Davey's arm shot into the air almost before the magistrate had stopped speaking

''Ee started it yer lordship . . . 'Ee gev me the finger!' The Senior Magistrate glared over his glasses.

'Silence there! You'll have your chance to speak later!' Having stamped his authority, he then turned to one of his younger colleagues and muttered: 'Finger? What does he mean, finger?'

'It's a provocative gesture designed to show one's disdain for another,' muttered the younger. 'One extends a third finger and jabs the air . . . so.' He performed the action under the bench and out of view. The Chief magistrate frowned.

'And its meaning?' The younger's cheeks coloured lightly and he cleared his throat before answering.

'Er . . . well, put crudely . . . up your arse . . .' he said in an embarrassed *sotto voce*.

'Ahh,' said the Senior Magistrate, nodding his head, 'I see.' And seeing, his mind drifted back some fifty odd years to a public school shower room where a strapping fifth-former had cornered a small fair haired fresher.

Yes, his memory supplied. *Banana Ffyffe-Farquhar . . . Big brute . . . but quite handsome with it if I remember rightly.*

'It's another one of those annoying Americanisms I'm afraid,' said the younger, interrupting the senior's train of thought

'What? Yes, well it would be wouldn't it,' retorted the senior. 'They all seem to be anally obsessed, with their constant referrals to 'ass' this and 'ass' that . . .'

The third magistrate, a middle-aged, pearl-bedecked, twin-setted woman with a tight blue rinse perm intervened.

'Nothing known for Terence William Albert Turner but;' she said, consulting a thin sheaf of paper in her hand, 'the other defendant, one David Ignatius Montgomery Parker . . . A spell in an Approved School and one . . . no, two, non-custodial sentences for receiving and one for handling stolen lead from a church roof.' The Senior Magistrate nodded and turned his fierce glare on the defendants' heads.

'Terence William Albert Turner, do you have

anything to say in your defence before we pass sentence?'

'What defence, we put free goals past you . . . scouse gett,' muttered the second head.

'Not really sir,' said the first head, after directing a withering glare at Head Number Two, 'except that this little berk,' he nodded towards the other head, 'tried to kick seven shades of shit out of me wheel chair.' The second head swivelled to face Head Number One.

'You gev me the finger first!' it shouted.

'Silence!' roared the Senior Magistrate, who then turned and consulted his colleagues briefly, before turning back towards the dock to address Head Number One.

'Terence William Albert Turner it would appear that although you were one of the main culprits in what developed into a dangerously incendiary public disorder disturbance, your actions – reprehensible though they were – were the result of a degree of provocation. Therefore you will pay a fine of £50 and are bound over for a period of 12 months. Any further breaches of the peace within this stipulated period will result in a custodial sentence. Do you understand?' T.W.A.T. nodded.

'Yes sir.'

'David Ignatius Montgomery Parker, have you anything to say in your defence before we pass sentence?'

Davey pursed his lips in thought.

'Well, 'ee called me shortarse your lordship . . . an 'ee tole me to fetch me sister, Snow White.' Head Number One swivelled in his direction.

'No I didn't. I told you to go an fetch yer six brothers . . . you little shit!'

'Silence! The senior magistrate yelled. He then turned and entered into a lengthy discussion with his fellow magistrates before once again addressing the heads in the dock.

'David Ignatius Montgomery Parker,' he intoned, 'you are not unknown to the Court, and it is our considered opinion that your actions contributed much to the sorry scenes of yesterday afternoon.

There could have easily been a large-scale riot as a result of your loutish behaviour. This court will not,' he snarled grimly, 'tolerate such behaviour, and will continue to do everything in its power to stamp out such antisocial actions.' He turned briefly to his fellows on the bench, who nodded gravely in agreement.

'One hundred pounds fine and thirty days in jail . . . suspended for one year.'

Davey groaned, then added wearily:

'Right, fanks yer lordship . . .' The Senior Magistrate briefly turned his eyes heavenwards and sighed lightly.

'Mr Parker,' he said tiredly, 'I am not a lord . . . a simple Sir will suffice . . .'

'Fank you . . . simple sir . . .'
'One hundred and fifty pounds!'
'Wot'd I say?' Wot'd I say?'

10

In the People's Dispensary for Sick Animals on Ordsal Lane in Salford, Penelope was happily humming 'how much is that doggie in the window,' when the phone rang insistently.

She waddled over to a desk cluttered with amongst the usual office paraphernalia, three kennel-shaped collection boxes, a stack of mini coasters depicting pictures of cute little kittens and a life-sized rubber chameleon – evidently used as a drawing pin cushion.

She batted the chameleon to one side and picked up the telephone receiver.

'Hello, People's Dispensary for Sick Animals,' she almost sang down the line. 'How may I help you? Yes. We are sometimes referred to as the Dog's Home . . . Yes I am afraid that it is sometimes necessary to put them to sleep . . . when the poor loves are very sick, or old, or injured . . . Pardon, what was that? You want to apply for the job of what? Well Really! We are not looking for an, executioner, as you put it! Our animals are humanely put to sleep by trained and dedicated professionals!'

A slight pause, then: 'How?' she said, with a rising tone of alarm and the beginnings of a tremor in her voice and treble chin. 'We give them a needle of course . . . What? NO WE MOST CERTAINLY DO NOT USE BASEBALL BATS! THE VERY IDEA! YOU . . . YOU . . . BEAST!' she cried, slamming the receiver down and dissolving into floods of tears.

Davey replaced the handset. He was bored. Grounded without a penny in his pocket and thanks to his court appearance, very much in Zelda's bad books. She'd hit the roof when he confessed to his night in the cells and the subsequent hefty fine.

'A 'undred and fifty quid!' she'd yelled. ''Ow in Mary's name are we gonna pay a 'undred and fifty bleedin quid!'

He certainly hadn't helped matters when he then suggested that it could be lumped in with her outstanding soliciting fines, and would just add up to another County Court Judgement and an extension to their current credit black list.

She'd given him a withering look, muttered 'my penance', and stormed off to an afternoon bingo session at *Clayton Conservative Club*.

So, now here he was . . . bored. If he'd had two thumbs he would have twiddled them. Instead, he shifted irritably on the settee and sighed.

'No money to go out; an a busted bleedin telly anall.' He glared at the dead box in the corner. The dead box stared back blankly.

'Must be sumfin to do ter pass the time,' he muttered to the silent room.

'Cud 'ave a read I suppose,' he mused to himself, eying an untidy clutch of papers and magazines sprouting from a bulging paper rack. He considered the idea for a moment, and then rejected it. Too much hassle holding and turning the pages with one hand. And anyway, his reading wasn't really very clever. He looked around the room, then said: 'I spy wiv my likkul eye . . . sumfin beginnin wiv . . . ruh. Yeah that's it, ruh fer radio!'

He slipped down from his seat, and made his way over to the dull, black plastic stacker system, resting under the window on a rickety MFI deluxe system support unit. He reached out and jabbed a finger at the On button. The deluxe system support unit threw a trembling fit, and then settled back into its usual state of imminent collapse, as tinny music assailed his ears.

'Crap,' he muttered, extending his finger and jabbing a tuning button. The deluxe system support unit quivered like a highly strung thoroughbred – quite a feat really, since it only cost 50 pence on a pub car boot sale – then stilled, as a soothing voice said:

'Welcome back to Your Life in Their Hands. This week Doctor Kilmoor has received an urgent plea from Russia, where the ailing President is seen to continually fall down. Russian doctors are baffled. Is it the Vodka? Or is it something altogether more serious? Perhaps even a deadly brain toomoor!' (Sound of balalaika music, followed by jet engines, ambulance sirens and car horns and a thickly accented Russian voice):

'Welcome Doctor Kilmoor. The Russian people are in your most capable hands.' (Doctor Kilmoor manages to insert a self-deprecating shrug into his Martha's Vineyard voice).

'My hands are a gift from God comrade doctor. I am . . . but a tool.'

The rough Russian voice is filled with admiration.

'But what a tool doctor . . . what a tool!'

'Enough!' said the good doctor, metaphorically rolling up his sleeves. 'My patient; is he ready?'

'Yes doctor; follow me to the theatre . . .' (Stirring music followed by the sounds of a respirator and the hypnotic pinging of a life support monitor).

'Wow!' said a well-impressed Davey. 'I 'ope 'ee can do the business, or 'oo knows, we might end up wiv world war free!'

(Sounds of ticking clock followed by slow, heavy music . . . followed by a nurse's voice):

'Your brow doctor, allow me . . .'

'Thank you nurse, that's much better. And

now . . . I'm going in . . . Saw!'

(Sharp buzzing noise that is then slowed and becomes quite laboured).

'Right nurse, you may now remove the cranium. Ahh, it's as I thought . . . a toomoor!'

(Heavy chords of music, followed by hushed tones of the Announcer):

'So, doctor Kilmoor's worst fears are realised. Can he save the desperately ill President; or will Russia be plunged into turmoil thru the toomoor? Tune in tomorrow for the next gripping installment of Your Life in Their Hands; brought to you by the makers of Moggymix the purrrfect treat for your purrrfect pet.' (Light jingle and fade out).

'Phew! Must remember to listen to that tomorrer,' said Davey as he jabbed the tuning button and the room was filled with the clippity-clop of hooves and western guitar music, followed by the creak of bat winged doors, a heavy measured tread and the jingle of spurs. The tinkling renderings from a tinny piano suddenly stop, as does a low hubbub of general conversation. A tremulous voice says:

'It's Pecos Pete . . . and he looks to be in an ornery mood!'

'That's right pardner I'm in an ornery mood all right. I'm lookin fer the dirty sidewinder that took liberties with missy Prissy the poor widder woman school teacher over by Hicksville.'

'Well then,' said a sneering oily voice, 'I

114

reckon you would be lookin fer me, Black Hat Bart from over by Rattler Creek . . .'

(Sound of several chairs being hurriedly drawn back). 'Yeahh!' shouted Davey, drawing a forefinger gun from his side and advancing on the radio with narrowed eyes.

'Reach fer yer iron Black Hat,' said a steely-voiced Pecos Pete.

'Yeah!' yelled Davey into the radio. 'Fill yer 'and you sonoffa bitch!' Two shots immediately rang out and were followed by an ominous thud as of a falling body.

'This should cover the cost of the funeral,' said Pecos Pete to the sound of several heavy coins being tossed onto wooden floorboards, the jingle of spurs and creak of bat-wing doors.

'Yeah, go an bury 'im deep up on gumboot 'ill!' snarled Davey, blowing the smoke from his finger gun as the tinny piano struck up again.

In the excitement he hadn't heard the door open and wasn't aware of Zelda regarding him with arms on hips and a sour prune expression on her face.

11

At Fifty-seven years of age, Father John James had encountered more crises of faith than Don King had had bad hair days. And he was having another one of them now. As he knelt at the side of the bed he closed his eyes and murmured: 'Forgive me Father for I know now what I do.'

He sighed lightly and concluded with a *'pater, et filius, et spiritu sancti* amen, before heaving himself to his feet, pulling back the duvet – and slipping into the hot and ample arms of Agnes, his faithful housekeeper.

Several hours – and if not a Cardinal sin, then at least a Bishop sin – later, he opened his eyes to a gentle sunbeam that dripped through the slightly drawn curtains, slid across the darkened room and disappeared into the gaping mouth of a snoring Agnes. 'Forgive me Father for I have sinned,' he murmured devoutly looking into the abyss.

Breakfast, as usual after his increasingly regular tumbles from grace, was a somewhat strained affair. Agnes, recognising his *mea culpa* mood kept her own council – apart from offering a muted 'good morning', as he slid into his seat at the breakfast table.

Later, and heavy with the guilt that always resulted from his capitulation to carnal cravings, he stumbled through the day, his mind only partly in gear. There was a visit to Clayton Drop-In Centre where he half-heartedly discussed the setting up of a bingo session for local pensioners.

He then called on a terminally ill parishioner to offer hollow words of comfort, and in the early afternoon he dropped in at the neighbouring St Annes, in Ancoats, where he went through the weekly ritual of tea and arrowroot biscuits with the borderline senile Father O'Malley. An apparently aimless conversation that covered among the usual trips down an assortment of memory lanes – the rights and wrongs of contraception, women Bishops in the Church of England and the efficacy or lack of it of Guinness brewed in England as opposed to its spiritual home in Ireland – finally concluded at four o'clock.

Ritual complete he said his farewells and after mouthing the usual 'see you next week' at the vestry door, he climbed into his car, pulled the door shut, sighed heavily, started up the engine and pulled off.

He turned left onto Every Street with the intention of taking the second right onto Ashton New Road, but instead, and almost of its own volition, his right hand pulled down on the steering wheel, and the car slid into the first right, dipping down onto Russell Street and a little oasis of green.

There, he braked, switched off the engine and climbed out.

This was the area where he had spent much of his childhood. He had passed it many times during the last couple of years as he had driven to and from his visits with Father O'Malley, and because his mind had usually been occupied with matters parochial, he had not given it much more than a fleeting thought or two.

Today, a slowly blossoming bud of nostalgia, perhaps fuelled by the old priest's innocent vocal meanderings had begun to insinuate itself into the dark undergrowth of his troubled mind.

The area, bordered by Every Street on one side and the *River Medlock* on another, had once been a little bustling island of life. There were the two hundred-yard long three storey flats of Ledge Avenue and Star Avenue.

There was Tetlow Street, cobbled Taunton Street and Taunton Street flats, Broxstead Street and Morris Road.

There was Titley's Corner Shop and Barnett's Chip Shop, where as a kid he used to queue for six pennoth of chips and a buttered barmcake for his dinner on his way home from St Anne's boys school at just gone noon.

There were three green-clad two-armed gas lampposts stiffly to attention, sentinels against the night and nighttime fears.

There was Russell Street playground with its

rickety swings and creaking roundabouts. And there was the cinder croft, legacy of a German bomb, where he and the other kids had stripped off coats or jerseys to use as goal posts and played football for hours on end until dusk descended about their sweating heads.

And now? Now there was nothing. Not a cobble . . . not a slate . . . not a brick . . . not a nail. Nothing. It was as if several generations had sunk beneath the coarse grass to lie dreaming for all eternity beneath a blanket of indifference.

He smiled thinly then sighed again. All those houses, he thought. All those houses, all those people tucked into such a tight little space. And when he thought of the people, he thought of the girls.

He thought of Charmaine Stewart, Margaret Hampson, Hannah Crowther, Maureen Jones, Elsie Cunningham and Hazel Bather.

The brief relationships, between the ages of seven and 17, marked by degrees of intensity, from the pre-hormonal platonic, to the heavy breathing, clumsy fumbling, not quite so innocent.

They were all still there in his memory banks, their girlish forms and sweet faces frozen in time. Each one of them had, he realised, contributed a silver or gold thread that was permanently woven into the plainer fabric of his distant youth. *Odd*, he thought, *how I remember them so well, while the boys I knew are mostly just blurred images in black and white. Then again*, he added mentally, *perhaps it's not so odd at all. Perhaps the attraction to the female of the species had always been there.*

With a slight sense of shock he realised that he could have ended up loving any one of them and if any one of those embryonic relationships had developed into a full-blown romance he almost certainly would not have set foot upon the path that had ultimately led to Church and God. *It was there all the time*, he thought. *Why did I deny it? Why did I push it aside? Why did I choose the Seminary instead of the local Palais?*

He shook his head to dislodge the insidious thoughts and drag himself back to the here and now. 'When was I here last?' He muttered. 'Ah yes': The last time he had been here was some five years ago. A time when his faith still held firm, and when the seeds of doubt were many seasons away from germination.

He had pulled up to witness the demolition of Taunton Street. He had sat quietly in his car and watched as they killed his little piece of Ancoats. Their metal monster, impatient for the carnage, had roared and panted, polluting the crisp clean autumn air with the stench of its blue-black breath. Unleashed, it had trundled forward to pounce upon its victim.

Yes, he remembered now. The terraced row had sat forlorn, neglected, dejected. He saw again the steel ball, heavy, thick, uncaring, as it hovered above the head of Number 1.

He remembered he had winced as it came crashing down. The metal monster had then coughed and wheezed as it retrieved its bludgeon for another blow. He had half expected to see gouts of warm red blood spurt from the savage wound. Instead, just broken, splintered ribs and a weary groan. The house was dead.

The monster had pounced again and again, chuckling with each crushing blow. The victim's insides were now laid bare for all to see. Obscene, unnatural, for it was not meant to be. Faded flowered wallpaper, layers thick, flapping in the breeze. Nervous twitch of something newly dead.

From the cocoon that was his car he had watched for most of the day.

Watched in isolation as the metal beast bit, crushed, tore and gobbled up a hundred years of life. He had seen the crown-topped Victorian chimney pots tumble with slow dignity beneath the New Elizabethan hammer. He had watched until it had come the turn of Number 33 – the last house in the street. The house that nestled next to the high brick wall that separated it from a twenty-foot drop to the turgid foam-flecked litter-choked waters of the *River Medlock*.

The house that was most important to him. It was the house where he had spent some early years, his Nana and Granddad's house.

She was a large forever aproned woman with

peach soft, if finely wrinkled skin, who was famed throughout the family for her home made seventy percent proof Christmas puddings. Puddings that were concocted in a zinc tub, mixed with a large wooden ladle, and sprinkled sparingly with silver sixpences, before being wrapped in white muslin cloth then tied with string ready for distribution.

He, like quite a few in yesteryear Ancoats, was second generation Italian. He had once had his own little ice cream business, where he used to tour the streets in his horse drawn wagon selling cornets, wafers and halfpenny lollies.

Later, not long before he died from bowel cancer, he moved on to work for Jimmy Street's Removal Company, where he often brought home furniture and bits and pieces left behind by customers. There was a hulking solid oak brass handled Dresser with bowed drawers and a huge mirror that many years later was shipped over to Australia by one of the far flung cousins (who turned down an offer of several thousand dollars from a dealer for it).

There was a pair of delicate pale green translucent china lidded urns with orchard scenes that showed a pair of young lovers reclining languidly beneath the boughs of an apple tree. And there was the dark mahogany upright piano that nobody knew how to play, that, cringingly un-tuned, sat for years in the front parlour.

He was always, it seemed, white-shirted,

starch-collared, waist-coated, with a gold Albert chain and pocket watch; a watch that seemed the size of half a crown in his huge gnarled hands.

Yes, his Nana and Grandad's house. A house always ringing to the shouts and laughter of many cousins, grown now and scattered like dandelion seeds to the four winds. A house that had been a home while his father worked away and his mother held down a full time job at Stevenson's Box Works then later at Ferranti's – where a heavy knock against a piece of plant had kick started breast cancer that later spread.

He had shut his eyes, and once again had seen the patterned cracks on the flaking plaster of his bedroom ceiling dancing in the flickering glow cast by the gently sighing gas lamp that stood guard outside his window. He heard again the heavy official knocking in the dead of night. His father's calm voice muted from below accepting the news from Ancoats Hospital. His mam had gone. Crushing; even though half expected.

He heard the slow heavy footsteps on the stairs. He saw the shadowy figure at the foot of his bed, heard the soft words 'your mam's gone' – then heard again his own reply of 'yes, I know.'

Then, five years or so ago, he had turned around and left, left a little part of who he was lying in the dust. Now he turned around, climbed back behind the wheel and left, left behind nothing – for he realised that who he was then all those many years gone by bore very little, or no relation, to who he was now.

12

Davey studied the black zig-zag of the kneeling Zelda's hair roots with casual disinterest as she tied double bows in his trainers' laces.

'There,' she grunted rising to her feet and stepping back a pace, eyed him up critically. She took in the United socks (folded over four times), the baggy (below the knee) white shorts, the iridescent goalie's jersey (to fit an eight year old – with the left arm neatly folded and pinned to the chest), and his lucky flat cap flopping over his ears and almost into his eyes.

As she looked at him she felt a momentary feeling of, what? Motherly tenderness? Annoyed with herself for allowing such an alien emotion to slip into her head, she said a little over-harshly, as she handed him his sports bag containing his civvies: 'Right, that'll do. Piss off – and be back for half eight. We're on at nine tonight.' Davey nodded obediently. He was on his best behaviour.

As the door closed behind him she shook her head, sighed deeply and repeated the personal mantra that she had come to accept as the embodiment of a price she had to pay for a dissolute and very sinful life. 'My penance, when will it ever end,' she murmured.

Ten Acres Lane sports hall was packed out for the East Manchester five-a-side knock-outs, with teams from 32 pubs battling it out for the right to take on the cream of South Manchester in the All-Manchester final at the *G-Mex Exhibition Centre*.

In their changing room Davey sat quietly in one corner and studied his team mates. They were a good bunch of lads, in fact, with his mam gone and his brother Arthur thousands of miles away in Canada they were the closest things he had to family.

He wasn't a sentimental person but he felt a little warm glow in the pit of his stomach as he listened to the banter – Tommy taking the piss out of Billy's knobbly knees and Billy replying that if the ginger streak of piss didn't shut it he would 'rip is ed off and gob down is froat.'

Yes they were good lads. Black haired pug nosed Billy was 'ard as nails' and had a temper that had landed him in Strangeways nick once – but he was sound as a pound when it came to mates. If you ever found yourself in a tight corner, then Billy was the man to have at your side, no messin.

Tommy and him went back the furthest. His own disability and Tommy's speech impediment had somehow laid the foundations for a mutual friendship. They had shared good times (a few) over the years and plenty of shit times. You knew where you were with Tommy.

Davey glanced across at Curtley and Fred, who were passing a ball back and forward between them. Curtley had moved into Beswick when he was eight or nine. His mam and dad were from Barbados and even now, after all these years she still dressed in bright West Indian clothes and spoke with an Island lilt. Curtley had partnered 'out of colour' a couple of years ago and he and his 'wife' Donna had a gorgeous little coffee coloured angel, Millie, who Davey always made a big fuss of whenever he went round to their flat.

Fred was a newcomer. The other lads were wary of him at first because He didn't fit the East Manchester identikit. He was decidedly middle class, and had never dropped an 'aitch' in his life. He was a bit of a brainy bastard with a dry turn of wit that sometimes, in the early days especially, almost got him into bovver – mostly with Billy, who usually spoke and thought in plain no nonsense black and white.

The little man's warm thoughts were interrupted as Fred suddenly picked up the ball that he and Curtley had been playing with and said:

'Right lads listen up . . . we can piss this lot. Brunswick Bruisers! More like Brunswick Bum Boys!'

'Yeth!' we're Bethick Redths!' shouted Tommy.

'Yo!' said Curtley.

'Reds rule!' screamed berserker Billy.

'Kick arse an gimme five!' yelled Davey, slipping to his feet and bending over for the ritual kick up the bum followed by a not very high five.

'Game plan,' said Fred earnestly. 'Get the ball up quick to Curtley. Billy, you chop the bastards whenever you get the chance. Davey you get your kite or anything else you can in front of everything.'

Tactics sorted they filed out to face their destiny.

'Here we are then,' boomed the MC into his microphone. 'Thirty-two teams started. Two are left. So let's hear it for the *Queen Vic's* Bessswick Redzzzs and the Brrrrunswick Brrruiserzzzs!'

The general polite applause was amplified in two small tightly packed pockets of fan fervour. Tightly packed that is, except for the Reds section, where a very large balaclava clad man in a navy blue overcoat sat in the middle of a little oasis of space.

'Bury em *Brunswick*!' yelled the Bruiser's fans. The Bruisers grinned and pumped their fists up and down. The Reds – to shouts of 'Leave em dead Reds!' – lined up in front of their fans and with a show of cool confidence that wiped the grins off the Bruiser's faces, bowed stylishly. One-nil to the Reds before the game had even kicked off.

Five seconds after kick-off, *Brunswick's* tricky star player found himself on his back looking up at a bright little constellation of stars that danced prettily among the floodlights on the high ceiling – as Billy the Red, with a look of angelic innocence on his face back-pedalled into his own half. 'Tweet', foul.

Five minutes and three 'tweets' later, Tricky hobbled off to be replaced by a nervous looking sub.

The game ebbed and flowed. To the groans of the Red's contingent, Curtley missed his three customary early sitters, while the Bruiser's fans cursed as Davey managed to get various parts of his anatomy in front of a similar number of shots.

Half time came and went with the game scoreless, as did most of the second half. Then breakthrough: Curtley fluked one off his shin, and the reds were in front. And so it stayed – until with seconds to go Tommy of the gangly legs brought a Bruiser down in front of goal. 'Tweet' penalty.

'Yeeahhh!' screamed the Bruiser contingent.

'Aaarrghh Shit!' moaned the Reds fans (with the exception of the big man in the balaclava, who had been warned by his mother about using foul language).

Davey's eyes narrowed under the floppy brim of his lucky cap. He rose slightly onto the balls of his feet, toes spread for purchase, ready to spring into action.

This was it. One-Nil to the Beswick Reds, seconds away from the whistle – and a place in the final. His enemy took two steps back behind the ball, all the time locking into cold eye contact and smiling thinly, dismissively.

Under the cap, Davey, body pulsing up and down like a spider ready to pounce, smiled back. The enemy broke eye contact to glance at the referee. The referee gave the okay and – 'thwack', the ball flashed towards the corner of the net on Davey's armless side (t'was ever thus).

He sprang. Missile and anti-missile missile merged with an explosive face to straining face meaty 'spplatt'. The ball cannoned out of play, the referee blew his whistle and a tiny prone figure with blood gushing from its nose, was jumped upon by four berserker red-shirted madmen, while the little Reds contingent yelled 'DIMP...imp! DIMP...imp! DIMP...imp!' In glorious unison – but for one slightly out of sync, excited bass voice, that lagged a little behind the rest.

Back in the flat Zelda studied the swollen red nose with the same level of casual disinterest that Davey had shown earlier when he had managed to extricate himself from under a pile of bodies.

'It's no big deal,' he had muttered, 'it's me job.'

'See you've bin usein yer 'ead agen Van der Saar.' Davey sighed lightly.

''Eees not bin our goalie fer yonks now,' he said patiently – as one does when discussing football with the non-interested female of the species.

129

'Whatever,' she muttered, with a shrug. He was not to be put off.

'Anyway. Yeah, you shuuda seen it. It was brill!' She stifled a yawn. He didn't notice.

'One-nil, almost time, an what do yuh fink 'appened?' She shook her head slowly.

'You know what, I really can't imagine.'

'That daft Tommy only gives away a bloody penalty, that's what!'

'Really'

'Yeah!'

'Right. An oh, by the way, talkin of blood . . .' Davey frowned (sudden changes of tack always threw him).

'What?'

'I'm sick of puttin yer jersey in cold soak. Why don't you get a red one, save me some work?' Davey gave her a look that men reserve for women who ask daft questions relating to the people's game.

'Can't wear a red jersey.'

'Why not?'

'Cos . . . Cos goalies as ter wear green . . . or, or, jazzy jerseys . . .Fought everyone knew that . . .'

She shrugged her thin shoulders, effectively consigning the topic to history and donned her school marm voice.

'Right, come on then. If we're late agen Mr Mason will do is bleedin nut.' Davey scowled. He did not like 'Mr Mason' one little bit. Nobody did.

Not even, Davey suspected, Mrs Mason. In fact, if nudged he would go so far as to say that Charlie Mason was a 24 carat gold-plated twat.

''Ee's a pratt. 'Ee's allus callin me names.'

'Mebee so,' said Zelda evenly, 'but 'ee's the pratt that pays us wages. So come on, shift yer arse.'

She had known Charlie Mason, in a business sense, for a number of years. Baby oil and hand relief was his bag. And it took him ages! Ninety-nine change hands wasn't in it! Still, it was a small price to pay for three nights a week work behind the bar at his club. And she'd even managed to twist his member into taking on Davey as a pot collector.

Quite an achievement that she often thought bearing in mind the little berk's situation...

13

Patronised in the main by prostitutes, pimps, pushers, piss and smack heads – plus the odd party of a stag or hen persuasion, and sandwiched between the *Aphrodite Adult Sex Shop and Mullett's Funeral Parlour* (known locally as the Fish and Stiff shop), the *Blue Cockatoo* was not the most salubrious of establishments.

The decor was Curry House Red Flock. The lighting was dim (in keeping with the bulk of the clientèle) and the ambiance was reminiscent of a Moss Side Shebeen – all dark suspicion with undertones of 'who you lookin at?'

At the moment, about half of the thirty or so customers were looking at Miss Pussy Galore, Exotic Dancer (and Sidney), in action on the first of a three night stint. Interest ranged from the casual to the under-the-table-rapid wrist action-glazed eyed riveted. She was a big girl. And Sidney was a big snake.

Behind the bar Zelda broke off from polishing glasses and nodded towards the stage where Pussy was entering into a particularly suggestive bump and grind sequence.

'She's a big girl,' Zelda opined. Mr Mason wiped the back of a pudgy paw across his mouth.

'Do you know how to make five pounds of ugly fat look attractive Zelda?' he asked, not taking his eyes off the performance on stage.

'No Mr Mason, how do you make five pounds of ugly fat look attractive?' she said dutifully to the side of his head.

'You stick a bleedin nipple on it!' She chuckled obediently while thinking *Oh oh! Ee's gettin 'orny. Looks like it's late away again tonight*. Meanwhile on his rounds to collect empty pots and glasses, Davey glanced back towards the bar and checked the clock. Ten-twenty five.

"Ee'l be goin ter the bog in five minutes,' he muttered to himself. And he was right. Davey knew that Charlie Mason was a bully, a blusterer, a grease ball, and a philanderer. He also knew that Charlie Mason loved to pontificate, loved to preach to all and sundry on one of his pet topics.

It might be the need to cram every 'coon' onto a leaking banana boat and send em back where they came from. It might be sympathy for any 'pakie' bashers, coz after all everyone knew that pakies were into raping white women, so a good bashin was well called for whenever the opportunity arose. He was also a self-proclaimed expert on bodily functions.

'Every night at ten-thirty I 'ave a crap,' was one of his standard conversational gambits – regardless of the level of company present. 'A good dump,' he would usually add, 'clears the 'ead an 'elps you to get a good nights kip.'

Davey made his way casually over to the bar, reached up, placed the two empty pots on the counter and slipped off smartly to the staff toilets. Inside, he quickly removed a small wad of tissue paper from a pocket and placed it gently between his lips as he lifted the toilet seat.

He laid the tissue on the cracked porcelain bowl and gingerly lowered the seat until it rested lightly on the package. Satisfied, he nodded.

'Right pratt! Let's see what you fink of that

then!' he muttered, as he backed out of the cubicle, pulled the door shut and returned to his pot collecting duties.

At ten-thirty one Mr Mason snapped on the engaged sign, dropped his trousers, slid his underpants to his knees and plonked his flabby posterior onto the seat. He didn't hear the tiny tissue wrapped glass capsule shatter.

'Like a submarine down a slipway.' he grunted, as he launched a number two.

At ten-thirty six Davey was humming a little tune to himself, as a red-faced Mr Mason returned to the bar.

'You all right Mr Mason, you look a bit flushed?' Zelda asked, feigning interest.

'Me guts, must be a bit off or somefin,' he said as he moved down the bar and poured himself a glass of soda water.

As he passed by clutching three empty pots, Davey caught the response.

'Yeah, an they'll be off termorrer an Sundee night anall,' he chuckled to himself.

'What you chunnerin on at?' said Zelda suspiciously.

'Nuffin. Nuffin at all,' he replied, his face a picture of innocence. She was not convinced.

'Yer up to sumfin you likkul gett. I can tell.' Davey scuttled away.

A relatively appreciative audience clapped – mostly with two hands – as Miss Pussy Galore and

Sidney exited stage right and made their way to the backstage changing room.

Cabaret over, the *Blue Cockatoo* clientèle reverted to type; the pissheads drank studiously, the pushers whispered sweet somethings to the shitheads and the hookers made eyes at anything that was not comatose.

'Liked yer act,' Zelda said pleasantly later to Pussy, who was perched on a high stool on the other side of the bar.

'Thanks,' said Pussy. 'Your boss must have liked it too; he's asked me back in a couple of weeks.'

'Did he? When did he say that then?'

'Oh he came into the dressing room a few minutes ago . . . when I was changing.' Zelda frowned.

'You want to watch out fer 'im you know.' Pussy's pencilled eyebrows rose a millimetre.

'Thanks, I will,' she said, as she sipped delicately at the straw in her glass of coke.

'Yer not from round 'ere are you?'

'No. I'm from Alsager.'

'That's a fair way; you goin back tonight?'

'I was going to, but Mr Mason offered me a room at his place for the night.' Zelda frowned again as she studied Pussy's face. Not much goin on in there, looks like all er assets are crammed into that 40 Double D cup, she thought. Still, she seemed a decent enough kid.

135

'Look, you don't really want to do that . . . 'ee's a pig.' Pussy's eyebrows rose again and her blue eyes opened wider.

'But I thought he was married . . .'

''Ee is, but they 'ave separate bedrooms . . . so I 'ear.'

'Oh.'

'Look, I tell you what, why don't you kip down at my flat. There's a spare bedroom.'

'You sure?'

'Course, no problem.' Pussy grinned.

'Great, I'll jus–' she broke off suddenly and glanced down quickly.

'Sidney! You get back in your bag you naughty boy!' Zelda leaned over the bar, cautiously.

'It's the zip. It's broken,' said Pussy apologetically, sliding off her stool and pushing a half emergent Sidney back into the well-worn holdall at her feet.

'Is 'ee dangerous?' said Zelda warily.

'Dangerous? No he's a big softee really. He's just nosy . . . wants to know what's goin on . . . don't you baby?' she cooed.

Back in the flat, Davey, as he glanced down warily at the holdall, was not a happy chappy.

'What if it gets 'ungry in the night an goes lookin fer a snack?'

'Don't be daft,' Zelda sneered. 'it don't eat people . . . does it?' she asked with a hint of interest in her voice. Pussy smiled and shook her head.

'Course not. He likes chicken pate', I mould it into little mouse shapes for him.'

'Yeah. Well it's all right fer you two, yer big . . . an that bag is bust!' said Davey, unconvinced. Zelda got to her feet and without a word left the room. A few seconds later she came back in carrying a large red holdall.

'You can put 'im in this. It's got a strong zip.' Davey did a quick double-take and bridled.

'That's me United bag!'

'So? 'Ee's not goin ter run off with it is 'ee?'

'No, but . . .'

'An you don't want 'im slivverin around in the night do you?' Davey looked down at his treasured bag, then across at the battered green holdall where, through the busted zip, a large triangular head sporting cold black eyes seemed to be studying him with hungry intent.

'I'm goin ter bed,' he mumbled, 'an make sure you close the door proper when you come in.'

Pussy's name, it transpired, was Sharron. She lived with her mother, who was looking after her one-year old son, Leonardo, while Sharron was on the road. Leonardo's dad had done a runner and left her up to her 40DD's in debt.

'He's a bastard!' said Sharron.

'Aren't they all!' Zelda said with feeling.

Next day: 'No way! That dirty arse fings not stayin; it crapped in me bag last night!'

Zelda was adamant.

'Yes it does. Sharron's got a coupla days hostess work in a Blackpool casino next week . . . an they don't let snakes in; not unless they're the two-legged kind, with plenty of dosh.' The wit was wasted as it sailed over his head .

'She can tek it 'ome an let 'er mam look after it.'

'Can't. 'Er mam's allergic to it.' Davey snorted.

'Oh aye. I'll bet she is.' Zelda was being Zelda and definitely having none of it.

'I've told 'er I'll look after it. It'll be some decent company fer me fer a change.' Davey tried one last tack.

'Me bag. We've got trainin on Mundee. I need it fer me kit!'

'You can take Sidney's old bag.'

'That rotten old fing!'

Zelda sighed.

'Look don't argue. She's a decent kid, she needs a break.'

''Ark at you, all nice an kind . . . '

'What!'

'Nuffin . . . I woz jus sayin . . .'

Saturday night, 10:25 pm – and Davey was in a bad mood. He put two little tissue-wrapped parcels under the toilet seat.

Ten-thirty five pm:

'You not feelin too good Mr Mason?'

'Me guts again,' he whined, mopping a florid face with a large more or less white handkerchief. 'Can't understand it. I'll 'ave ter get ter the quacks on Monday mornin. Smells like sumfin crawled up me jaxie and bleedin died . . .'

Sunday night: 10:35 pm.

'No better Mr Mason?'

'No. I'm definitely goin ter the quacks in the mornin. I'll probably end up 'avin to 'ave an internal and a bloody barium enema an a bastard x-ray!' he whinged pathetically. Zelda seized the opportunity.

'Do you want me to stay on tonight?'

'No. I'm not in any mood fer it; you piss off when we shut up shop.'

His ill humour was not improved an hour later when Pussy came on for her final stint. He had had plans for her, and now it was too late – even if he could get her on her own.

'Bleedin guts!' he moaned to himself.

Up on the stage the taped bump and grind music was in full swing. The skimpy top was lying discarded on the stage and Sidney's tail – to a chorus of lusty cheers – had slid between Pussy's g-stringed legs; when suddenly, events took a turn for the worse.

One second Pussy's face was a picture of pre-orgasmic ecstasy, the next, her half closed eyes shot open and her low 'yes,yes,yes', turned into a 120 decibel 'OWWW!' as Sidney buried his sharp little fangs into a kneecap.

Pussy's 'Oww!' was followed by an immediate (and literal) knee jerk reaction – and Sidney took gracefully to the air, to land with a heavy thump on a stage side table; the occupants of which did not hang around to get acquainted. Two brasses leapt screaming to their feet and backed into the table behind, which, as it overturned to the sound of smashing glasses and startled yells saw its occupants exit sideways to collide with other tables . . . which were overturned to the sound of smashing glasses and startled yells, which . . .

Amid the pandemonium, a stunned Sidney flopped to the floor, and went slideabout. This did nothing to ease the situation.

'What the bleedin!' an agitated Mr Mason yelled.

'Arrghhh! Let me out!' screamed a panic stricken woman.

'Gerrofff me fukin 'ead!' pleaded a muffled male voice, 'I can't breeve!' These relatively lucid auditory exclamations were punctuated with many sound bites of a less determinate nature as Pussy jumped down from the stage and limped in pursuit of a pissed off Sidney.

'Sidney! Sidney! Where are you baby?' Then: 'There you are!' as she pulled him out from under an upturned table.

'There, there baby,' she cooed, running her hands along his quivering body in a soothing motion. 'I don't understand it,' she said to a white-faced patron standing at a safe distance, 'he's never done anything like that before.'

As she spoke, her stroking hand suddenly stopped above Sidney's tail. 'What the . . .' she said, as her fingers rubbed against the edges of a two inch square of green plastic tape. 'No wonder he's so ratty!' she yelled. 'Some bastard's taped his arse up!'

Sidney probably winced as she tore the offending item off. Davey did wince, as he picked his way over broken glass on his way to the relative safety of the staff toilets.

'You likkul gett!' Zelda was spitting fevvers.

'It crapped in me bag,' mumbled Davey.

'It crapped in me bag,' she mimicked in a mocking voice.

'Well it did . . .'

'Do you know the bleedin trouble you caused! One poor bloke in an oxygen tent, nearly suffocated by some fat bint 'oo fell on is 'ead . . . People treated fer shock . . . Sharron's 'ad a tetnus jab in the arse . . . an Mr Mason's threatenin to cut the goolies off 'oo ever ee can find to blame fer all the damage.'

'Not my fault, I dint know the daft fing would bloody go an bite 'er leg did I . . .'

'You'd get ratty if someone taped your arse up . . . and he's not a daft thing!' said a still miffed

Miss Pussy as she stroked Sidney's head.

'Yeah,' Davey admitted slowly and grudgingly, 'but then I wunt go an crap in someone's best sports bag would I . . .'

14

Davey didn't ask much from life . . . mainly because he knew that asking would be pretty much a definite waste of time.

Yes, he would like to have a squillion quid in the bank, own a chain of betting shops and a brewery and be a major shareholder in United, but he was not so daft as to think that any of those things could ever happen.

No, his much earlier desire to be the first five-foot one-armed professional goalie had taught him that dreams were okay – as long as you confined them to a dim little corner at the back of your head and didn't allow them to slide down to lodge like prickly burrs in your heart.

He was happy enough to take his pleasures, such as they were, from wherever they cropped up. In this respect there were four places where he was at his happiest: in goals for the Beswick Reds; in a packed crowd at Old Trafford; in a pub with a full pint in his hand. And now, on his way to number four: a betting shop. As he opened the flat door and stepped out onto the communal landing – and froze in his tracks. A strangled 'Arrgghh!' burst from his throat as, what to the casual observer, appeared to be the result of a sexual liaison between a long haired rat and a muddy brown mop head, filled his vision. A mere two feet away the demon dog, Benji, lips drawn back over needle sharp teeth was coiled ready to pounce.

'Yipyipyipyip!' piped the dirty mop head. His face suddenly drained of colour, Davey backed into the hallway clutching at his empty sleeve. Benji, sensing he held the upper paw, grinned evilly and charged across the threshold in pursuit.

'No!' pleaded Davey. 'Good doggie, go away!' Benji's body stiffened and the little pink bow in his hair bounced up and down as he let loose a blood curdling 'yipyipyipyipyip!' before launching him self forward.

As flesh and blood seeking teeth fastened onto his trouser cuff, Davey screamed, stumbled backwards and came hard up against the handle of a door.

'No! Gerroff!' he yelled shaking his leg in an effort to dislodge the beast – but the death grip only tightened and the tiny coal black eyes fixed him with icy cold intent.

Davey lifted his leg and shook it again. Benji,

dangling two-foot from the floor, snarled and snuffled his defiance. As the door handle stabbed between his shoulder blades some kind of survival instinct suddenly kicked in.

It was the spare bedroom door. Without taking his eyes off the horrible apparition that was hell bent on tearing him to pieces, he groped behind his back, grabbed the handle, twisted it down, thrust his weight against the wood and in one smooth movement, swivelled round and kicked out sideways.

There was a ripping sound as his trouser cuff shredded, and a small furry object was catapulted into the spare room to land in a flopping heap, before scrabbling to its feet and charging back in a determined skittering run.

Heart in mouth, Davey slammed the door shut and was rewarded with a meaty thunk as a woolly head slammed against the solid barrier. There was a few seconds of silence – but for the pounding of blood in his ears – before: 'Yipyipyipyipyip!' then a few more seconds silence, followed by: 'Yip?' This questioning yip gave way seconds later to another frenzied bout of 'yipping', which ended, very suddenly, with a startled 'Yi–'

Knees weak with the aftermath of panic, Davey held on tightly to the handle; leaned heavily against the door and strained his ears for any sound coming from the bedroom. There was nothing, except, perhaps, a slight slithering noise as of something sliding slowly across a carpet.

'Serves you right,' he whispered through dry lips. 'I tole you to go away, so it's yer own fault.' Slowly, he released his grip on the door handle, turned and on his way to the front door, said a little silent prayer of thanks to Zelda, who had let Fred out of his bag earlier to have a little stretch.

The betting shop was fairly quiet, with only four or five punters intent on lining Mr William Hill's mega deep pockets. After a quick glance around the room Davey wandered over to an array of wall boards that had racing pages pinned to them.

At one of these notice boards a large middle-aged man was chewing a pencil while studying the form. As Davey came up behind him the punter took the pencil from his mouth, and leaning forward, put a tick next to the name of one of the horses displayed on the racing paper. Davey leaned to one side and mouthed the name slowly:

'Sweet Nuffins'. He tutted loudly and shook his head.

Distracted by the noise, the punter turned around quickly, then seeing no one; turned back to the board and began to write out a bet.

Davey tutted again – louder.

'What the . . .' said the man as he spun round and bumped into the little figure.

'What's your game then?' Davey looked up into a face that only a mother and the boss of an

Ugly Model Agency could possibly love.

'No chance that one mister.' The large man frowned.

'What you on about?' Davey shook his head slowly.

'Won't last the distance.'

'Bollocks, come on like a train last time out, only two furlongs less than today!' Davey nodded sagely.

'Oh aye, BUT . . .'

'But what?' Davey tapped the side of his nose.

'Tek me word for it mister . . . fade int last furlong.'

The punter peered down intently into the small face.

''Ere, you a jock or somefin?'

'No I'm English me,' said Davey seriously. The punter pulled a wry face.

'Very funny, I meant are you a jockey?' Davey shunted quickly into fairy tale cover up mode.

'Er, no . . . used to be though . . . long time ago, till . . .' he indicated his empty shirt sleeve.

'What 'appened?' said the punter as he noticed for the first time that Davey only had one arm.

''Orse went mad an bit it off . . .' The big man's eyes widened.

'Bleedin 'ell, you don't say!'

'Yeah,' said Davey, warming nicely to the occasion. 'Stopped me career good an proper it did.' Cudda bin a top rider anall . . .' The man nodded sympathetically.

'No shit. Still, keep yer ear to the ground though do you. Get inside info?' Davey nodded slowly. 'So, what you reckon's got the best chance in this one then?'

Davey stepped to the side and looked up at the board. His lips moved slowly as he struggled with the list of names – until one leapt out at him.

'Davetherave,' he said firmly.

'Bollocks!' snorted the big man. 'It's a bleedin nag, it's got no form at all, look,' he pointed to the form card, 'nowhere, nowhere, pulled up!''

'Come on like the clappers,' said Davey confidently. The big punter looked from the form page to Davey's open face, then back to the page.

'Twenty to one,' he muttered. 'Twenty to bloody one . . . surely not . . .' Davey tapped the side of his nose again.

'Yeah trus me . . . I useta be a jockey y'know.'

Making up his mind, the man tore his slip in half and wrote out a new one.

'Davetherave a tenner on the snout.' Davey nodded wisely as the punter took his bet to the cashier's window and handed it over. That done he came back to Davey's side to wait for the off.

'Get much info do you?' asked the punter casually as they watched the runners and riders make their way down to the starting gate.

'Er, yeah. Me an er, Lester, as a reglar

chat . . .'

'Lester! You mean Lester Piggott?' said the big man turning quickly not believing his own ears.

'Yeah. Mates me an Lester; an Billie Carson . . .'

'Billie? You mean Willie?'

'Er yeah . . . but 'is mates call 'im Billie . . .'

'Y'don't say!'

'Yeah . . . not many people know that . . .'

'Y'don't say!'

'Yeah,' said Davey enthusiastically, 'ee even invited me over to watch that Question of Sport fing when 'ee was on it . . .y'know, when 'ee an Willie Beaumont was captains like . . . a few years back.'

'Billy.'

'What?'

''Is name is Billy Beaumont . . . '

'Oh aye . . . it is but . . . 'is mates–'

'Don't tell me . . . 'is mates call 'im Willie, right?'

'Yeah that's right.'

'You sure you're not tekkin the piss . . .' said the punter with an edge beginning to creep into his voice, and his scarred face taking on the stressed appearance of a butcher's chopping block.

'Er no . . . not me mister. I don't tell lies. Me mam brought me up ter be 'onest she did . . . nun she was me ole mam . . .'

'Y'what!'

'What?'

'Yer mam was a nun! 'Ow could yer mam be a nun; nuns don't get wed.'

'Er, well she dint get married . . .'

'You mean ter tell me yer mam, a nun, 'ad you . . . an on the wrong side of the blankets anall!'

'Er, no,' Davey said slowly, as the realisation that he was perhaps digging himself a dirty great hole began to dawn. 'She stopped bein a nun. She kunt stand all that no torkin. Liked a gossip did me old mam . . . That an the bells . . .'

'The bells?' said the big man struggling to keep a firm grip on an exchange that was rapidly sliding into the surreal.

'Yeah, all them church bells . . . they give 'er 'eadaches.'

The big man closed his eyes briefly and shook his head as if to re-align a faulty neural connection, or eject a foreign mental object.

'The mind; it bleedin boggles!'

'Yeah, it does dunt it?' said Davey matter-of-factly.

'Yer old man; not a defrocked priest was he?'

'Course not. Merchant seaman he was.'

The big man's eyed narrowed as suspicion tip-toed up and took a slow, tentative, yet soon to get serious, grip. He was about to put voice to his doubts, when he was interrupted by the monitor announcement of the off.

As the race unfolded two things became abundantly clear: Sweet Nothings was a flier and

Davetherave was – stretching it somewhat – at best, a trier.

The race commentator's voice rose in pitch as they entered the home straight.

'Well into the last furlong now!' he shouted 'And Sweet Nothings is romping home followed by Memphis Belle in second, Julie's Pride, Northern Lights, Romany Prince and tailing off last Davetherave . . .'

Davey inched towards the door as the big punter slowly turned, and began to build up a head of steam that, if unchecked, would probably become sufficient to hurl the *Flying Scotsman* from London to Edinburgh at Mach 3.

'Davetherave! I'll give you Davethebleedinrave! C'mere you likkul twat!'

'Nnngghhh!' said Davey as he snatched open the door and shot out onto the precinct.

'Aaarrgghhh!' yelled the big man, as he followed in lumbering purple-faced pursuit.

15

After he had pounded through the precinct Davey crossed over Grey Mare Lane and ducked through empty stalls on the Market, before doubling back on the blind side and catching sight of sanctuary in the shape of Saint Brigid's church.

With a quick look over his shoulder he barrelled through the double doors, and, panting, slid into one of the back pews. For a minute amid the calm cool silence his ears strained to pick up any sounds of pursuit. Nothing. Relaxing slightly, he looked around the dim, empty interior. The church was lit only by weak sunlight that filtered through three small stained glass windows that fronted onto Grey Mare Lane. One of these displayed a nativity scene in carmine red and indigo blue. It had apparently been used for air gun target practice, and as a result of this, the beatific face of the Virgin Mary looked lovingly down on an infant Jesus who sported a neat round hole between his innocent eyes.

As his panic slowly subsided, Davey forced himself to breathe deeply and slowly. As he did so, his nose caught the faint but heavy lingering odour of incense and the sharp tang of melted candle wax – smells that hadn't entered into his consciousness for quite some time.

In his youth of course, Ethel had dragged him along to mass every Sunday; but nowadays he was far from being a regular frequenter of church. Even so; today, those barely remembered smells of incense and candle wax, triggered a slow trickle of religious memory that morphed into a gradual feeling of calmness. His breathing eased, he took a quick look backwards towards the doors; and allowed himself a loud sigh of relief – just as Father James entered through the vestry door.

The priest's face took on a slightly startled look as the apparently empty church, proved not to be. He narrowed his eyes and peered through the early afternoon gloom and at first, saw nothing. Then a sudden movement caught his eye. It was the top of someone's head in one of the rear pews.

He froze in his tracks, for it was a sad sign of the times that a Church, whether it was Catholic or Protestant, was these days no longer looked upon as sacrosanct by the lower elements of society. He had heard plenty of stories of break-ins and serious assaults carried out on priests and vicars by thieves and drug addicts in search of anything to sell for a profit or a quick fix. Squinting through his glasses, he fixed on the interloper's head.

It's a child! he thought with a little surge of relief. Still it paid to be careful. Cautiously, he made his way up the aisle; then, seeing who it was, he smiled.

'Oh it's you Davey!' he said, sliding into the pew alongside the little man. 'Not seen you here since. . . well since your mam's Requiem if I'm not mistaken.' Davey looked up into the priest's kindly face and nodded.

'Erm no farver . . . I sorta fell out wiv God a bit then.' The little man looked down at his trainer-clad feet then began to swing them slowly backwards and forwards.

'Did you now?' said Father James quietly taking in the little sign of embarrassment. Davey nodded.

'Yeah. Dint seem fair ter me, tekkin me mam like that. Dint deserve all that pain . . . she 'ad a 'ard life y'know . . .'

The priest returned the little man's nod, and as he did so, Davey's words at the time of the funeral slipped back into his head. Davey could have asked God why He had seen fit to rip away the only anchor in his storm tossed life. Instead he had knelt at the altar with his single hand held out over the altar rail in a poignant parody of prayer, and had said: 'Look after me mam . . . she dint deserve what she got.'

'Yes,' said the priest softly. 'A hard life. Good woman . . . good woman . . . Had a quiet dignity about her . . . born of faith I suppose . . .'

'It were a nice funeral though,' Davey said brightly.

'What? Oh yes it was,' said Father James. 'Very well attended. She was a very well liked woman.'

As he spoke, the priest's mind slid back to a re-enactment of a scene on the day, as Ethel's remains had entered the church and when, because of Davey's insistence that he be one of the bearers, the coffin had almost walked down the aisle. The foot end had been balanced on the little man's head and secured by a strap that ran around the casket and fitted under his chin. The other bearers were trying, without much success, to even things up by bending their knees – but this only leant an added air of surrealism to the proceedings. Surrealism compounded by the sight of the usually deadpanned undertaker Mr Mullett – for whom the word 'lugubrious' was surely penned – scuttling along sideways in Davey's wake with a panic-stricken look on his face and hands outstretched ready to catch the casket in case of calamity.

'Yeah, she was a good kafflic all right.' Father James shuddered slightly as the memory faded and he was drawn back to the present.

'What? Oh . . . yes she was . . . better than most.'

'Yeah. So, what you reckon, she's up there now, in 'eaven?'

'Well, yes, I suppose she is Davey . . . I suppose she is.'

'What you reckon it's like then?'

'Pardon?'

'Up there in 'eaven. What you reckon it's like?' The priest shook his head slowly.

'Well, we don't really know Davey.' The little man nodded.

'Yeah. Funny that int it. All we know about 'eaven is there is these big pearly gate fings an everyone swans about in like, white gowns wiv grins on their faces fer ever an ever.' The priest smiled thinly. 'But 'ell, that's diffrent int it,' said Davey seriously. 'We know all about that. There's flamin fire all over the show an there's these millions of likkul imp fings wiv long tails an 'orns on their 'eads 'oo go around eatin babies an stickin red 'ot forks up people's bums. Funny that int it?' The priest smiled thinly.

'What, sticking forks up people's bums?' he said lightly.

'No, not that. Funny that we don't know much about 'eaven – but we do about 'ell.'

The priest turned to look down into the little open face.

'I'll tell you what I think shall I Davey?' Davey nodded eagerly. 'I think the concept of eternal happiness is an esoteric one.' Davey's brow creased and he pursed his lips. 'I mean,' said the priest quickly, 'it's a bit soft and woolly. It's a thing of the mind – whereas the thought of everlasting agony is one that everyone can grasp; it's sharp and very much to the point because it's a thing of the body, like burning your fingers or a nagging toothache. So that's why the bible and the Christian Church have a lot to say about the agony of eternal damnation and the pain meted out in Hell. It helps to keep people focused on being good.'

Davey's eyebrows knitted in concentration then relaxed.

'Oh right,' he said slowly, 'it's like puttin the frighteners on.'

'Bluntly put – but true nevertheless Davey.'

'What about uvver religions though, those that don't 'ave an 'ell ter worry about? 'Ow do their bosses put the frightners on them then?'

'Well, there's Buddhism. It believes that you go through many reincarnations . . . that you are re-born many times and,' he added, 'in many forms.'

'What? Like you could be a woman or a rabbit?'

'Indeed.'

'Right then,' said Davey, 'what'd you like ter be when you come back next time?'

'Well,' said the priest, 'I suppose if it really did work that way – and I'm not saying it does mind – I suppose I would want to be someone or something that didn't have to torment itself with moral issues all the time.'

'Eh?'

'Someone or something that could just accept things as they were and get on with it.'

'Oh, right; like a . . . a big lump of rock or sumfin?'

'A big lump of rock? Well yes, why not. Just being, not feeling. Not letting anyone down, not getting caught up in the mad whirlpool of life.' Davey considered this for a few seconds, then screwed his face up and shook his head slowly from side to side.

'Yeah, but a bit borin though eh Farver, jus sittin there for like a million years lookin at the same fing all the time?'

Father James sighed lightly.

'Yes, you're right of course Davey. That really wouldn't do at all, just switching off. Too selfish; much too selfish.'

'Yeah, I suppose.' The priest nodded then turned towards his companion.

'And what about you Davey, what would you like to be?'

Davey pumped his cheeks up then blew the air out slowly.

'Well…I fink I would be . . . a bloke agen, but five foot eight tall . . . an wiv two arms of course.'

'What, that all? Five foot eight and two arms?'
'Yeah.'

'Why not six foot three?' The little man shrugged.

'Naw. Me mam said me dad was five foot eight, so that'd do fer me. If I was too big everyone would keep lookin at me an I've 'ad enough of that already fank you very much.'

'Ah, I see. So you'd be just normal . . .' *Oh no*, the priest thought, *I shouldn't have said that, what will he think of me!* He was relieved when Davey's answer came back without so much as a hint of bitterness in it.

'Yeah, that'd do fer me.'

'Good. And why not; too many people would want to be someone special, someone rich or famous, or able to do just what they liked, without having to consider the consequences.'

'Yeah, I suppose. Mind you a few quid in me pocket now an agen would be nice . . .' Father James smiled.

'Well, I guess that would be all right, as long as it wasn't too much and led to you looking down on those not so well off.'

'Naw, I wouldn't do that, don't fink.'

No, I don't think you would, the priest thought. *You'd be happy with just enough for a pint and a fag and a few bob left over for a little flutter.*

'Good. That would mean – if you were a Buddhist of course – that you would be taking a positive into your next life and that in each reincarnation . . . life . . . you would hopefully improve until you reach a state of spiritual perfection that they call Nirvana.'

'That would be good then wunt it?'

'Yes of course. However, if you do something bad in one life, you have to pay for it somehow in the next. So, going back to your question about hell; their hell is right here on earth.'

'Bloody 'ell!' said the little man tapping his fingers against his chest; 'I musta bin a right swine in me last life then!' Father James allowed a wry little smile to form on his lips.

'I shouldn't worry too much about that Davey you're not a Buddhist anyway are you?'

'Well, no, yer right there Farver; but then, like I said; I'm not really anyfin . . .' Father James nodded.

'So,' he said, in an effort to bring the meandering theological discussion back onto the straight and narrow, 'you've lost your faith then?'

'Yeah, suppose so.' Father James nodded again.

'I think I can understand that . . . yes indeed . . . can happen to us all . . . can't it . . . oh yes,' he sighed, looking down at the toes of his shiny black shoes. 'Oh yes indeed . . .'

Davey was not, at the best of times, blessed with an intuitive nature; but here and now, something in the priest's voice made a connection.

'What. You mean you anall?' Father James glanced down at his little companion, sighed heavily and smiled lightly.

'If you only knew . . .'

'Mus be 'ard fer you; you bein a priest anall.'

'Indeed it is, but;' the priest added with a tinge of conviction, 'we must both of us seek God's help to overcome our doubts.'

'Yeah, well, easier said than done fer me Farver, what wiv the way fings are . . .' The priest 'hmmmed' in sympathy.

'Yes, you have had more than your fair share of crosses to bear . . .'

'Y'can say that agen! Yuh wunt believe all the shi—bad moufin I've 'ad ter tek. Bullied rotten me . . . just coz I'm likkul, an only got one arm . . .' Father James nodded slowly twice to emphasise his sympathy.

'People can be very cruel Davey . . . very cruel.'

'Yeah they can. Me ole mam though,' he mused after a few seconds, 'she looked after me . . . when people usedta tek the pi–mick, at me bein likkul. "Davey", she usedta say, "you are not a dwarf; you are the world's smallest giant." Good that weren't it?' The priest smiled.

'It was indeed. Must have made you feel better.'

'Yeah it did a bit. Yeah. Then five minutes later she'd be rakklin me earole fer doin sumfin wrong – an then when I cried, she'd give me luvs! Wimmin eh!'

'Yes. Women eh!' said the priest with a fair amount of feeling. Davey nodded in agreement.

'Yeah, an then there's my Zelda. I never know where I am wiv er. One minute she's effin an jeffin at me fer sumfin, then the next it's like I'm not even in the same room!' Father James tutted softly.

'Yes, I can see how that kind of thing would be very confusing to someone like . . . I mean . . . yes,' he trailed off lamely. Then in a firmer voice he added: 'Mind you, your Zelda is another woman that's had a hard and troubled life . . . I think. So perhaps you should make some kind of allowance for that.' Davey considered this for a couple of seconds.

'Yeah, maybe.' Then: 'Our Arfur, 'ee said

wimmin come from the planet Zogg . . . cept fer is missis 'oo come from the planet Moo, 'ee said, coz she were a bit of a cow. Yeah space creatures wiv like, alien brains. What you fink?'

Father James leaned forward, dropped his chin onto a fist, and stared ahead and above the altar, where a crucified Christ gazed down at him with what appeared to be a quizzical look upon his thorn-crowned, bloodied face.

'What you fink?'

'Pardon?'

'Bout wimmin cumin from the planet Zogg?

The priest dropped his eyes from the gaunt pale face, sighed lightly, and, placing both hands on the back of the pew in front, seemed to study his white knuckles for a few seconds.

'The bible says,' he said flatly, 'that God took one of Adam's ribs while he slept and fashioned Eve, the first woman from it.'

'Musta 'urt that.'

'Hurt?'

'Yeah.'

'Possibly.'

'Why dint 'ee jus snap 'is fingers then; stead of goin to all that trouble?'

Father James eased himself back into the pew and turned to face his companion.

'It didn't necessarily happen that way Davey,' he said quietly. 'It was probably a symbolic account.' Davey nodded in mute incomprehension.

'Oh.'

'Yes,' said the priest. 'To quote an old song: "things that you are liable to read in your bible – it aint necessarily so."'

'Oh.'

'No. Anyway;' said the priest with forced good humour and in an effort to lighten the mood by steering the conversation down a less painful avenue, 'what about the football then?'

'What United?'

'No, your five a side team; going well I hear.'

'Yeah, we're int final of the All-Manchister pub five-a-sides!'

'And you're in goals?'

'Yeah.'

'Amazing.'

'Yeah it is. Tommy an Curtley aint too bril – but I can usually pull us frew.'

The priest took in the open face and the words that carried no hint of conceit or sarcasm for his team-mates abilities or lack of them. *What you see is pretty much what you get*, he thought. True he was to a degree skewered to a specific and horrific point in the past – but he was essentially a creature of the here and now. Yesterday to him was history, tomorrow a mystery. Today is his present . . . even though for him, it bestowed precious few gifts.

Father James felt a sudden rush of shame for his own weakness, selfishness, and his petty self-centred mental bleatings. I will try to do better he thought as he turned his gaze back towards the pale crucified shepherd of men.

The resolution's birth was then followed immediately by another conception. As he looked up into the pale bloodied face, he thought: *Confession*.

'Yes.' he murmured, 'Confession.'

'What?'

The priest sucked in and let out a deep breath, before turning to face his little companion again.

'Confession,' he said, 'is good for the soul.'

'Oh yeah, so they say,' said Davey with a distinct lack of enthusiasm. Undeterred the priest continued.

'When was the last time you went to Confession Davey?' The little man puffed out his cheeks and swung his feet back and forth.

'Pff, must be years ago I fink . . .'

'What, before your mam died?'

'Yeah . . . suppose so . . .'

'Wouldn't you like to seek God's forgiveness for your sins since?' Davey frowned.

'Don't know bout that Farver. Y'know what I said bout losin me faith an all that.' The priest smiled lightly.

'Yes I know what you said Davey . . . and I think I can understand why you feel that way. I myself haven't been for several weeks.' A look of surprise blossomed on the little man's face.

'What, you go ter Confession!' Father James nodded.

'Of course . . . priests sin as well you know.'

'Yeah? Well; yeah; priests is only youman I suppose.'

'Oh yes, very human,' said Father James, 'with all that that implies.'

Davey thought about this for several seconds then accepted it as fact. Then another thought slowly emerged.

'You're a priest right.'

'Yes of course.'

'An you listen to ordinary people 'oo want ter confess.'

'Yes?'

'Then 'oo do you confess to?' Father James smiled gently and glanced up briefly towards the rugged cross and its bloodied prisoner.

'To God of course . . . and to another priest.'

'Oh right,' said Davey. 'Must be a bit 'ard that, you bein a priest an 'avin ter confess to anuvver priest like.' The priest shook his head lightly.

'Normally it's not a problem.'

'Right.' Then: ''Oo does your confession then?'

'The parish priest at St Annes.'

'Oh, right.'

Father James sensed that Davey was prepared to let it rest there. He needs a little prod, he thought.

'Of course a priest's sins are usually no big deal when placed alongside the evils at large in the world today. No,' he continued, 'it's usually a case of Pride, or Envy, or Sloth, but sometimes . . .' He paused to make sure he had Davey's attention. 'Sometimes a priest is guilty of the sin of Omission,' Davey pursed his lips.

'What's that then when it's at 'ome?'

'What?' said the priest in apparent innocent inquiry?

'That sin of O . . . Omission fing?'

Father James looked into the open face and widely spaced blue eyes, and felt a sudden creeping tremor of doubt. *I'm using him* he thought. *I'm weak and I'm using him. I want to lighten my burden by dumping on his little shoulders. But,* countered the little voice in his head, *It won't be a burden to him. He's a simple soul. He'll accept it and won't judge. He'll probably forget about it as soon as something more important – like United's next home match crowds it out of his mind . . . plough on regardless*. So he did.

'Well. You understand about confession and having sins forgiven?'

'Yeah, suppose so.' The priest nodded and looked deeply into the trusting eyes.

'You know that one can only be forgiven for those sins that one confesses and that one must be truly sorry for those sins?'

'Yeah I remember that from Catechism at school yonks ago.'

'Yes good; well . . . a sin of Omission is where you don't confess a particular sin or sins on purpose.' Davey nodded slowly.

'Right . . . so . . . you wunt be forgiven would yuh . . . for them sins you dint own up to!'

'That's right Davey. But the fact that you deliberately did not confess those sins becomes a sin itself – the Sin of Omission.'

'Right, I geddit! Well yuh learn sumfin every day eh Farver!' Another prod needed.

'I'm afraid that's one of my sins Davey – the Sin of Omission . . .'

'Is it?'

'Yes,' said the priest. Before adding a little too forcefully: 'There are things that I just cannot find the strength to confess to another priest!'

'Oh Right.' Deep breath and Big prod.

'Tell you what Davey; why don't you and I go into the Confessional and we'll hear each other's confessions!' Davey's eyes opened wider.

'What. You tell me your sins anall!'

'Yes, why not!'

'Well . . . what about 'Im?'

'Who?'

'Y'know, '*Im*,' whispered Davey again, in italics, while nodding towards the silent witness on the cross. The priest smiled lightly.

'He will understand I'm sure.'

'But I'm not a priest . . . not even a real kafflic anymore.'

'That's all right Davey. You can trust me. I wouldn't ask you to do anything that was wrong would I?'

'No, course not,' said the little man.

'Well then?' said the priest, turning his body square on to his companion to reinforce his request. Davey thought about it for a few seconds – seconds that seemed much longer to the priest – then said:

'Yeah okay, why not!' Emotion washed over the priest's face.

'Thank you Davey!' Davey shrugged.

'No big deal Farver.'

'No, of course it isn't. But you do realise that anything that is said in the Confessional must go no further don't you Davey?'

'Yeah course . . . sacrid innit . . .'

'Indeed it is Davey,' said Father James.

Together in the dim light they slid out of the pew, and made their way over to the dark oak varnished, Confessional, that sat between painted portrayals of Stations Six and Seven of The Cross.

'You take that side,' said Father James, as he opened the priest's door and stepped into the dark, slightly musty interior.

Inside, he lowered himself onto the padded chair that sat at right angles to the rectangular gauze curtain that separated the two halves of the box. With a curious mixture of relief and trepidation he heard the other door creak open. This was followed by a heavy stumbled entry, a quiet muttering and a soft shush as knees made contact with the leather covered, foam filled kneeling form.

Father James swallowed nervously and wiped a hand across his brow. *Right*, he thought, *I've come this far, so just a bit further and I'll be able to share this awful burden. Then, once that's done, perhaps I can begin to see a way forward.* He swallowed again.

'Right Davey . . . you first . . . if that's all right?'

'Right.' Then silence.

'When you are ready my son . . .'

'Right. I was jus tryin ter remember 'ow it goes.'

'Forgive me Father for I have sinned . . .'

'Oh yeah. Got it. Forgive me Farver for I have sinned, it as been . . . yonks since me last confession.'

There then followed a brief recital of transgressions that included the liberation of money and cigs from Zelda's handbag; the telling of several porkies to a mixed bag of people; occasions of near falling down inebriation; an addiction to the gee-gees; over-use of bad and profane language; a bizarre tale of feeding a Maltese terrier to a python – and finally, an eye-popping, somewhat muddled recital of depravity, involving two prostitutes a bottle of Japanese scotch and a sopping wet window leather.

'That's all I fink farver . . .'

With an effort the priest dragged his mind away from a salacious but horribly compelling mental image conjured up by Davey's final admission.

'What? Oh yes. For your penance say two Hail Mary's and three Our Father's.'

'Right then . . .'

'Pardon?' said Father James, still wrestling with the eviction of carnal images.

'Your turn.'

The priest took a deep breath, wet his lips and ran a sweaty finger around the inside of his suddenly tight dog collar.

Right, no going back now he thought before clearing his throat and swallowing once more.

'It has been five weeks since my last confession,' he whispered. 'And at that confession I compounded earlier sins of Omission by not confessing to . . .' He paused then rushed on, 'Indulging in sins of the flesh!'

'What?'

'With my housekeeper! Sins of the flesh! SEX!' This last word was chased from his mouth by a strangled sob of guilt.

'Oh right,' said Davey matter of factly.

Father James was confused by the tone of Davey's voice. Here he was confessing to an awful sin and the little man treated it as lightly as if he, the grievous sinner, had confessed to a liking for second helpings from the dessert trolley!

'You don't understand!' the priest whispered fiercely. 'I'm a priest! I can't indulge in . . . in Sins of the Flesh!'

'Yeah, well me neever . . . really . . .' said Davey with a mental shrug of his shoulders. Father James, well wound up in Penitence mode, appeared not to have heard Davey's words.

'It goes against all my vows, the very nature of the priesthood,' he agonised. 'How can I stand up in the pulpit and lecture people on the sins of the world when I'm no better than the basest sinner! I'm supposed to set an example!' he finished with a bitter whisper.

There followed a few moments of silence in the dark, broken only on the priest's side by a pounding heart in the cathedral of his chest, and a heavy rasping of breath. Then, from the other side of the Confessional, a soft low key response:

'I suppose you could jack it in . . .' Breath caught on full intake, then released slowly.

'Jack it in?' said Father James, as though he was a dyslexic mentally struggling to make sense of a jumble of vowels and consonants that swam before his eyes.

'Yeah. If it's givin you so much grief . . . stop bein a priest.'

'Stop being a priest . . .' He ran the words over his tongue then through his mind. As simple as that . . . stop being a priest.

In the confessional silence reigned. And this silence was one of many kinds of silences.

There is the silence in the head that follows a sharp intake of breath. The silence outside the bedroom window when one wakes, and knows without looking, that the rooftops and ground are covered with freshly fallen snow. The comfortable silence that fills the gaps between words for long married couples. The aching silence that keeps fallen out lovers apart. The gracious silence that spans five heartbeats following a welcome compliment. The compassionate silence displayed in the wake of dreadful news. And the silence that is the virtue of fools. And in the few heartbeats after the little man's bald statement, and his own surprised response, those four little words became truly worthy of another kind of silence; a *sacra silentio* – a sacred silence.

'Why not?' said Davey. And as the priest squeezed his eyes tightly shut in an abortive effort to concentrate on that "why not", there came instead a kaleidoscopic burst of colour, which was closely followed by a mental image of him waving to St Paul, as they passed on opposite sides, and in different directions, on the road to Damascus.

'Is that it then?'

Father James shook his head and the image wavered and like a heat-hazed mirage faded out of existence.

'Pardon?' he said in a voice that had miraculously lost its ragged edge.

'Y'got any more sins?'

'More sins? No, no more sins Davey . . . Thank you . . . thank you very much!'

'S'okay.'

'Yes. Yes it is, isn't it!' said Father James.

'Right then, for yer penance say three 'ail Mary's one Our Farver an . . . an go ter City's next four 'ome games.'

'Thank you Davey!' said the priest as a soft shush of air signalled the little man rising to his feet on the other side of the Confessional. This sound was followed by the creak of a door opening, and a stumbled exit.

'Oh, and by the way Davey;' said the priest lightly through the gauze curtain, 'I am a City fan, you know.'

'It dunt make any difference really,' said a guileless voice as the door closed.

Father James sat for a long while after the patter of little footsteps on terrazzo tiles had faded away. So there it was then. The words had been spoken.

Feared for their life-changing implication, they had lodged unformed somewhere in the back of his mind for a long time, and now thanks, to the simple logic of a simple soul they had been dragged out to proclaim in red neon-lit foot-high capital letters. STOP BEING A PRIEST.

In the Confessional Father James rose from his seat, reached forward in the dark, and with a firm push of the door, emerged into a brighter world; his horror grown mild and his darkness miraculously transformed into blessed light.

16

Well, has he been a good boy then?' asked Pussy, as Zelda ushered her through the front door and led her into the living room.

'No trouble at all,' said Zelda. 'Ee's in the spare bedroom. I let 'im 'ave the run of it a couple of times rather than keep 'im cooped up in is bag all the time.' Pussy smiled in appreciation as Zelda waved her in the direction of an easy chair.

'Thanks Zelda, I'm dead lucky to have someone to look after him at such short notice.' Zelda shrugged her bony shoulders.

'No probs. Anyway, c'mon, what 'appened in Blackpool?'

'It was real good. It was a really smart place. Showed the *Blue Cockatoo* up a bit I can tell you!'

'Wouldn't 'ave to be up to much to do that,' said Zelda.

'No, you're not wrong there. Anyway I left my

mobile number with the manager and he's going to let me know when something else crops up. Shouldn't be more than a week or two at most, he reckons.'

'Let's 'ope so,' Zelda said. 'Anyfin's better than 'avin to strip off an parade about on a stage for a load of slobberin male shits.'

'Yes I suppose so,' said Pussy, not completely convinced, 'but dancing does bring in some very useful cash; and the way things are at the moment every little bit helps what with having no man bringing any money in.'

'Yeah, well, believe me,' Zelda replied sourly, while mentally shaking her head at Pussy's use of the word dancing, 'once yer looks start to fade that 'useful' cash will begin to dry up before you even know–'

'Yeah, she's right there!' Davey butted in as he made his way in from the kitchen and plonked himself down on an armchair. Zelda turned round in her chair and gave him a withering look.

'Make yerself useful,' she said, 'go an fetch Sidney. 'Ee's in yer bag in the spare room. And by the way,' she said turning back to Pussy, 'don't you worry about Sidney, we'll be glad to look after 'im agen, 'ee's no bother.'

Davey pulled a face, muttered something under his breath, then climbed down from the armchair and left the room. Seconds later he struggled back in carrying his Man U bag. Pussy's face lit up.

'Hello baby,' she cooed as she unzipped the bag and a head the size of a small shovel popped out. 'Did you miss your momma then baby?' Sidney slid further out of the bag and flicked his tongue against her fingers. Davey sat down quickly and eased his legs up onto the chair.

'Here baby,' Pussy said, 'momma's got a little treat for you.' She reached into her coat pocket and took out a handkerchief. 'It's your favourite!' she sang, as she un-wrapped a pate' mouse and held it out. Sidney 'sniffed' it, but apparently was not very impressed.

''Ee mustn't be 'ungry,' Davey said casually as Pussy eased Sidney fully out of the bag.

'I'm not surprised, look at the little tummy on him!' said Pussy. Zelda glanced quickly across at Davey.

''Ave you bin feedin 'im?' she asked. Davey looked a little sheepish.

'Well,' he muttered, 'I did give 'im a tin of, er, 'ot dogs.' Zelda studied the bulge in Sidney's middle.

'You did tek 'em out of the tin first I suppose?' Davey snorted.

'I'm not bloody stew-pid yuh know!'

Charlie wiped his hands on his trousers legs, picked up the phone and dialled. As the number rang and rang he muttered, 'C'mon! C'mon!' He was on the verge of hanging up and spitting out a colourful curse, when the receiver was picked up at the other end.

'Yess!' he mouthed silently. Then: 'Hello Tony? It's me Charlie, Charlie Mason from the *Blue Cockatoo*. How are you mate?'

Charlie was using his best buddy-buddy voice as, for some time, he had been desperately keen to claw his way up the local villains' ladder by breaking into the inner circle of the Quality Street gang.

'Listen, Tony;' he oiled down the line, 'I really enjoyed that poker school the other week and I thought maybe you and the lads might like to come over to my club this week for another good session . . . free booze an snacks of course.'

Fingers crossed he listened for a few moments to the voice on the other end of the line.

'No problem,' he said, 'the club's closed on a Wensdee. There'll only be you, me and the lads; plus one or two discreet bar staff to keep the refreshments comin. What do you say Tony?' Charlie held his breath then mouthed another silent 'Yesss!' when Tony agreed.

'Great,' said Charlie, 'you contact the others Tony an we'll all meet over at the club say, nine sharp on Wensdee.'

Time and venue agreed, Charlie left his mobile number in case of hitches and with an overly familiar, 'cheers mate!' he hung up.

Unlike the existing members of the Quality

Street gang, Mrs Mason's little boy was no Big Time Charlie. The Gang had their fingers in all manner of juicy Manchester pies. Tony Morrelli and his brother Vincent ran the doors in just about every pub and club of note. Eddie (Fagin) Carter operated a string of up to 20 'professional' lifters, who between them did their level best to strip every major store in the city of their better lines of merchandise. Jimmy (Wheels) Murphy and his associates could put their hands on a cut price Merc, Jag or Beamer for customers from home or abroad at very short notice – and with no nasty comebacks relating to such tiresome trivialities as registration documents or marks of identification.

Although they operated independently in their own particular spheres of expertise, they did, on occasion, team up under the 'Quality Street' umbrella to fund and or assist in any projects that were too complex or logistically out of individual reach.

Charlie Mason was small time. He had the club. He also owned a car breakers yard off Ashton Old Road, and it was this facility that had initially attracted Jimmy Murphy who, on occasion, needed to dispose of a vehicle or indulge in a quick spot of ringing. Charlie had always obliged for a cut price; and recently, for an introduction to the mysteries of the – admittedly outer edges – of the inner circle.

With the initial groundwork for the game laid, Charlie picked up the phone the next day and punched in a number.

'Zelda, that you? Right, listen, I want you over the club Tomorrer night. I'm organising a private poker game with some very important people. Be there for arf-eight till maybe arf-twelve. I'll book a taxi to take you 'ome an there's twenty-five quid in it for you. Oh yeah; and you might as well bring stumpy wiv you. I might find sumfin for 'im to do.'

Zelda put the phone down.

'It's Mr Mason,' she said. ''Ee wants us over at the club Wensdee night at arf-eight till about arf-twelve.'

'It dunt open Wensdee night,' said Davey looking up with a distinct lack of interest from the sports pages of the *Manchester Evening News*.

'I know that; 'ee's got a special card do on for a few of is big time mates.' Davey scowled. He didn't like Charlie Mason; so, by definition, he reckoned his 'mates' would also be arseholes.

'What's 'ee want me for?' Zelda shrugged her thin shoulders. It was a mystery to her too.

'I can't for the life of me fink,' she said shaking her head, 'but 'ee does, so we're goin.' Davey pushed the paper to one side.

'''Ow much?' Zelda placed her hands on her hips and looked down on him with a scowl on her face.

'Is that all you fink about – 'ow much?'

'Yeah. 'Ow much?'

'Fifteen quid.'

178

'I want a fiver.'

'Right.' Davey did a quick double take. She hadn't argued.

'Must be goin soft in er old age,' he mused to himself as he unfolded the paper and thumbed over to the racing pages with a view to turning an out of the blue fiver into a whole bunch of crinkly brown tenners.

The games room at the *Blue Cockatoo* contained a pool table, a dartboard, a high level television set resting on a wide wooden shelf, and half a dozen smallish rectangular tables and a dozen chairs. In the centre of the room two of the tables had been pushed together and were covered with a well-worn green baize cloth.

Sitting in the centre of the baize was a large wooden cigar box with the legend *King Edward* printed on the lid. Two other tables; which were also pushed together, were laid out with an assortment of crisps and nuts in small round plastic bowls and half a dozen mixed bottles of coke and lemonade. These tables had five chairs arranged around them, two at each side and one at one end.

Zelda studied the layout critically, stepped forward and rearranged the small bottles. Satisfied, she returned to the tiny bar that was a right-angled extension to the larger club bar.

'Pushin the boat out a bit in't 'ee?' said Davey, dipping his fingers into a bowl of peanuts. Zelda bridled.

'Arrgh geroff! I've jus spent ages layin them out. Keep yer sticky likkul fingers off!'

'Yeah, yeah, keep yer keks on,' said Davey coolly as he made his way over to the bar. (He was in a bit of a cocky mood since he had screwed a fiver out of her without a fight). 'Pull us a swift arf before is nibbs comes back in, eh?'

Zelda pursed her lips and through gritted teeth, put him firmly in his place.

'Don't you push it you likkul pratt! Get behind this bar an wash some glasses out, now!' Chastened, he mumbled something under his breath and did as ordered. He'd just finished when Charlie Mason pushed open the games room door.

'Everyfin in order?' he asked, casting a critical eye around the room.

'Spot on boss,' Zelda said cheerily. Charlie smiled thinly.

'Not quite,' he said, crooking his forefinger in Davey's direction, 'you, lofty, nip frew into the club an get arf a dozen of them long cushions off the back rests an bring em ere.' Puzzled, Davey left and a minute later struggled back through the door with two of the three-foot long back rests.

'Put 'em down there,' said Charlie, pointing to a spot some six feet from the back wall and in line with the pool table. 'And put the others next to 'em comin back this way,' he indicated.

After laying out the six cushions Davey looked

quizzically at Charlie.

'Right that should do it,' said Charlie, 'now piss off outer the way behind the bar.' Zelda hissed at Davey and signalled urgently.

'Move it,' she mouthed, just as a harsh buzzing from across the dimly lit main room signalled a new arrival.

Charlie slicked back his thinning, greasy, dyed black hair, and with a quick glance around, made his way to the main door. Seconds later there was the muffled sound of greeting and he came back into the small room followed by two short, stocky, swarthy men. He didn't bother with any introductions.

'Take a pew lads,' he signalled with an elaborate sweep of an arm towards the baize covered tables, 'while I get us some liquid refreshment.' He nodded towards the two men. 'Scotch and a dash of soda, if I remember right?' Both returned his nod. Charlie snapped his fingers.

'Scotch and a dash of soda, three doubles . . . an none of that cheap house shit!' he added with a *hey only the best for my guests*, tone to his voice.

Zelda opened a cupboard under the bar counter and took out a three-quarters full bottle of Chivas Regal. She poured the drinks, added the mixer and placed the glasses onto a tin tray. She was about to make her way over to the seated men when Charlie stopped her.

'No, let stumpy bring 'em over,' he said

smiling thinly. Zelda handed Davey the tray and gripping it carefully by the edge he made his way through the hatchway opening. As soon as they saw him the two swarthy men reacted with slight surprise. He hadn't been visible from behind the bar.

Charlie grinned as Davey placed the tray down with exaggerated care on the green baize.

"Ee's not much use,' he smirked, 'but I keep 'im for the freak value.'

Back behind the bar Zelda's normally hard face turned even stonier.

'Slimey bastard!' she muttered, as a red-cheeked Davey made his way back to her side.

Zelda kept her eyes on the seated men, while out of sight she pushed the whiskey bottle over towards him. Puzzled, he looked up as she pushed a glass over too.

'What?' he mouthed.

'Drink,' she whispered. Davey grinned, reached out and making sure not to produce any glugging sounds from the bottle, he very quietly poured himself a treble.

'Slimey bastard!' Zelda repeated, as Davey necked the scotch in one. He was about to reach for the bottle again when she elbowed him none too lightly in the ear.

'One!' she mouthed – just as the jarring note of the front door buzzer sounded.

Charlie ushered the two newcomers into the

room, where they exchanged quick greetings with the others.

Where the two latin-looking men were very similar in appearance – medium height, middle forties; the newcomers were very much 'unalike'. Jimmy Murphy was well into middle age and well over average height and girth. He was second generation Irish and it showed in his ginger hair and ruddy complexion. Thirty-something Eddie Carter was tall and whippet thin. His light brown hair was shaved to a half-inch stubble, and a large, crescent-shaped scar; like an upside down grin or, perhaps – more reflective of the man's demeanour – a shark's mouth, traversed his crown. His nose had migrated sideways in both directions and one of his front teeth had been replaced with a gold implant.

'Drinks?' said Charlie as the men took their seats.

'Rum and pep,' boomed Jimmy.

'Jack Daniels, neat,' said the thin man, his pale blue eyes stabbing into Charlie's face. Suddenly uncomfortable, Charlie turned away from the unnerving stare, and forgetting to snap his fingers, said: 'Rum an pep an a JD . . . neat.'

Behind the bar Zelda nodded and busied herself with the order. When it was done, Davey reached for the tray, but she knocked his hand aside and slid quickly out and on her way, as Charlie opened his mouth to speak. Too late. He frowned as she put the tray down and spun on her heels.

'Bloody 'ell Charlie! Few miles on the clock there!' said Jimmy to Zelda's retreating back. Charlie laughed.

'Three times round I reckon; but she gives a fukin good J Arfur.'

Behind the bar, Davey filled a liquor glass with Jack Daniels and pushed it over to her. She nodded, ducked down to open a cupboard and following his earlier example downed the drink in one.

After a couple of minutes' small talk Charlie put on his MC's voice.

'Right gents, same rules as last time,' he said, as he reached for and opened the cigar box and removed four stacks of casino chips coloured white, blue, red and black. 'White's a deep sea diver, blue a cock'n en, red a score an black a nifty,' he intoned, as he split the colours equally into five identical stacks and pushed one of these over to each of the other four players.

'These'll cost you a grand each,' he said. They all reached into their jacket pockets and took out thick sealed envelopes, each one with their own name written on the outside. These were placed in the centre of the table. If Charlie had been dexterous enough he would have patted himself on the back. *I'm a natural at this* he thought. *I'll 'ave 'em eatin out of me 'ands by arf twelve.*

'Okay;' he said in a very business-like voice, 'minimum bet a fiver, five-card stud. Last game starts no later than midnight. Oh . . . and no pound coins!' he added with a little chuckle as he looked at Eddie. The Morrelli's and Jimmy Murphy laughed. It was common knowledge in the local underworld that Eddie had fronted a break in on a *Group 6* warehouse and walked off with almost 100,000 pound coins that were helpfully bagged and left sitting on a loading bay.

Eddie did not laugh; instead he fixed Charlie with a cold gimlet-eyed stare that carried not too deep or subtle undertones of crunching nose cartilage and the brittle snap of breaking bones.

Behind the bar and well removed from the action, Zelda and Davey stealthily topped up their glasses. She was still quietly seething. *Bastards*, she thought. *I've moved in circles where you lot wouldn't get the bleedin time of day. Tekkin the piss out of us makes you feel sumfin special does it – arse 'oles*. She looked down at Davey who, from his calm expression, appeared to have mentally shrugged off the earlier slight and consigned it to the back of his mind, where it nestled with a myriad others. *It's ok for me to call you names; I'm the one 'oo as the grief of lookin after you*, she thought, as she placed a hand lightly on his shoulder.

'What?' he said in surprised reaction to the unusually gentle touch.

'Nothin,' she answered quickly, whipping her hand away.

As the game progressed Charlie's pile of chips – and his air of OTT *bon homie* – grew steadily.

'Hey lofty, anuvver round of drinks, an bring that box of King Eddie's off the shelf,' he ordered. Davey delivered the tray of glasses and the cigar box, and was about to return to his stool behind the bar when Charlie held out a checking hand.

'Whoa, 'ang on stumpy, cumeer a minit!' He made a beckoning gesture with his forefinger.

'Boss?' said Davey as he approached slowly.

'Cumeer. I'm not goin to bite you,' said Charlie, glancing round at the others and grinning hugely. Davey looked quickly back towards Zelda, who gave a little shrug of her bony shoulders.

'We're goin to tek a likkul break in a minute so yer goin to provide a spot of light entertainment fer us,' Charlie said casually. Davey looked bemused.

'I can't sing,' he said.

'No, an I bet yer not much of a juggler eever!' crowed Charlie.

Davey swallowed nervously and took another quick look back towards Zelda. She seemed very far away as she stood red faced behind the bar.

'Naw. You don't need to sing . . . or juggle . . . or dance,' said Charlie, sliding back his chair and climbing to his feet. 'Just go and stand over by them cushions you brought in before.' Davey frowned, but did as he was told.

'Right gents,' said Charlie to the seated players, 'I'll bet anyone a nifty that I can toss the likkul bleeder the furthest!' The others grinned and climbed to their feet.

186

'I'll 'ave a piece of that!' chirped Jimmy, flipping a black chip into the centre of the table, before spitting on his hands and rubbing them together like a punter about to heft a huge hammer and ring the bell at a county fayre. Charlie matched the fifty, as a stricken Davey looked around for an escape route. There wasn't one.

The five men advanced on the little figure.

'I, er . . .' said Davey, looking wildly left and right.

'It's all right,' said Charlie greasily, as he spun Davey around and hooked one hairy paw around his trouser belt and with the other grabbed a handful of shirt collar.

'On the count of three,' said Tony. Charlie tightened his grip.

'Whoa! We need a referee,' Jimmy chimed in. 'Someone as ter check ow far ee gets tossed.' Charlie eased his grip.

'Yeah, right; 'ow about you Vinny?' said Charlie. 'You won't be 'avin a go will you . . . what wiv yer dodgy ticker?' Vincent scowled. His 'dodgy ticker' was common knowledge, but he didn't appreciate some smart arse who he hardly knew bringing it up lightly in company.

'Yeah, right,' said Vincent; mentally adding that if it was a close run thing, then Mr Smart Arse could be sure of finding himself out of pocket.

'Okay, on the count of three,' intoned Tony, as Vincent took up a position alongside the mats.

'One.' Charlie hoisted Davey off the deck and swung him backwards, then forwards. 'Two.' Davey squeezed his eyes tightly shut. 'Three!' Charlie heaved and grunted. Davey yelled 'Nnngghhh!' as he flew through the air, then 'Ummmpphh!' as he landed with a thump belly down some seven feet onto the cushions.

'Yeah!' crowed Charlie, pumping a fist up and down. Jimmy sniffed disdainfully.

'Move outer the way an let the dog see the rabbit,' he said, as a disoriented Davey staggered back to the starting line, and Vinny moved to the point where Davey's head had made the furthest indentation in the row of cushions.

'Okay, on the count of three,' intoned Tony. 'One.' Jimmy hoisted Davey off the deck and swung him backwards then forwards. 'Two.' Davey squeezed his eyes tightly shut. 'Three!' Jimmy grunted and heaved. Davey did a verbal replay as he flew through the air and landed with a thump belly down – a good head short of his last little trip.

'Yeah!' crowed Charlie, whirling to face Vincent.

'Yeah,' said Vincent, a trifle sourly as the little projectile struggled to his feet and limped back.

'I've 'urt me knee,' Davey moaned. Nobody paid him any attention. The four newcomers were coldly eying a smirking Charlie who was strutting around in a little circle pumping a fist up and down while crowing:

'And are there any uvver takers wiv the bokkel to take on the champ!'

The drink, a few winning hands, and the fact that he appeared to be the champion tosser, had gone very much to his head.

'Yeah, go on I'll give it a shot.' Davey groaned as Tony stepped forward. Charlie stopped his little dance and looked from Tony then across to his brother Vincent and his eyes narrowed slightly.

'Just a minute . . .' Davey looked up, a flicker of hope in his eyes.

'What?' said Tony.

'Look; don't tek this the wrong way Tony;' Charlie said, 'but blood an water an all that . . .'

'What you on about, blood and water?'

'Well . . . you know . . . you and Vinny are bruvvers like . . .' Tony scowled as the words and their implication registered.

'You tryin ter say me an Vinny are cheats?' Charlie, a bead or two of sweat suddenly sprouting on his upper lip backed off smartly.

'Jesus Tony! Course not! Course not! Vinny can ref, no problem!'

Tony's scowl stayed firmly in place and his voice took on a flinty edge.

'Our family comes from Napoli and we don't take kindly to anyone questioning our honour.' Things suddenly went very quiet and Charlie squirmed as a horrible mental image of himself sitting on a powder keg farting sparks leapt into his head. Behind the bar Zelda's mouth creased into a wolfish grin.

'Wriggle you bastard,' she murmured.

More beads of sweat sprouted on Charlie's greasy forehead and ran down into his eyes. He wiped the back of a slightly trembling pudgy paw across his eyebrows and swallowed nervously.

'Apologies Tony,' he croaked. 'The drink, you know; got a bit carried away.' Tony's scowl stayed firmly in place but he cut a bit of edge from his voice.

'Yeah, right, so let's get on wiv it.' Charlie took a relieved breath and smiled weakly.

'Sure Tony, be my guest.' He extended an open palm in the direction of the little figure. Resigned to his fate, Davey limped over to the starting line.

'On the count of three,' intoned Eddie. 'One.' Tony hoisted and swung. 'Two.' Davey, hoping for a happy landing, kept his eyes open. 'Three!' Davey clamped his jaws shut as he took to the air. As he came in for a landing Vinny casually slid his marker foot backwards, so that it rested neatly in line with Davey's head on touchdown.

'Dead 'eat!' said Vinny, turning to face the starting line. Charlie opened his mouth; then shut it quickly as Tony inclined his head and raised his eyebrows as if inviting a response. Charlie grinned weakly.

'Good throw mate,' he managed.

'Looks like we need a decider,' said Tony brightly. Charlie's nod lacked any trace of enthusiasm.

'And I've got a ton that sez Tony wins,' Eddie drawled.

'Me to,' said a grinning Jimmy.

'Pity I 'ave to stay neutral,' said Vinny – the epitome of fair play and Corinthian spirit.

Charlie began to sweat again – while behind the bar, Zelda offered a silent little prayer of thanks to the God of Retribution.

Trapped, Charlie put on a pale imitation of a brave face.

'Course, no probs lads; off you go Tony mate.' Tony stepped up to the mark. Davey sighed in resignation as he was hoisted off his feet and swung backwards and forwards. 'One.' Then; 'Urrrk' as instead of another swing he was tossed forward to land about five feet onto the cushions.

'Oh dear, not very good that one,' said Tony. 'Still I think it might be good enough,' he added, looking squarely into Charlie's sweating face, as the little man limped back.

'I've 'urt me knee!' said Davey.

'Shut the fuk up!' snarled Charlie, as he leaned forward, took a handful of Davey's waistband in one sweaty mitt and a lump of collar with the other, and hoisted him off his feet. Charlie swung.

'One,' intoned Vincent. 'Two,' Charlie swung,

191

'Three!' Charlie swung – and lost his grip on Davey's collar.

'Owww!' yelled Davey as he pitched forward onto his head.

'Slipped,' muttered Charlie; then as he looked into a trio of faces that reminded him suddenly of circling sharks, he muttered: 'Still fair do's eh, 'ee did go forward . . . a likkul bit . . .' Tony smiled.

'Well that's very sporting of you . . . *mate*.' He made the last word sound anything but matey; more like 'slimeball' or 'pervert' or 'dogshit'.

'Ah well, you win some you lose some, eh,' Charlie said weakly, as he made his way back to the table to pay out.

'Don't worry about me!' Davey muttered sourly as he struggled to his feet and hobbled back to the sanctuary of the bar.

'You all right?' Zelda frowned, as she realised with more than a *frisson* of surprise that she had just experienced a little twinge of concern on his behalf.

Davey gave a fair impression of a wounded soldier struggling back from the front line.

'I've 'urt me knee,' he said, rolling up his trouser leg to gently probe the injury. 'It's all red,' he whinged.

Zelda bent forward

"Ere, let me see,' she said, probing a little pink patch on his knee.

'Owww!'

192

'Don't be such a mard arse. It's just a likkel bit of a knock.'

'Yeah. Well it's all right fer you. It weren't you they was tossin around like a sacka bleedin spuds!' She backed off.

'Yeah. Well do you want a double whisky . . . to tek away the pain?'

'Yeah!'

Zelda shook her head slowly. In some ways she was glad that he was a bit thick. As he was, she could guarantee a roof over her head for the foreseeable future. But then, leaving aside self-interest, she often also thought that intelligence would be a curse for him. He'd have the ability to agonise over the cruel twists of fate that conspired to leave him stunted and disabled.

Yes; he had a little moan about his lot now and again – but as soon as he lit a fag, or supped a pint, or a nag went in, or United won, he'd shunt any trace of self-pity well into a weed choked siding at the back of his mind. She envied him this ability mightily; but increasingly – and to her considerable annoyance – she was pleased for him.

Pleased that he could move from cloying quicksand to solid ground with no more than a gentle mental skip.

Back at the table the cards had resumed. As the night wore on the game ebbed and flowed. Charlie won a couple of largish pots; then very prudently folded on a couple of more when he held strong hands. It wouldn't do to antagonise his guests further he decided; and especially not Eddie, who unnerved him with his gimlet-eyed gaze.

The conversation, lubricated with liberal libations, eventually turned to work and Charlie dropped a number of unsubtle hints that he would be pleased to offer his services in any way the inner circle deemed appropriate. It was after one such hint that Eddie gave him the intro he had craved for so long.

'There's one likkul job you could do,' Eddie said casually as he scanned the cards he held in his gold-ringed, tattooed-knuckled fist.

'Just say the word Eddie mate!' Eddie lifted his gaze from his cards to Charlie's eager face.

'Smiffield Market; you know it?' Charlie nodded

'Yeah, Openshaw, off Ashton Old Road.'

'Right, well, there's a fruit an veg unit, Robert Timpkin and Co in 'all B.' Charlie nodded.

'Ask fer Keiff Timpkin and tell 'im yer 'ere on be-arf of Mr Brown. 'Ees got a consignment of ten cases of avocados from Israel. You pick 'em up, bring 'em back 'ere, an I'll send someone over for 'em at twelve noon tomorrer.'

Avocados? Charlie was disappointed. He was looking for something a fair bit more substantial; a fair bit more big time than being a fruit and veg delivery boy! What a downer. What a soddin downer!

He was so instantly down in fact, that he almost didn't catch the words: 'Special avocados.' Eddie's thin lips peeled back over his teeth. 'They're made of wax wiv, very special centres.'

The big mental downer was suddenly elbowed out of the way by a much brawnier interloper – personal fear. *Oh shit!* Charlie thought. *Coke or heroin . . . shit!* He grinned wanly and muttered weakly.

'Oh right . . . no probs, mate.'

'No there better not be,' said Eddie coldly. 'Cos if there is I'll be very upset. It's a very expensive consignment.' Charlie swallowed noisily.

Midnight signalled the last hand. Charlie stacked a full house with two hundred quid in the pot. He just wanted to get the game done with. *Drugs is fukin 'eavy*, he thought. *I mean, bent motors, bit of receivin 'ere and there, no problem – but fukin drugs . . .*

The game over, they tallied up. Everyone – except Charlie, who was down nearly five hundred – was a bit in front. He took his loss with a show of nonchalance. He had other more important things on his mind.

When his guests had gone he sat for a few minutes at the table while Zelda and Davey tidied up. When Zelda went through to the main bar to phone for their taxi, he called Davey over.

'Eh Stumpy.'

'Boss?'

'I've got a likkul job fer you in the morning . . .
Its werf a fiver fer you.'

'Boss?'

'Be outside yer flats at seven. You can come
wiv me to pick up some . . . stuff . . . from Smiffield
market.'

17

Charlie opened the passenger door to a bleary-
eyed Davey.

'C'mon move it!' he ordered, as   Davey
climbed awkwardly in. 'I want to get this over an
done wiv quick as nick.'

''Oo's Nick?' said Davey innocently. Charlie
shot his companion a sour look, slid the gear stick
into first and pulled out into the road. His bottle
was beginning to twitch again.

Don't like it he thought for the umpteenth
time since he had heaved himself out of bed at half-
five. *Don't like it one likkul bit*. He'd managed to get
himself sucked into a shit situation. So, now he had
to make the best of it somehow.

He glanced across at his little passenger. *Yeah*
he thought *that's the best fing. I'll just 'ang back
and keep me eyes peeled and let stumpy load up.
That way if the cops pounce I'll 'ave a good chance*

196

to leg it.

The drive over to Smithfield Market took ten minutes. Minutes that were, in Charlie's case, spent agonising over the possible dire consequences that could ensue should things go avocado pear shaped. Davey dozed.

As he pulled up at the site security cabin Charlie's mood was not improved when he spotted a police car nearby. It was then that he remembered that there was a traffic police yard directly behind the market.

'Shit!' He groaned.

'Boss?'

'Nuffin. I was just finkin somefin . . .'

'Musta bin a bad fought . . .' Charlie's caustic response was cut off by the approach of the security guard.

'Timpkin and Co, Hall B,' said Charlie in his best posh voice. The guard nodded and raised the barrier.

'This end, first 'all on the left.'

Charlie parked the car up, and with Davey in tow entered the open ended, high ceilinged hall.

Even at this relatively early hour it was busy, with a dozen or so men and women going about their business, raising roller shutters and moving quantities of fruit and veg from place to place on stacker and hand trucks.

Charlie clocked each and every one with a jaundiced eye. *Could be pigs*, he thought, as he pulled up outside a half opened roller shutter that had the name Timpkin & Co painted in white peeling block letters on a high level dark green fascia board.

"Ullo, anyone there?' Charlie peered under the roller shutter into a dimly lit interior that contained an assortment of stacked boxes and bulging sacks.

'Yeah. 'Oo you lookin for?' Charlie jumped as a tall thin man wearing a grubby light brown overall coat emerged from the camouflaged background of a stack of potato bags.

'Er, Keif Timpkin; I've come to pick up a delivery for a Mr Brown.' The thin man nodded.

'Avocado's, right?' Charlie nodded back.

'They're over there. Ten boxes.'

'Right. That it then?' Charlie muttered, as he ducked under the shutter.

'Yeah just sign this delivery note, tek the pink slip an load em up.' Charlie signed the name John Smith, took the pink copy, turned, and beckoned Davey over.

'Those ten cardboard boxes; load 'em up.' Davey walked through under the shutter, crossed over to the stack of cartons and lifted one.

'It's 'eavy. Give us a 'and.' Charlie scowled.

'Tough. Jus get on wiv it . . . if you want yer fiver.'

Ten minutes later, as Charlie kept a watching brief from a safe distance, the ten cartons were loaded onto the folded down rear bench seat of the car. Job done, a sweating Davey slid into the front passenger seat and lit up a fag. Charlie approached warily, throwing anxious glances left and right.

'See anyone suspicious?' he muttered as he thumbed open the driver's door. Davey shrugged and exhaled a lungful of smoke.

'No, only you.'

'Very funny.' Charlie climbed in, slammed the door and took a quick look in the rear-view mirror.

'I can't see out the back.' Davey shrugged again.

'It was the only way I could get 'em all in.'

'Right. Well let's get the fuk outer ere.'

At the security hut he held the delivery note out of the window. The guard gave it a quick glance and lifted the barrier. Charlie turned the car right onto Ashton Old Road, and after about four hundred yards, pulled into a petrol station on the left.

He didn't really need any fuel, but decided it was a good idea to give it a few minutes to check for any unwelcome attention from the law.

''Ere,' he said, taking a ten pound note from his back pocket, 'put a tenner's worth in.' Davey opened the passenger door. ''Old on dummy!' Davey stopped. 'You can't put petrol in wiv a bleedin fag in yer mouf!'

'Oh, right.' Davey leaned over and placed his cigarette on the rim of an open ashtray at the side of the handbrake.

'Bleedin dummy!' Charlie muttered, as his little passenger moved to the back of the car and began to fuel her up. He had just finished and was on his way to the shop when a police car pulled in behind Charlie's vehicle. In the driver's seat, Charlie casually glanced in the wing mirror – and almost had a coronary.

'Jesus Christ!' he moaned, as in the mirror he saw the car door open, and a pair of size twelve's plant themselves firmly onto the deck. His already twitching bottle blew a long wet ppffttt as he quickly switched on the ignition, shot off the forecourt and turned sharp left back onto the Old Road.

In the shop, Davey paid the cashier, turned to leave and ran smack into a very large traffic cop.

'Whoa!' The cop said, grinning.

'Sorry mate!' Davey did a smart sidestep and exited toot sweet. Cops always made him nervous. Outside he did a quick double take and scratched his head.

'Where's 'ee gone?' he quizzed the empty space where a minute earlier he had climbed out of the car. Behind him the cop emerged stripping the wrapper off a Mars bar.

'Lost somethin?' the cop asked, with a distinct lack of interest.

'Er, yeah, me lift.'

'Looks like yer walkin then,' said the cop

though a mouthful of chocolate, as he strolled over to his car and climbed in.

Davey scratched his head again.

'Why's 'ee done a runner?' he mused. Then a thought struck him: *Bollocks 'ee's got me bleedin fiver!*

Charlie put his foot down and was almost half way to Ashton Under Lyne before his thumping ticker had slowed down to something like its normal rate.

'No sign,' he muttered, glancing for the tenth time into his wing mirror. 'Thank Chr– WHAT THE!' His heart leapt up into his throat as a burst of flame, fanned by the car's heater blower, licked hungrily at his left leg. *FIRE!* his brain screamed as his eyes battened onto an appalling sight.

A mini mountain of debris – that included a half smoked cig, two empty Big Mac cartons, an assortment of toffee wrappers, three empty Hamlet packets and a month old copy of the *Daily Sport* – was well and truly alight!

Panicked, he reached over and wildly flailed at the flames with his left hand. Unfortunately this only assisted the bellows action of the heater blower to fan the pretty red and orange flames higher.

'Arrggghh!' he yelled as his jacket sleeve caught alight. 'Whhooaa!' he screamed as the car smacked into a kerb, mounted it and smashed into a very injudiciously placed lamppost.

The abrupt deceleration from 40 to zero produced an interesting reaction in the animate and inanimate objects in the vehicle's interior. Charlie's body – because he made a point of cocking a snoop at The Law by not wearing his seatbelt – shot forward and his forehead came into sharp and bloody contact with the steering wheel. Then, as, in a daze he jerked himself back away from the pain inflicting object – he was just in time to meet a box of avocado's travelling in the opposite direction. This smashed into the back of his head on that wee bony bit just behind his left ear. Lights out.

'W-w-where am I?' A concussed Charlie looked up through blurred eyes into a sea of disembodied legs.

'Lie still mate,' said an equally disembodied voice. 'An ambulance and a fire engine are on the way.'

'Me avocado's!' said Charlie. 'Where's me avocado's!'

'Feedin the fire by the look of it,' said another disembodied voice to the accompaniment of sirens from rapidly approaching emergency vehicles.

The police arrived as Charlie was being loaded into the ambulance.

'As 'ee said anythin about what 'appened?' asked one of the officers as he absently picked up a melted, vaguely pear-shaped lump of wax that had a bit of polythene sticking out of its centre.

'Not really,' said the ambulance driver. "Ee jus keeps on mutterin somethin about a likkul twat.'

18

Davey opened the door to a smiling Mr Smith. Surprised and a little ungraciously – he was still peed off about his fiver – he said: 'What you want?' Mr Smith's smile stayed firmly fixed as he doffed his trilby.

'My appointment with Sister O'Flerhity . . . I am a little early perhaps?' he added, raising his left wrist to within six inches of his eyes and squinting at the face of his watch. Davey sighed.

'Early? Yeah yer early all right!' he muttered, adding under his breath, 'bout five days early . . . bloody nutter.' Mr Smith, poised on the chilly side of the doorstep, looked on expectantly. Davey sighed again.

'You've just missed 'er, she's gone to Asda fer some . . . bandages an . . . plasters an fings . . .' Mr Smith's smile faded quicker than England's dreams of winning the World Cup.

'Oh dear, I was so looking forward to doing a little doctoring too . . .' he murmured, raising his tatty doctor's bag to his chest and patting it lovingly. Davey was about to say 'tough titty' and then slam the door, when the seeds of a cunning plan began to germinate. She would be gone for at least another hour or more, so why not take advantage and let the nutter in if he was so keen on doing a bit of doctoring?' He nodded, and smiled thinly.

'You might as well come in then an wait fer a bit,' he offered, stepping to one side. Mr Smith's smile re-emerged from behind a cloudy countenance as he stepped lightly over the threshold.

'While yer 'ere,' said Davey casually, 'you can take a quick look at me. I'm not feelin so clever terday . . .' Mr Smith's smile increased in intensity by 500 watts.

'Certainly young man, shall we go through to the operating theatre?'

Inside the 'operating theatre', the good doctor placed his bag on a coffee table, removed his topcoat, turned to the patient and, rubbing his hands together in anticipation, said: 'Now then young man, what seems to be the trouble; it's not that nasty constipation again is it?'

'NO!' said Davey in alarm. 'No, that's well sorted, fanks to you doc. It's, it's me 'ead. I, I get a bit dizzy sometimes.'

'Ahhh!' said Mr Smith nodding wisely. 'Sounds very much like a circulatory problem. I'm sure I have something in my bag that will tackle that.' Davey watched as the doctor snapped open the catch on his case and began to rummage inside.

'Oh by the way doc,' the patient said casually, 'Sister O'Flerhity said that when you come I should ask you for the usual likkul donation . . .' Davey held his breath as Mr Smith looked up.

'Yes, of course young man, I'm always pleased to contribute to Sister O'Flerhity's practice funds. Twenty pounds be sufficient?' The patient expelled a silent breath.

'Er, yeah, that would be great,' said Davey licking his lips as the doctor fished out his wallet, removed, and held out a crisp twenty pound note.

'I'll give it to 'er later,' the patient said, as he took the money, folded it carefully twice between his third and fourth finger and thumb and slipped it into his shirt pocket.

As Mr Smith returned to rummaging in his bag Davey performed a little skip of delight behind his back. All that remained now was to go through with the charade — and with no enema involved that couldn't be too much bother. Once that was done he'd get rid of the nutter and he'd be twenty quid in pocket with Zelda none the wiser. Brilliant!

'Ah, yes, these should do the trick.' Davey looked on as Mr Smith fished out three little purplish lozenge-shaped tablets from his bag, folded two of them in a sheet of paper that he ripped from a notepad and handed them over to his patient.

'Put these away and take one a day for the next two days.' Davey took the folded paper and placed it in his shirt pocket with the twenty pound note.

'What about the uvver one? He asked.

'Ah, yes, take this one now,' said the doctor. Davey held out his hand and took the pill.

'I tek this now?' he said, opening his hand and studying the tablet that had the letters VGR stamped on it.

'Certainly young man.' Davey was not so sure; after all he was dealing with a nutter wasn't he? It could be poison or sumfing.

'Wot's the vee gee are for?' he asked suspiciously.

'Er, um, very good relief,' said Mr Smith.

'You sure it's okay?' said Davey still not convinced.

'Certainly!' beamed Mr Smith. 'Sort the problem out in no time,' he added, while trying to remember where he had got them from. *Ah yes*, he thought. *In the Flying Horse a few months back . . . paid forty pounds for six of them . . . chap said they were perfect for getting the blood to flow to vital parts . . .*

Davey decided that it was in his best interest to play along. He popped the pill into his mouth and with a little difficulty forced it down.

'That it then . . . doctor?' Mr Smith nodded.

'Right, well I'll tell 'er you called . . .' Mr Smith

smiled, but made no move to leave.

'I'll wait for a while, if you don't mind. I do want to discuss, er, other matters.' Davey mentally rapped himself on the forehead with a fist and frowned. He could guess what the 'other matters' were likely to be.

'She may be a long time.' Mr Smith smiled.

'That's all right young man; I'm not in any great hurry.' Davey frowned again. He hadn't bargained for the nutter wanting to hang on.

'Right; well I've got to nip out fer a bit,' he said thinking of the twenty in his pocket and the chance to turn it into big money at the bookies before Zelda came back and pinched it off him.

'Fine,' said Mr Smith. 'I'll just sit here and wait.' Davey shrugged.

'Right then, I'll be back in a bit,' he muttered, making his way to the door. Mr Smith smiled sweetly at Davey's back. He was well made up with his diagnosis and administration. *Another grateful patient placed firmly back on the road to health and vitality,* he thought proudly as he plonked himself down on a chair.

Half an hour later a deflated little figure heralded his return with the slamming of a door.

'Bloody useless Nags!' he muttered. 'You still 'ere?' he added, hoping for a distinct lack of response.

'Yes,' was the bright answer from behind the operating room door.

'Shit!' Davey whispered. His cunning plan was swiftly running out of cunning. *She'll skin me alive,* he thought; then: *unless . . . unless, I can keep the nutter torkin; then 'ee might ferget about the twenty* It was a water-logged straw to a drowning man in a swirling maelstrom.

He composed himself, opened the O.R. door and said breezily: 'You might as well come frew to the parlour, an I'll mek you a cuppa, an you can tell me all about doctorin an all that stuff.'

'That would be most pleasant,' said Mr Smith as he followed Davey into the next room.

'Tek a pew an I'll put the kekkul on.' Mr Smith sat down and studied his surroundings as Davey made his way into the kitchen. He had barely had time to scan the room when a loud 'Ooohhh!' followed immediately by the thud of what sounded suspiciously like a falling body, caused him to jump in alarm.

'Oh dear!' said a worried Mr Smith springing to his feet and hurrying to investigate.

Two minutes later he had managed to drag a white faced Davey back into the living room, and heave him onto the settee.

'My bag,' he muttered. 'Must get my stethoscope . . . could have a major crisis on my hands . . . at last!'

Hands sweaty with anticipation, he retrieved his stethoscope, and, bending forward, he placed the pad on Davey's chest – over the breast pocket.

Nothing. Nothing? How could there be nothing? Suddenly panicked, Mr Smith snatched the pad from Davey's chest, shook it vigorously and applied it to his own. There! Yes a thump-thump-thump. It was not very loud admittedly – but there was a definite thump-thump-thump. He put the pad back on his patient's chest. Nothing!

'Uh-oh! Uh-oh! Uh-oh! He wailed executing the opening steps of a little Saint Vitus dance of agitation, as a nasty thought bored its way to the surface of his brain. In a sudden state of turmoil the steps kicked up a gear or two.

'Wrong pills! Wrong pills! Malpractice! Malpractice!' he cried; unaware that a combination of ear wax, folded shirt sleeve, paper packet and twenty pound note, were conspiring to muffle completely any sign of life.

'Uh-oh! Uh-oh! Uh-oh! Got to go! Go now! Malpractice!' The slamming of the door did nothing to disturb the little figure on the settee that lay with only a large throbbing bulge in its trousers to indicate that life still existed.

'Wake up you dozy likkul sod.' Zelda shook his shoulder roughly and was rewarded with a little groan.

'What? What?' Davey opened his eyes and groaned again. 'I fainted.' Zelda's mouth pruned.

'Oh yeah; you lay down on the settee an fainted.'

'No. I was in the kit . . . Are you on yer own?'

'Course I'm on me own. You fink I brought Brad Pitt back from Asda with me!' Davey heaved himself up into a sitting position.

'Was Mr Smiff 'ere?'

'Mr Smith? Not since last Wensdee. You bin dreamin?'

'Yeah. Must a bin,' said Davey with a little hint of relief in his voice. He gingerly climbed to his feet and with an exaggerated John Wayne swagger, took a few tentative steps towards the bathroom, where he intended to flush the remaining evidence of Mr Smith's visit down the loo. Zelda, hands on hips, watched his slow exit.

'Why you walkin like you've bin buggered by a bleedin bull elephant?' she asked.

'Er, me leg's a bit stiff,' he mumbled.

Zelda shook her head as she made her way into the kitchen with the grocery bags. A minute later after the flushing of the toilet he joined her and made his way over to the sink to get a glass of water. As she began to unpack the bags she was suddenly startled by the sharp sound of breaking glass, followed closely by an 'Ooohhh!' and a heavy dull thud.

'What the bloody . . .' she whirled round to see him stretched out on the floor in an apparent dead faint.

Five minutes later, and on the settee, he opened his eyes and groaned.

'Ah yer back with us then.' Zelda's peroxide blond head loomed over him and a thin bright red-nailed hand reached out to adjust a damp facecloth on his forehead.

'Fainted agen,' said Davey matter-of-factly.

Zelda's gaze slid down from his face to his swollen groin.

'Yeah, well; if you will persist in 'avin pervy foughts an getting a stiffy on . . . it's yer own fault.' He was well indignant.

'It's not me!' he insisted. 'It's me todger, it's got a bleedin mind of its . . . oooohhhh!'

Hubert (not surprisingly) was still sitting in his usual chair at the table as a distraught Mr Smith barrelled into the dining room, reached for a bottle of brandy that sat on a silver salver on top of a cabinet, and poured a very large drink.

He drained the glass, coughed, refilled it with trembling hands and downed it again before collapsing into a chair opposite his silent companion.

'Wrong pills Hubert! Wrong pills! Uh-oh! Uh-oh! Uh-oh!' Across the table Hubert's empty eye sockets seemed to radiate an accusing stare.

'Malpractice!' Moaned Mr Smith. Hubert's stare seemed to intensify and his lipless mouth appeared to be on the verge of uttering crushing condemnation.

The accused lowered his eyes away from the

terrible, one-time friendly visage and whimpered. So this is what it had come down to! A life dedicated to the well-being of his fellow man; a life of service to those in need of his ministrations, gone. Just like that, with the pop of a pill!

The GMC would strike him off. The world would condemn him for a malpractitioner. They would take away his beloved instruments and his pills – they would take away the only reason he had to live!

'What to do!' What to do! He wailed. Then, almost before the brooding air had gobbled up the tortured words, the answer crept into his head. Wrong pills, he thought . . . Now right pills . . . Suddenly he was calmer. He reached for his bag, snapped open the catch and turned the contents out onto the dining table.

There was his stethoscope, three spatulas, a tin of sticking plasters, two elastic knee bandages, a notepad – and twenty assorted bottles of pills.

Three days later, when examining the contents of Mr Smith's stomach, the pathologist was heard to exclaim: 'I've seen some drug cocktails in my time; but this one's got just about everything from Aspirin to Zantac via Viagra and Smarties!'

19

With a puzzled look on her face, Zelda replaced the receiver.

'What?' said Davey.

'That was Mrs Mason.'

'So?'

'Mr Mason . . . 'ees bin arrested.'

'What for?'

'Drug smugglin . . .' Davey's eyes widened then his mouth sprouted a sudden grin.

'Good! Serve the bastard right . . . way 'ee teks the piss outer me.' Then, as suddenly as the grin had blossomed it faded and died.

'Shit!'

'What?'

'I'll proberly never get me fiver now!' Zelda shook her head.

'Never mind yer fiver you div. 'Ee was arrested when 'is car crashed yesterday. You know, the car you was in . . . with the avocados . . . avocados full of cocaine . . .' Davey's eyes widened again.

'Cocaine! Shit!'

'Yeah, shit; an you cudda bin in it up to yer likkul neck if 'ee 'adn't of left you standin at that garrige.' Davey whistled softly.

"Ee'l proberly get bail,' he said, all hope of getting his fiver not quite dashed.

'Not accordin to Mrs Mason, she says 'ee refused it for some reason.'

'Shit.'

'Yeah well,' said Zelda with a rising note of brightness in her voice, 'Mrs Mason wants to meet me over at the club tomorrer afternoon. She reckons coz she dunt know anythin about runnin it, that I could take it on with 'er 'elp!' Davey perked up instantly.

'Yeah great! Then you could do a sneaky an get me fiver back outer the till eh?'

Frumpy, dumpy and 40, Marjorie Mason, felt that all her previous birthdays had pitched up at once. She had been married to Charlie Mason for eight years. Eight years of being an underpaid skivvy. Eight years of him chasing young skirt and playing the 'big time Charlie'.

Eight years that had gradually sandpapered away any silly notions of eternal connubial bliss.

'Ee's a prick,' her mother had said through a shower of crumbs from a slice of wedding cake; cake that had somehow remained undamaged – even after falling off the back of a lorry.

'Yes, a prick!' Marjorie spat the words into the empty air as she slid into the driver's seat of her clapped out Corsa. 'A prick that is going to be out of my hair for a good few years!'

She had on occasion – particularly in the early

214

years of the marriage – asked him to let her take part in the running of the *Blue Cockatoo*. He had always slapped her down with some sneering remark relating to a woman's place being in the home looking after her lord and master and not getting ideas above her station.

'Well I've got plenty of ideas now prick!' she mouthed into her rear-view mirror as she reversed into a parking space in the little car park behind the club and killed the engine. The name, for a start. She was a big fan of Country music.

Once she got his name removed from the licence – and as a convicted drug dealer that shouldn't prove too difficult – she would turf out all the pimps, pushers, prostitutes and piss heads, and re-name the place *The MCC* (Manchester Country Club).

She would extend the dance floor, re-decorate and open a little in-club shop, selling tapes, CD's, DVD's, stetsons, checked shirts, tassled leather skirts and cowboy boots. She would even look to bring in a dance teacher who could lead the new members in all the latest dance steps.

Yes, she thought, as she made her way round the front to meet Zelda, *the little worm is now well on the turn*.

Inside, Zelda was delighted.

'So I can be the manageress an 'ave a real say in the runnin of the place?' Marjorie nodded.

'Certainly, you're the one with the club and

bar experience. I'll look after all the financial dealings, like takings and bills and booking the turns and you can handle all the rest. You can even hire, and if necessary, fire your own staff.' Zelda shook her head in wonder.

'Wow! So I can take on anyone, like even if they're not like very experienced?' Marjorie shrugged.

'That's up to you Zelda, you're the boss it's your responsibility.' Zelda nodded slowly in wonder at the turn of events.

'Well in that case,' she said, 'there's this likkul guy I look after, I'll bring 'im in to do some pot collectin . . . if that's okay?'

'You mean Stumpy — by the way what's his real name?'

'It's Davey,' said Zelda in slight surprise. 'How do you know about 'im?'

'Oh, I've heard the Prick going on about him from time to time.'

'Oh, then you probably won't want 'im 'ere then eh?' Marjorie smiled and shook her head.

'Not at all, anyone who can get up my dear husband's greasy nose is all right by me . . . and anyway it looks as though your Davey is the one to thank for the way things are turning out.'

'What do you mean?' said Zelda frowning. 'How does 'ee come into it?'

'The car crash that got the Prick nabbed; it was caused by a fire that was started by a lit cigarette that had somehow fallen into a pile of rubbish.' Zelda shrugged her bony shoulders and looked none the wiser.

'And?'

'The Prick doesn't smoke cigarettes, he's into cheap cigars; your Davey, the Prick picked him up that morning didn't he?'

'Yeah?'

'He smokes cigarettes, doesn't he?'

'Well yeah, 'ee's always nickin me f . . .' Zelda's eyes widened as realisation began to dawn.

'Davey! Bloody 'ell! The likkul sod's done somefin right fer a change!' Marjorie grinned.

'That's right the little sod has. Oh, and by the way, according to his solicitor Charlie keeps referring to him as a "likkul twat", so I reckon he's all right by me.' Zelda put her hand to her mouth to stifle a belly laugh.

'I don't believe it! So I've got 'im to fank fer all this,' she said, indicating the club with a sweep of her bony arms.

'It certainly looks that way,' said Marjorie, as she cast her eyes slowly around the dim interior. 'All this, as you call it, might not look up to much just now, but once we've got stuck in and transformed it, we'll both have something to really thank your little Davey for.'

'Wow! An I'll really be a boss wiv a proper wage anall?' Marjorie laughed lightly.

'Of course, and if things work out and we

make decent profits, then maybe there would be some kind of bonus scheme at the end of the year.' Zelda shook her head again. Things like this didn't happen to her. Surely it was too good to be true – this remarkable change of fortune. She had to test it out, she was, after all, so much more used to kicks in the teeth than kind words and helping hands. Squaring her shoulders she took a deep breath and thought *here goes*.

'But you don't even know me,' she said firmly. 'I could rip you off or make a cock up of fings . . .' Marjorie smiled.

'I'm not stupid. I know you've got a, shall we say, chequered history.' Zelda felt a sudden churning in the pit of her stomach, and the faint smile that had taken up permanent residence over the last few minutes faded from her thin lips.

'It's all right,' Marjorie assured her, 'he told me a few things about you, and as you can imagine, knowing the kind of maggot he is, he wasn't very complimentary. But I know you really run the place and whatever things he called you, thief or dummy weren't included in them. No. I reckon we'll make a good team.'

Zelda's sick feeling passed quickly, but was then replaced by a little nagging feeling of doubt.

'But what if 'ee gets off with it, an 'ee kyboshes all yer plans?' Marjorie shook her head.

'No chance, my uncle, Jeremy, is a Local Magistrate. I've already discussed things with him.

He reckons the Prick will definitely go down for at least two or three years, and that's only if he comes clean and implicates the others. Believe me he's so shit scared of getting his kneecaps blown off that he'll end up carrying the can on his own. Should end up with at least five years.'

Later, back at Fort Beswick, Zelda sported a huge grin. Davey was non-plussed. He couldn't remember, in all the time he had known her, ever seeing a real smile on her kite. If her lips did occasionally twitch upwards it was usually the pre-cursor to some sarky remark, or a weary, slow spelling out of some perfectly simple matter that he didn't apparently have the nous to grasp.

'What you so 'appy about?'

'A proper job an a proper wage, that's what.' Her smile grew even bigger and was matched by Davey's growing sense of wonder.

'Wow!' he said, almost as much for the startling transformation as for the promise of some very welcome extra cash coming in.

'Mrs Mason reckons 'ee's goin to get at least four or five years. Oh,' she paused, and took something from her pocket. 'Seein as 'ow I'm in such a good mood, 'ere, cop for this.' Davey did a little jig of delight as he clutched the crumpled fiver to his chest.

Later, as she outlined Marjorie's plans he was even perkier.

'Cowboy 'ats an boots!' he crowed.

'Yeah all the staff will wear em. It's all part of the . . .' she was about to say 'ambiance', but thought better of it, instead she said, 'style of the club.' Davey opened his mouth to say something, but she cut him off. 'An no, before you ask, no six shooters . . .'

That night Davey dreamt he was Pecos Pete facing down an ornery Black Hat Bart, who bore more than a passing resemblance to an erstwhile club owner and little person baiter.

For the next few days Zelda was busy conferring with Marjorie regarding the refurbishment.

Each time she returned to the flat she rattled on *ad-nauseum* about bat-wing doors, jugs of beer, spittoons (decorative only) sawdust, fiddle players and general 'he ha slap my thigh-ness'. Her startling transmogrification from acid-tongued harridan to happy-go-lucky flatmate/carer was a constant source of wonder to him. She seemed to have given up slagging him off and she even asked him what he fancied at meal times.!

'I don't get it;' he mused, 'it's like she's grateful fer sumfin I've done . . .'

As there was no further mention of pistols, Davey soon got bored. And anyway, he had more important things on his mind . . . like the five-a-side final at the *G-Mex Exhibition Centre* where the Reds were to appear in under a fortnight, along with a number of other five-a-side teams in the warm ups to the Northern Senior Ex-Pro's competition.

20

In the *Derby Arms* a short, thickset late middle-aged man, wearing a baseball cap and Japanese General glasses was animatedly watching a horse race unfold on Channel Four.

'C'mon me likkul beauty!' he yelled. 'C'mon me darlin!' Tony, pass me me whip!' The barman grinned, leaned over the bar and handed the punter an imaginary goad. The little man cracked the whip three times at the galloping horses.

'C'mon baby! C'mon baby! ARRGGHH YOU USELESS THREE-LEGGED BASTARD!' The barman picked up and began to polish a glass as the punter turned away from the screen and violently shredded a blue betting slip.

'I take it yer nag come second then Kipper?'

'Fuk off an give us another pint.'

'Charmin as ever,' said the barman, as he reached up and took a pint glass down from the shelf.

That little tableau complete, it was followed by another that was being played out at the other end of the vault, where four tanked-up youths were playing Knob-End pool.

Two teams, of two usually tipsy players, risked this unusual version that decreed that when a ball was potted, the next player on the opposing team was obliged to place the end of his todger in the jaws of a mousetrap on the edge of the table. Howls of pain and riotous bellows of crude laughter followed each eye-watering SNAP!

Fortunately for the long term well-being of each player's family jewels the chances of a clear-up in this game were extremely remote as all the contestants were sufficiently in their cups to preclude any one of them potting more than one or two balls on the trot.

Once the distraction from the game had tailed off, and four limping inebriates had filed out — possibly to enter into a game of acrotwats by clambering up scaffolding or tightrope walking high walls — the Beswick Reds returned to a discussion of tactics to use against the enemy, the *Pig and Ferret*, from Poynton.

'Do we know,' asked Billy, 'oo I 'ave ter clatter?' Captain Fred — who had gained the esteemed position of captain mainly due to the fact that he was "heducated" (he had spent a year as a Sociology student at Manchester Uni before dropping out) and could talk proper — nodded.

'Yeah I've seen them. They've got a little bastard with ginger hair . . . fancies himself as

Scholesy.'

'Sorted,' said Billy. Tactics concluded they moved on to the serious matter of downing a few jars.

'Your shout Dimp,' said Fred, indicating his empty pint pot. Davey nodded, climbed down from his stool and made his way over towards the bar. As he approached it he noticed a late middle-aged, balding man, in a black leather jacket who was smiling at him.

'Y'all right?' said Davey, wondering if he knew the other from somewhere.

'Yes. You?' Davey nodded.

'Yeah.' Then: 'Do I know you?' The man's smile remained enigmatic.

'No, I don't think so – but I know you David Ignatius Montgomery Parker.' This response was met with a little shrug, for Davey was aware that he was quite well known in these parts, what with him being something of a footballing phenomenon – that, and of course, because there weren't many one-armed dwarfs in Beswick, Openshaw or Clayton.

After he had made the necessary trips to and from the bar to transport the refreshments, Davey hitched himself up onto his stool and turning slightly, nodded in the direction of the man in the leather jacket.

''Oo's 'ee?' he said to no-one in particular. 'Im wiv the baldy 'ead an levver jacket?' Fred looked over Davey's shoulder.

'Don't know,' he said, 'except I think he's some sort of writer or something . . .'

'Yeah? Well 'ee sez 'ee knows me an I don't know 'im from bleedin Adam,' said Davey.

'Yeah, well he would know you big man,' Fred replied. 'You're bleedin famous aint you!' Davey grinned and nodded.

'Yeah, suppose so.'

Three pints down the line their banter was interrupted when the vault door swung open and a tall grey-haired, pinch-faced man strode stiffly into the room.

'Uh Oh, Billy!' said Fred, who was facing the door, 'It's your old man.' Billy turned slowly on his stool.

'Shit!' he muttered, 'that's put a bleedin dampener on it.'

At 26, Billy White was the oldest of five brothers and two sisters. The others had all been born in the Manchester area, whereas he had been a toddler when his parents had moved across from Belfast to escape "the troubles". He was followed by Bill at 23, William at 20, Willy at 18 and Will at 15. Spread between the boys was the two girls, who didn't really matter (probably because their mother had put her foot down firmly and refused to have them named Billy or any other derivative thereof).

As can perhaps be gleaned, Billy's dad (Billy) was old school Orange. When he spoke, it was with muted thunder from the pulpit. When he moved, it was with ramrod stiffness.

Nobody had ever seen him out, even on the stickiest summer day, without a collar and tie on. It was rumoured that he kept a signed photograph of Ian Paisley in a frame on a bedside table, and that he saluted it every night before turning out the bedroom light.

Some wags even said that if Mrs White wanted to turn him on all she had to do was slip on his orange sash and don his bowler hat and Bill's yer uncle – he would be standing stiffly to attention.

'All right Da?' said Billy with forced cheerfulness.

'I am!' boomed Billy as he strode over to the table. Billy smiled weakly at his approach.

'What you doin up 'ere then Da? You usually stay int *Manchister*.' Billy glowered.

'It's full of painted women, giggling and squealing!' was the 85-decibel reply. The reds looked on blankly.

'Oh right!' said Billy. 'Linda wotsits 'en night innit . . . male stripper.' Billy's face darkened.

'Abomination! Sodom and Gomorrah!' (90 decibels and rising) Davey jumped in his seat, and several pint glasses on the bar shelf performed a nervous little rattling shimmy.

'Whoa Da!' said Billy, making a calm down motion with both hands. 'It's just a bit of fun . . .'

'FUN!' roared Billy, his face turning a deeper

shade of puce.

'Yeah;' Curtley butt in (unwisely), 'maybe your girls is down there anall getting an eyeful, eh Billy?'

'Ohhhshit! Ohhhshit!' muttered Billy as Billy lunged forward, bent, and shook Curtley none too gently by the throat.

'My girls are God fearing girls you heathen!'

'Uuurrkkk!'

'Da! Da!' pleaded Billy. 'Let go of 'im now, 'ee's turnin blue!'

Billy relaxed slightly and removed his grip, but his eyes were still ablaze with righteous outrage. Curtley swallowed painfully and massaged his throat.

'Nutter!' he croaked. 'An I'm not an 'eathen eever, I'm an Anglican.'

'Next door to a Papist!' mouthed Billy, shooting him a look of utter disdain.

'Enough Da! No more religion right!' said Billy forcefully.

'You want a pint, fine I'm buyin, but no more religion right?' Billy took a deep breath.

'Guinness,' he said, straightening his tie, easing an inch of crisp white shirt sleeve out of each arm of his immaculate charcoal grey suit, adjusting his Union Jack cufflinks and parking himself on a stool between Davey and Fred.

Billy's lively arrival proved to be an immediate and bazzing conversation stopper. Curtley, Fred and Tommy developed a sudden and intense interest in their pint pots; lifting, sipping, studying and then reverentially placing them gently back on the table.

Davey looked from one to the other, then, as Billy returned from the bar carrying a pint of Guinness – and in much the same way that Joan of Ark's jailer could have exhibited a marked lack of sensitivity by asking if she would like a flame grilled steak for her last meal – said lightly by way of casual conversation: 'So mister White, you're an Oranger are yuh then?'

The next hour – which included a history lesson taking in the Battle of the Boyne, the heroics of the Apprentice Boys, the murderous duplicity of the IRA, the INLA, the Real IRA, various other Fenian splinter groups and the mealy-mouthed treachery of certain Unionist politicians – took three hours to pass. Dirty jokes, tales of loose women and swearing were out.

They thought they were on safe ground with United; but it transpired that Old Billy held the view that they were still a Catholic-rooted club, and that how any son of his could betray his heritage by supporting "fenians" was a dagger thrust to his heart. So that was United well and truly off the agenda too.

The only good thing to come out of the session was the news that Billy Senior had managed to wangle a free coach from the Maynes' Bus Company – where he worked as a driver.

This meant the team and the supporters could

be driven down to the *G-Mex Exhibition Centre* in style and then be driven back, hopefully in triumph, to *The Derby* for after-match celebrations that were set to include cheese and tomato, ham and tomato and egg and tomato butties (the landlord's wife had a veg stall on Grey Mare Lane market), Bury black pudding and hot pot with brown sauce and pickled red cabbage.

The next strained half hour or so limped along with the occasional brief foray into short (safe) conversations that were kicked off with questions such as: 'Flipping cold terday int it? 'Did yer see Corrie lass night?' and 'I don't care what anyone sez, Bodies bitter int what it useta be is it?'

Eventually, even toothache has to stop. Billy senior drained his pot, checked his watch, straightened his tie and rose to his feet.

'I'm away now,' he said. 'The abominations in the *Manchester* will have run their filthy course.'

'Right Da,' said Billy, pushing his stool back and standing loosely to attention. 'I'll see yuh later.' Billy nodded and turned on his heel.

'Fank Christ fer that!' Billy muttered to Billy's retreating back, as his old man made his way over to and out of the vault door.

'Bit of a card 'im int 'ee?' said Davey as the door shushed to. Billy pulled a face.

'Yeah, the King of bleedin Clubs!'

'Fukin nutter if you ask me!' said Curtley, raising a hand to massage his throat. 'Cudda frokkled me . . . fukin nutter.'

'Fink yerself lucky,' Billy answered lightly. 'Cuppla years back one bloke ended up wiv is 'ead in a sling fer two munfs after makin some crack about the size of our Maureen's threpnee bits.'

'Well, she has got a fair old pair on her,' said Fred. Billy scowled. He wasn't sure about Fred. All right he seemed one of the lads, but he talked posh and didn't come from round here, not really; and on top of all that he was one of them huniversity wallies . . . liked to see themselves as one of the proles . . . all brothers under the skin, an all that shite.

He'd pitched up one night at the *Queen Vic* about two years ago, and after a couple of pints he'd made a point of starting a conversation with Davey, just like to prove that he was a man of the people and that the big man's problems were kinda like . . . invisible.

Still, Davey reckoned he was okay and, Billy had to admit, once Fred had joined in on a few kickabouts on the spare ground outside Barmouth Street Swimming Baths, he turned out to be a decent enough player.

In fact, it was Fred who'd suggested they put together a proper five-a-side team in the first place. So yeah, ee was probably okay. That didn't mean ee shouldn't ave is card marked though.

'Yeah, an you'll be suckin yer dinner frew a fukin straw if 'ee ever catches you anywhere near 'er,' Billy said coolly. His doubts about Fred as a bloke might have faded, but he had his suspicions regarding the captain's intentions towards his sister.

He also knew that Maureen's lack of resistance to almost anything in strides that was accompanied by a reasonably well-stuffed wallet was common knowledge to all and sundry (with the obvious exception of her Da).

21

In the vestry at Saint Brigid's, a sober suited and dog collar-less John James stared at the large black suitcase that contained his meagre personal possessions.

'So this is it,' he said quietly to himself. 'I'm really going to do it.'

He knew in his own heart that he was not a brave man. A brave man would not have buried his doubts under a mountain of pious prayer. And when that mountain had finally crumbled, a brave man would not have agonised and deliberated *ad nauseum*. No, a brave man would have acted decisively before nagging doubt had developed into full-blown crisis.

He had plugged those cracks of doubt with tissues of delusion. Knowing even as he did so that they were sure to disintegrate and the buttress of his faith come tumbling down like the walls of Jericho.

Yes, he was weak; but there comes a time in the life of every weak man when he is faced with stark and unavoidable choice – In his case it was "Accept" or "Change". He had finally chosen Change.

He had composed and posted a letter to the Bishop yesterday. In it he had apologised for the suddenness of his resignation.

He had also assured the Bishop that his actions would in no way rebound to the detriment of the Church, as they were not connected with anything relating to impropriety with children (a topic that was increasingly rearing its ugly head within the Catholic Church these days).

Instead he had cited a slow but gathering feeling of non-fulfillment; an increasing desire to step down from the pulpit and away from the comfortable, ordered life of the priesthood and into the unsure – but exciting – secular world.

He didn't actually confess to having already sampled a little of what was on offer in that secular world; but he thought that the Bishop, who was a very well grounded man, would have no difficulty in reading between the lines.

Forty-five year old Agnes Williams had been

taken aback when he had suggested the drastic course of action.

She had been a widow for over five years, and in spite of the recent (and now quite regular) plunges from grace with Father James, she still considered herself to be a stalwart of The Faith.

The idea of being responsible for depriving the Church of a long serving and dedicated servant had caused her more than a little consternation, and led to her quizzing him deeply as to his resolve. He had fielded her questions honestly and without any apparent wavering regarding his intent.

'Are you one hundred percent sure?' she had said earnestly. When he had smiled and nodded, she instantly abandoned any further notion of trying to deter him. This was what she had secretly yearned for, but had never had the strength to suggest.

She had told him of the smallholding lying between Llanfyllin and Lake Vyrnwy in North Wales. It had come down to her after the death of her mother some nine months earlier, and was now being run by a manager, but she had the option of taking over at short notice should she wish to do so. And now she did.

'It will be a shock to your system,' she warned. 'It's hard work and often very dirty work. Long hours, not much pay . . .' He had grinned.

'It's what I want and need after years of being wrapped in cotton wool and isolated from the world at large.'

So, here he was – after twenty-odd years of commitment to the faith and several more years of snowballing doubt – on the brink of a momentous change of direction that would colour the rest of his life. And all thanks in no small way to a life-defining conversation with a little one-armed man.

He would soon be on his way to pick her up from her little two-bedroomed terrace house in nearby Manipur Street, and from there they would be taken to Piccadilly train station and on to a new life as a couple.

The taxi horn blared. He took a last look around the familiar room, bent, picked up the fairly light suitcase and made his way confidently to the door.

22

"Ow do I look then?' Zelda stood back a pace and took in the (on his head, fifteen gallon) ten gallon black cowboy hat, the black boot lace tie with the silver ruby-eyed bull's head fastener, the red and black check shirt, the wide black belt with silver buckle, and blue jeans tucked into tan cowboy boots. She made a conscious effort to smother the birth of a smile.

'You look like you just jumped off yer 'orse, especially with those pins,' she said, pointing to the natural bow in his little legs. He took it as a compliment, but then had a little whinge anyway.

'Why'd you get me a black 'at?'

'What's wrong with it?' Davey sighed and shook his head.

'Everyone knows that black 'ats are fer baddies, goodies wear white 'ats.'

'So, simple, be a baddy.' He pulled a little face.

'An me boots, they're too big. Me feet look like bleedin coal barges.' She looked down. He was right they did look out of proportion.

'They were the smallest we could get; an anyway, they'll stop you from fallin over when you get pissed.'

'Very funny,' he muttered clumping around the room.

'They'll be okay,' she offered, 'just stuff 'em with a bit of newspaper.'

'I suppose so,' he muttered, not too convinced.

The club redecorating and refurbishment had been rushed through in double-quick time with the sweetener of a bonus for the decorators and joiners.

The curry house flock had been consigned to history and replaced by adobe stucco, punctuated with brightly coloured cactus murals. The three foot high stage had been ripped out, and an eighteen inch high, much smaller version – large enough for a couple of musicians – had taken its place, and the small wooden dance floor had been enlarged to cater for big session line dancing.

The dim ceiling lighting, so conducive to previous nefarious activities involving banned substances, hookey gear and clandestine assignations, had been replaced by three suspended wagon wheels, each of which carried six bright down lighter fittings arranged around the rim.

Four high-level black spotlight bars with white, red or blue tinged filtered fittings covered the dance floor and stage area, while the bat wing entrance and the toilets signs were also picked out by down lighter spots.

All the new fittings had individual switches and dimmers that were controlled from behind the bar. Overall the transformation from dark back street shabeen to bright in yer face openness was, in Zelda's words, 'bleedin amazin!'

Zelda, Marjorie and Myrna the waitress, had been kitted out in red neckerchiefs, white blouses and tasselled brown suede waistcoats and skirts. The ensemble was then topped off with white calf-length cowboy boots.

Back in the flat, when she had first tried on her outfit, the words mutton and lamb had crossed Zelda's mind as she looked at the finished article in the bedroom mirror.

'But what the 'ell,' she had muttered to her reflection, 'mutton's good enough if you've got nowt else.' Saying the words, she realised with surprise that she meant it. Life had taken a turn for the better and where once, not long ago, any conversation with her mirror twin would have centred around sour discontent aimed at life's repeated smacks in the gob – now she could come over all philosophical!

'Times they are a changing!' she mouthed at her reflection – which nodded in agreement.

In an effort to get the new venture off to a flying start Marjorie had been busy spreading the word about the Wednesday night opening through her country and western loving friends and via the local press. She had also rung a number of C&W clubs throughout Lancashire, and these measures between them had resulted in almost fifty firm bookings, included among which was a twenty strong coach party from Accrington.

'It's a great start,' she said to Zelda, 'and once word gets around it can only get better.' Zelda agreed. In the time she had worked at the *Blue Cockatoo* she had never seen the place pull in more than thirty or forty maximum on any one night, and those that it did pull were, almost without exception, more like the crud than the cream of the crop. She was sure that forty and fifty-something year-old happy couples would certainly make a change from the usual simian browed short-fused pissheads she had had to put up with over the last year or so.

'I'm really up for this!' she said to Davey as the cab passed the new neon sign that proclaimed 'MCC' in electric blue two-foot high letters and pulled into the car park.

From his seat next to her in the back of the taxi Davey glanced across and marvelled again at the change. She was almost happy and for Zelda that was a mood shift of seismic proportions . . . no shit.

Marjorie greeted them at the door and was about to make a go on through gesture, but was stopped as Davey slid beneath her upraised arm.

As he pushed his way through the bat wing doors in the little reception area and entered the club proper, he tilted the stetson back on his head and gave a little whistle of appreciation.

'Wow!' he muttered, taking in the brightly painted orange-brown walls with their glowing green cacti stencils, the wagon wheel lighting, the rough round wooden tables and straight-backed chairs, the three fat brass (decorative) spittoons that squatted beneath a new brass bar rail and the alterations to the stage and dance floor.

'It's jus like a saloon!' he marvelled as Zelda and Marjorie came through to join him.

'Well, what you fink then?' asked Zelda.

'It's bloody ace!' he said as Marjorie grinned

down on him. She had never met him before and she hoped that the expression on her face when he moseyed through the front door hadn't offended him. Zelda had spotted her reaction and had given her a little smile and shake of the head that translated as, 'he's just a big soft kid'.

With an hour to go before opening, the band (in the shape of Brian and Eric) arrived and began to lug in and set up their gear. After they had tuned up Davey hitched up his jeans and sauntered over.

'Howdy.' he drawled.

'All right cock?' said Brian, the older of the two musicians. Davey frowned lightly.

'Yeah, I mean YEP.'

'Oh,' said Brian, 'you fink we should talk cowboy like?' Davey nodded.

'Course; it's part of the . . . style, int it?'

'Right then pardner', said Eric, the younger, 'ow about you mosey over to the bar and get us two arfs of bitter while we run frew a coupla numbers?' Davey tipped his hat back on his head.

'Cummin up,' he drawled.

'A coach just passed!' said Zelda twenty minutes later. 'It must be the Accrington lot.'

'Eight o'clock on the dot!' said an excited Marjorie, who then turned to Davey. 'Go and unlock the door,' she said. 'And when they come in you greet them right?'

'Me!'

'Yes you. It will be quite a . . . pleasant

surprise for them.' The little man shrugged, and turned to make his way towards the bat wing doors.

'Yeah,' muttered Zelda to his retreating back. 'One that should make a big impression all right.'

'Howdy folks!' Davey boomed to a series of startled looks.

'If you'll just step this way folks,' said Marjorie, 'and print your names in the membership book, we'll have your membership cards ready for when you leave later.'

With the Accrington party ushered in, Marjorie and Zelda made their way through to the bar to serve drinks, leaving Davey at Reception.

'Just greet anyone that comes in and ask them to sign in the book,' said Zelda. He was not too pleased.

'Aww! I want to come in.' Zelda pruned it.

'Just do it eh. Mrs Richards phoned up earlier, she's bin 'eld up coz their Shane just stuck a knittin neegul in a plug socket an fused all the electrics in the miggul of Eastenders. She'll be 'ere anytime now, but till she comes you're the receptionist, right?'

'Right,' he muttered hitching up his jeans.

Half an hour later, after he had greeted several new members and Mrs Richards turned up to relieve him of reception duties, he turned to make his way through to the club proper – just as the front door flew open and a large and decidedly tired and emotional man staggered in.

239

'Pint a bitter!' he ordered of Mrs Richards.

'No chance, yer pissed,' she replied.

''Oo's pished?'

'You are, an anyway it's members only.' The big man frowned and was about to argue the point when he noticed Davey.

'Fukin 'ell, if it int Billy the fukin likkul Kid!' Davey looked up into the bleary-eyed grinning face.

'Sorry pardner,' he drawled. 'The lady's right it's members only now.'

'That so?' said the big man, his voice hardening as the fact that he was going to be denied refreshment seeped into his fuddled brain. Davey shrugged.

'Yep,' he said.

'Yep?' Yep? What the fuks wiv yep? I want a drink an I want it pronto . . . savvy?'

It's a Mexican standoff, Davey thought, and it was, for about three seconds, until the drunk lumbered forward and like a man demanding his dinner on the table now from his little woman, brought a fist down with authority on the top of Davey's black hat.

'Ow!' said Davey as the hat concertina'd round his ears and over his eyes and his knees buckled.

'Bastard!' he yelled, as his legs straightened and he shot blindly forward in the direction of his attacker. 'Oooff!' said the big man as the little blur smacked into his groin, and then 'Aaarrghh!' as teeth like a steel bear trap locked onto his testicles. With suddenly watering eyes and an agony induced gaping mouth he looked down at the appalling sight of two cold diamond bright eyes above a snuffling nose staring up at him.

'Nooo!' he begged as the little apparition began to shake its head from side to side like a bull terrier worrying a fat rat. 'Please!' He pleaded. Davey relented and the drunk collapsed to his knees cupping his damaged jewels

'Pffftt! Pfftt!' 'Euuu!' spat Davey, trying to remove the odour of stale urine from his mouth.

'I'm corlin the law!' shouted Mrs Richards as Davey struggled to pull the battered hat up from his eyes and his victim staggered to his feet, turned, and limping heavily, shouldered his way out through the front door.

'It's all right,' Davey said in a voice that should have been accompanied by two hands dusting themselves off, 'ee's gone, bovver over.' Mrs Richards whistled in appreciation.

'Wow, that's some likkul party trick that is!'

'Yeah, well,' said Davey with another little metaphorical dusting of hands, 'when yer likkul you as ter use yer 'ead an yer teef, or else yer in the shit.'

'What's goin on? What's all the racket?' Zelda demanded batting aside the bat wing doors and striding through into the reception area.

'Nowt now!' said Mrs Richards. 'Some big

drunk just tried it on, but your Davey sorted it.' Zelda looked down at him with a little spark of surprised admiration in her eyes.

'What's 'appened to yer 'at?' she demanded in an attempt to mask any weakness.

'Nuffin. Jus got a bit bent,' he said coolly, before removing it, chomping on the rim and ramming a little fist up inside to pop the crown back up into place. Mrs Richards grinned.

'Don't you believe 'im Zelda, 'ee was brill; drunken bastard hobbled out of 'ere wiv tears streamin down is kite!'

'Ah!' said Zelda nodding. 'Bin ballbitin agen 'ave we?' Davey slapped the hat back on his head and grinned.

As the night wore on, his mood, buoyed by his earlier exploits, blossomed, and he strutted around chatting to all and sundry.

'Jus call me Dead Eye Dave,' he introduced himself to one couple from Accrington; while another couple was assured: 'Any problems just ask fer Durango Davey.'

'He seems to be getting right into it,' said Marjorie as she watched him slipping from table to table collecting pots and talking to the punters. Zelda nodded.

'Yeah 'ee's in 'is element.'

'Yes, he is and that's good. Everybody seems to appreciate it too. Looks like he could be our little trump card.' Zelda looked across from behind the bar and saw him holding court at a table full of grinning grey-haired grannies.

'Yeah,' she mused with a smile on her lips, 'looks like the likkul bugger's got 'em wrapped round a stubby likkul finger all right.'

Intoxicated on success, Davey ambled over to the band.

'Time to liven it up a bit boys,' he drawled. ''Ow about yuh do Achey Breaky Art?' Brian looked at Eric, Eric, the singer shrugged.

'Achey Breaky it is then,' he said clearing his throat.

Davey made his way to the centre of the brightly lit dance floor

'C'mon folks, line up fer the Achey Breaky!' he ordered, beckoning his new fan club to their feet.

'I better get out there and lead the line,' Marjorie said from behind the bar. Zelda nodded and as Marjorie made her way onto the dance floor said, 'Yeah', I fink that's a good idea. The likkul sod might only 'ave one arm, but 'ee's got two good left feet to make up fer it . . .'

As Eric launched into the song, the three lines of mostly middle-aged dancers, with Marjorie up front and Davey just behind, stepped into the routine. After half a minute of tripping over his oversized boots, Davey managed to more or less pick up the steps.

'Hey look at me Zelda!' he shouted over to the bar. 'I'm dancin!' She looked and she smiled. Big hat, big boots, pudgy little hand tucked into belt and a grin to shame a Cheshire Cat.

'Yeah,' she said to herself. 'Go on, enjoy.'

The Achey Breaky was followed by a number of other Country classics, all of which filled the dance floor with happy fans. From her position behind the bar Zelda marvelled at the change in atmosphere. Where once there had been a dark brooding, bordering on belligerence, now the place literally jumped and sparkled with *bon homie*. I don't ave to worry about flyin beer pots or punters getting glassed anymore she thought, as the dance set finished and the smiling, flush-faced dancers made their way back to their seats.

'Did it look like they were enjoying themselves?' asked a sweating Marjorie as she moved back over to the bar to order a cooling glass of lemonade.

'In spades!' said a grinning Zelda as she filled and handed over a fizzing glass. She was about to add a comment about Davey's contribution when she spotted him making a beeline for the bar with a stricken look on his kite.

'What?' she managed, before he turned and pointed to the bat wing doors at the top of the stairs.

'It's 'im!' Zelda turned to look in the direction of Davey's suddenly trembling arm.

He was tall and whippet thin. He had a mashed nose and under the glare of an overhead spotlight that bathed the double doors in white light, the crescent scar beneath his close cropped hair stood out like a king sized frown – a scar, that if one had the bottle to get all up front and personal, and hold an upturned pint pot over it, would be neatly hidden by the vessel's rim.

'What's 'ee want?' Davey asked. Zelda turned to Marjorie who had picked up on the tension in Davey's voice.

'I reckon 'ee wants a word with the boss.' Marjorie turned to Zelda.

'Who is he?'

''Ee's one of your dear 'usband's card buddies. An if I'm not mistaken 'ee'l want to 'ave a word about that likkul business with the avocado's.'

'Well then,' said Marjorie with a degree or two more nonchalance in her voice then she felt; 'I'd better go and have a word.'

'We'll come with you,' said Zelda taking a reluctant Davey firmly by the arm.

As the little delegation approached, the thin man's mouth creased into a smile just wide enough for the overhead spotlight to pick out a glint of gold between the thin lips.

'Evenin all,' he said in a voice that was very much at odds with the rattlesnake look in his eyes.

'It's members only,' said Zelda as Davey edged slightly behind her.

'Yeah, I know, your kind receptionist just signed me up.' Marjorie nodded.

'Fine, everyone's welcome,' she said, 'as long as they don't cause any trouble.' The tall man's face took on a hurt look – but his eyes stayed firmly flat and cold.

'Trouble? Me? No way, I'm just a Country fan. Though,' he added, 'I must confess there is another reason for my visit.' His gold tooth disappeared as he suddenly dropped the charade. 'I've also come to 'ave a quiet word about Charlie Mason. Your 'usband, I take it?' He nodded towards Marjorie.

'Yes,' she said returning the nod. 'He is . . . for now at least.'

'Ah, yeah, I can understand that . . . bit of a pratt int 'ee?'

'I've re-christened him the Prick.'

'Fits 'im well. Anyway I want you to pass a message on to 'im when you see 'im before the trial.' Marjorie shook her head lightly.

'If I see him you mean.'

'No; when you see 'im.' Marjorie looked into the dead eyes and decided - yes when I see him.

'Right; what message?'

'You can tell 'im that Eddie is very upset.'

'Okay, is that it, Eddie is very upset?'

'Yeah, and oh, you can add, that if 'ee doesn't keep is big gob shut 'ee'l find 'imself holdin up some fukin flyover over a motorway.'

'Right, flyover over a motorway . . . I'll make sure I give him that message mister . . . Eddie?' Eddie nodded.

'Very kind of you I'm sure. Now that's out of the way is it okay if I 'ave a drink an listen to the music?'

'Certainly. Enjoy. Davey, a pint for our new member – on the house.'

After he had placed a pint – very gently – on the table where Eddie had taken up residence, Davey returned to the bar.

'Ee gives me the creeps!' he said with a little theatrical shudder.

'Yeah, well, it's sorted now,' said Zelda, as she looked over to where Eddie was tapping a knobbly tattooed hand on the table in time to the music. 'Looks like 'ee is a Country fan just like 'ee said.'

For the next half hour or so Eddie nodded his head and tapped his fingers. He also took an interest in the comings and goings of Davey, as the little man scuttled between the tables picking up empty pots and glasses and then returning with refills on a tray that he balanced with his one hand over his head.

On one of Davey's passes, Eddie narrowed his eyes, stroked his chin thoughtfully and took a mobile phone out of a jacket pocket and keyed in a number.

'Hi, it's me, Eddie,' he said. 'Yeah,' he added after a few seconds. 'Like I said it was out of me 'ands, pratt that did the pickup ballsed it up. But like I said yesterday, I've managed to trawl around me contacts for some more.' He nodded into the phone for a few seconds. 'Yeah, I can get it to you in time for the event tomorrer night. And by the way, just as a likkul fank you fer your patience I might be able to bring along a likkul novelty addition to yer cast.'

A minute after he had rung off Eddie collared Davey on his way to the bar.

'Eh, lofty,' he said crooking his finger, 'c'mere a minute, I've got a likkul proposition fer yuh.'

'Forty quid!' Zelda said back at the bar a couple of minutes later, 'ee's givin you forty quid for two or three 'ours waitin on!'

'Yeah, I've got it already, in me back pocket!' Zelda frowned. *What 'ave you got yerself into now* she thought. She sighed loudly then said with a tired edge to her voice: 'C'mon, let's go an 'ave a wee chat with mister generous.'

'What's all this?' she asked. 'Forty quid for a couple of 'ours fetchin an carryin at some private do? Where's the catch?' Eddie smiled thinly.

'No catch; friend of mine is throwing a likkul party that 'ee wants to film, an 'ee needs some extra staff.'

'What kind of party; an why 'im?' she said pointing to Davey. Eddie smiled thinly.

'It's a, shall we say, historical dress party; Roman actually.'

'Orgy.'

'Well, yeah I suppose . . .'

'An why 'im?'

248

'Adds a bit of debauchery to it, 'avin a dwarf in a toga fillin up goblets . . .' Zelda turned it over in her head for a few seconds. The moral side of things didn't cause her any problems. Christ, she'd even played a leading role in one or two "productions" herself in her younger days.

No, that was okay, but what about him? It was another case of "freak value", like the dwarf throwing incident. Would he handle it okay? *'Ark at you*, a little voice chimed in her head*, all concerned like you was is mam*. Irritated by the voice, she kicked it into touch.

'Right,' she said, 'but I'm comin anall to make sure 'ee's treated right . . . an forty's not enough, 'ee wants another tenner.'

'Right; just one fing though . . .'

'What?'

'Make sure you stay be'ind the bleedin camera.'

Later, back in the flat, Davey was buzzing.

'That was bloody great!' he trilled to Zelda. And to top it all he had a windfall fifty quid in his back pocket!

And his mood didn't waver, even when later, from his bed, he saw the door open and Zelda was silhouetted in the frame with a seductive smile on her face and dressed in her nurse's uniform.

23

'It's 'ere!' said Davey as he rushed out onto the landing in response to the sharp double toot that drifted up from below. 'Hey an it's a big Lexus anall!' he shouted back through the open landing door. Zelda, smiling at his excitement, said 'Right, you run down, I'll be there in a minute . . . as soon as I pick a pair of shoes,' she added, opening the double wardrobe door.

Ten minutes later and Eddie, in the front seat next to his driver was probably thinking something along the lines of: Why is it that a man can ave a shave, shower, shampoo, shit, cut is toenails, polish is shoes, get dressed, make an eat a snack, an read the first six chapters of The Lord of the Rings, while a bleedin woman is still agonising over which pair of shoes goes with er dress?

Three impatient bouts of horn thumping later: 'Right I'm 'ere now. What's all the tootin for?' Eddie shook his head and sighed as Zelda opened the rear door and slid in beside Davey.

'Well, come on then,' she said. 'We've not got all night.' Eddie turned and fixed her with one of his best dead-eyed stares.

'Y'know,' he said casually, 'I've 'ad blokes kneecaps blown off fer givin me less grief.' Zelda didn't seem at all phased.

'Well, I'm only finkin of you. Don't want to keep yer bignob friend waitin do you?' Eddie turned back in his seat, fixed his eyes dead ahead and said: 'Tommy, Lyme Park, Disley, on yer way.'

'Wow! This is a posh area int it?' Davey said forty minutes later as he weighed up the huge detached Georgian or Tudor houses with their cricket-pitch sized immaculately manicured lawns, which slid past on either side. From her seat next to him Zelda nodded. *Yeah, posh* she thought, *an every one of them probably home to some slimy theivin gett who got is fortune by shittin on the shoulders of all those poor sods under im.*

'Are we nearly there yet?' Zelda, dragged out of her little red reverie, shook her head in mild exasperation.

'The world's only seven-year-old thirty-year-old,' she muttered.

'What?'

'It doesn't matter.'

'Next on the left Tommy, pull up by the iron gates,' Eddie ordered.

'Right boss . . . what now?'

'Get out an press the intercom, an when they answer say Ave Caesar.' Davey's eyes widened.

'Did you 'ear that! It's just like spies an fings int it!' Zelda yawned.

'Yeah, dead interestin.' Tommy slid out pressed the intercom button, and after a few seconds delay spoke the passwords into the speaker slot. The gates shushed open.

'Hey, that's neat int it!'

'Yeah,' yawn. Seconds later as the Lexus rolled though the gates and onto a long drive, where the crunching gravel under the car's tyres seemed to whisper money, money, money, Zelda, in spite of her intention to remain aloof, was well impressed. Two hundred yards away on a gentle grassy rise the three- storey house looked imperiously down its nose at them. Zelda's immediate impression was of a Dixieland mansion – all white columns and long veranda.

As they drew nearer, the gravel drive bisected an immaculately manicured lawn that rolled like a soft green ocean swell to lap against a set of five wide marble steps. *Magnolia and Honeysuckle is all it's missin*, she thought. *Oh, an a rockin chair an a table with a glass jug of chilled mint julep*, she added mentally. Davey was also impressed.

'Wow, that's some pad int it!'

'Yeah,' she conceded, before adding quietly: 'An I bet 'ee's still an arse 'ole.'

Tommy slid the Lexus to a stop opposite the marble steps, climbed out and went round the front of the car to open Eddie's door. When he made no move to do the same for the back seat passengers Zelda directed a sour look at the back of his head and opened the door herself.

'C'mon,' she said to Davey, 'let's see what you've got us into now.'

As they joined Eddie on the lowest step he looked down at Tommy.

'Tek the motor round the back an park it up wiv the others, then knock on the back door. They'll sort you out wiv some refreshments an you can join the uvver drivers fer a game of cards or summat. You two follow me . . . an don't try ter nick anyfin.'

Zelda half expected Eddie's knock to be answered by a po-faced butler, instead, the door was opened by a huge, shaven-headed, broken-nosed specimen, who would surely have been more at home in the Gorilla House at Chester Zoo.

The specimen, without so much as a grunt, ushered them into an elegantly decorated, richly carpeted and painting-hung entrance hall.

'Hey, what the. . .' Zelda spluttered, as the doorman relieved her of her handbag and clipped open the catch.

'Cameras,' Eddie said as the man rummaged through the bag's contents before handing it back and bending down, ran his hairy paws over Davey's pockets. Satisfied, he grunted 'this way,' and pulled open a pair of large dark oak, brass handled doors.

The room, if that was the correct term, was enormous. It was at least 15 metres long, eight metres wide and some four metres high. The walls were painted in a rich deep burnt sienna, which was briefly interrupted at a height of about two metres, by a white picture rail, from which a number of erotic reproduction paintings hung.

There was Poussin's *Rape of the Sabine Women* with its chaotic melee of bodies clothed in vivid blues and reds and pinks. There was a depiction of Zeus in the form of a great white bull about to seduce the beautiful Europa. There were paintings of naked laughing Wood Nymphs with breasts like little ripe apples, being chased through sylvan glades by leering horned Satyrs with hairy goat's legs and cloven hoofs and draped in spotted panther skins, from which huge bowed erections jutted.

And there were paintings of willowy women with flowers woven into their hair and draped in sheer gossamer wraps that offered tantalising glimpses of roseate nipples and a hint of shadow at the tops of their thighs.

Above, the ceiling was painted in rich swirling honey whorls, and there were three huge, cut glass chandeliers, that shot out bright shards of light which bounced back from a floor made up of six inch by three inch polished Indian Rosewood blocks set in a herringbone pattern.

On the floor, were a half dozen rectangular soft wool fringed *Medallion* and *Hamadan* style Persian rugs, decorated in blue, gold, ivory and brown, and a wild scattering of at least fifty plump silk cushions in riotous reds, blues and greens.

In the middle of the floor there was a five-metre long low trestle table draped with purple damask silk.

At the end of the room closest to the double doors and set beneath a large window masked by ruby red crushed suede curtains, there was a chaise longue upholstered in pink and green striped satin . . . and at the opposite end of the room, there was a little press of eight middle-aged, sandal-clad men dressed in ill-fitting togas that served to highlight flabby arms and pale white calves, who were delicately sipping colourless liquid from long-stemmed cocktail glasses.

Zelda was about to say 'bleedin ell!' when she was stopped by the doors at her back opening outwards.

'Eddie! Glad to see you got here early.' The man was tall and tanned. Zelda took in the thick, dark brown collar length hair and the whisper of grey at the temples. *A lady-killer in 'is day* she thought. But as she also took in the red, thick-veined nose and the straining lower buttons on his white shirt, she mentally added *but runnin to seed.* Eddie smiled an oily smile.

'Hey, you know me Charles, steady Eddie!' The tall man tilted his head sideways.

'Well, I'm thinking not so steady, when you cock up my delivery.' Eddie pulled a wry face.

'Like I said Charles, that likkul problem was out of me 'ands. And anyway,' he patted his jacket pocket, 'I've brought a little freebee as a way of apology.' Charles smiled and then apparently noticed Eddie's two companions for the first time.

'And that's not all you've brought by the look of it. What on earth do we have here?' Zelda's face flushed.

'This is me likkul surprise,' said Eddie, pulling Davey out from Zelda's side.

'My word!'

'Yeah. I fought 'ee would add a real touch of the surreal to yer movie. You can dress 'im up an use 'im to nip around serving the wine an stuff.' Charles smiled thinly and ran his eyes up and down Zelda.

'And yes . . . the other one . . . how on earth do I use her?'

'Ah, well, she insisted on being 'is minder. Just keep 'er be'ind the camera outer the way an she'll be no problem.'

Zelda's face flushed again, and she opened her mouth with the intention of letting the pair of shits have it with both barrels, when there was a movement behind Charles' back in the hall.

'Ah, the ladies,' said Charles clapping his hands together. He stepped to one side and a line of six "Cleopatra's" flowed into the room.

They were dressed in finest, almost see-through linen, dyed powder blue or palest pink, and each had long, black bead-threaded hair cut in a fringe that framed green malachite shadowed eyelids, black galena-lined lashes and eyebrows and red painted lips.

They were all elegantly slim of neck, arm and

ankle, but through their sheer thigh-length linen dresses their ample womanly curves, unbound by any form of undergarment, marked them out as juicily ripe for action.

Each carried a silver tray balanced on a red-nailed hand level with her shoulder. On these trays were fat black and green grapes, ripe figs, peaches, ruby cherries, roasted pheasant and wood pigeon in white sauce, quails eggs, oysters, little honey and almond cakes and cinnamon spiced pears soaked in red wine.

The line of women, cool and aloof, marched over to the low table and each bent and placed their tray on the purple clad surface. That done, they stood back in a line against a wall their heads bent, eyes downcast and alabaster arms folded, with each hand cupping a plump breast.

In spite of herself, Zelda was impressed – and she was even more impressed when two huge black men in skimpy loin skins and with arm and thigh muscles oiled and gleaming under the chandeliers' lights, marched into the room carrying silver trays containing eight pewter goblets and four large earthenware flagons that exuded a heady aroma of mulled wine and cinnamon. These were also placed on the low table, before the men turned and without a word exited through the double doors.

The little spell that held Zelda and Davey's mouths open was suddenly broken when Charles said urbanely: 'We'll leave them to get warmed up a bit before we start shooting,' and strode out of the room. Zelda, Davey and Eddie followed him into the hall where he ushered Zelda and Davey through another door that led off it, before popping his head in and saying: 'Find the little guy a toga,' and then, taking Eddie by the arm finished with: 'Come on, you and I have a little business to see to.'

This room, unlike the last one, was just a room. Normal sized, and normally decorated. So normal in every way . . . if one could ignore the two huge, semi-naked black men in loincloths, sat on a white leather sofa genteelly sipping coffee from tiny porcelain cups with little fingers crooked; oh . . . and the leopard that reclined at the feet of another – though much more richly clothed – Cleopatra, who sat in one of two white leather matching armchairs. This time Zelda did manage to say 'Bleedin ell!' The woman looked up and smiled.

'Quite,' she replied before adding: 'But it's a hell that pays well.' One of the two black men pursed his lips and made a little moue.

'Maybe for you sweetie, but then you're the big man's leading lady.' The other man mountain tutted twice then lisped: 'Ooo don't be bitchy Julie.' Julie's mouth twisted into another little moue.

'Yes, well it's all right for you Julie, but I'm going to catch my death one of these days parading around in next to nothing.' Zelda shook her head, while beside her a wide-eyed Davey looked on.

'You came with that Eddie did you?' said the

woman to Zelda.

'Yeah, 'ee's arranged for Davey 'ere to do some waitin on in yer film.' The woman's eyebrows arched.

'Has he now. And have you ever done any . . . film work . . . before Davey?' Davey shook his head.

'No missis.'

'You can call me Candy, Davey . . . and don't worry, as long as you don't trip up over the carpets or cushions you'll be okay.' Zelda nodded.

'I'm Zelda by the way . . . I kinda look after 'im,' she said, glancing across at her little companion.

'And we're the two Julies,' lisped one of the seated black men. Zelda frowned.

'Two Julies?'

'Julian and Julius,' Candy cut in. 'We call them the two Julies because they're a pair of prancing queens.'

'Bitch,' lisped Julius (or Julian).

Introductions over, Zelda wanted to know the score.

'So,' she said, 'how does this thing pan out then?' Candy grinned.

'You saw that sad bunch of tossers in there?' she said pointing towards the door. Zelda nodded.

'They each pay a couple of grand to ham it up like Caligula and cop as much pussy as they can handle, and Charles then gives them their own private copy of the movie for them to take away to drool over.'

'Rich tossers then?'

'Very.'

'An you an the girls?'

'We do all right. Charles pays good rates and there's usually some good tips.' One of the Julies snorted.

'Yes sweetie, all right for you lot, but why can't Charles invite some nice boys?' he said, wiggling his bare muscular shoulders, 'who might fancy a change from women?'

'Keep on like that Julie and I'll have to slap your face so hard you bitch!' said the other Julie.

'Now girls, don't get your knickers in a twist. And you Julie,' Candy said wagging a finger, 'stop winding her up, you know how jealous she gets.'

Davey followed the exchange but his mind wasn't really on it. Instead, he was looking at the leopard.

'That's a leopard int it?' he said to Candy.

'Her name's Phoebe, Charles got her from Namibia as an orphan cub. She's been here ever since. Getting on a bit now bless her; but she still looks the part. She normally has the run of a big pen in the grounds, but we bring her in for special productions.'

'Does she bite?' Candy smiled.

'Bite? No, but if she did it would only be one bite, wouldn't it Phoebe?' She reached down and scratched the big cat's head. Phoebe purred.

'You reckon she could do an Alsatian then?'

'Probably eat two for breakfast if she had a mind.' Davey nodded.

'Good, she's all right wiv me then.'

'Right, well down to business then; we've gotta get you kitted up for the part,' Candy said, as she climbed to her feet, beckoned Davey and made her way over to a large metal trunk that sat in a corner.

With a curious Davey at her side, she lifted up the lid and after a little rummage, pulled out a small pair of leather sandals.

'Try these on for size,' she said, before returning to the trunk. Davey shucked off his trainers and slipped his feet into the sandals.

'They're a bit tight,' he muttered. Zelda shook her head.

'Tek yer socks off dummy. You don't wear socks wiv sandals.' Davey squatted on the floor and did as he was told, while Candy selected something from the trunk and returned to his side.

'Here,' she said, 'this should fit . . . with a little adjustment.' Davey looked up and his eyebrows creased in a mega frown.

'That's a frock!' he said. 'I'm not wearin no bleedin frock!' Zelda stepped in.

'It's not a frock it's a toga . . . all the top Romans wore togas.'

'Don't care,' he replied obstinately, 'I'm no arse bandit, wearin a frock.' Zelda glanced across at the two Julies and made a little apologetic shrug.

'Sorry,' she said, 'ee lets 'is gob run away wiv itself sometimes.' Davey looked at the Julies.

'Oh, right, yeah sorry, no offence.' One of the Julies gave Davey a very slow wink and tilted his head coquettishly.

'No problem cutie,' he lisped. The other Julie frowned. With Davey slightly off guard, Zelda sighed heavily.

'Well then,' she said wearily, 'you better give Eddie is fifty back an we'll get on our way.'

'So, it's not really a frock then?' Davey shot back in immediate reply.

'No, like I said, it's a toga.'

'All right then.'

'Right. You better try it on then.'

'Right, where's the changing room?'

'Don't be so soft; nip be'ind there an I'll 'elp you put it on,' Zelda said, pointing to the empty armchair.

Candy held out the linen toga that was really a spare slave girl dress and Davey, still not convinced, took it reluctantly.

'Right,' she said, 'pop behind that chair and take everything off.' Davey's frown returned.

'What? Everyfin!'

'Fraid so, house rules, no underwear of any kind whatsoever.'

Muttering to himself, Davey, with Zelda close behind, slipped behind the chair.

'Right, that looks okay,' said Zelda a minute later as she looked down. A dis-embodied and far from convinced voice floated up.

'Yeah, well, if anyone laughs it's comin off.'

'Ooo yes!' said the flighty one of the Julies.

'There, that's fine, you look just like a Roman Emperor,' Candy said as he stepped out slowly.

'What about 'is arm though?' said Zelda pointing to the little stump. Candy shrugged.

'Doesn't matter, I suppose it adds a bit more to the . . . bizarreness.'

Any further discussion or protest was stopped dead by the door opening, and a toga'd up bright-eyed and lazily smiling Charles and Eddie entering.

Oh aye, looks like they've bin at the angel dust, thought Zelda, who had, in her day, had plenty of experience in that particular direction.

'Right, Ricky's been filming a few warm-up scenes, so let's get into the action,' Charles said.

'Okay gang,' said Candy, 'the Oscar's await.'

'Oo's the Oscars?' muttered Davey to Zelda. She didn't bother with an answer.

The little group trooped out into the hallway and made their way over to the open double doors that were fully folded back. In the hole that they would normally have filled, a slightly built middle-aged man with a jauntily set black beret on his head was panning a tripod-mounted halogen floodlit camera around the room's interior.

'Right,' said Charles, as they all — with the

exception of Zelda, who parked herself just behind the cameraman – made their way through the doorway, 'let's party!'

Inside, the action was warming up and Davey's eyes opened wider as he took in the scene.

The floor was covered in sprawling lovely – and not so lovely – semi naked bodies.

All of the men now wore half-face black masks that gave them an air of mysterious, if not handsome, anonymity.

Most of the slave girls' togas were very much off-the-shoulder, exposing plump, but firm, rouge-nippled breasts. Some were on their knees feeding grapes into open mouths, while others held pewter mugs in front of slack-lipped, bloated red faces.

One of the girls was performing a slow sinuous dance while two of the men, from semi sitting positions ran their hands up and down her tanned calves and thighs.

'Okay, you, little feller.' Davey's eyes snapped back from the scene to Charles' face.

'What?'

'Make your way over to the table and take one of those wine jugs around while Ricky films you.' With Candy, Phoebe and the Julies in tow, Charles then led the way to the chaise longue – while a grinning Eddie made a beeline for the action.

Davey glanced over to the open doorway and Zelda nodded, and made a little get on with it movement with a hand. Taking a deep breath, he stepped into the arena, then over a couple of writhing bodies and arrived at the low table.

The first two jugs he tried were empty. The third held a fair amount. He hoisted it and departed on his rounds. Nobody paid much attention to him, as he tipped the blood red liquid into proffered goblets. He relaxed a bit. *Piece of piss this*, he thought, *just fill the cups an fanny's yer bleedin aunt...quids in!*

'What could go bleedin wrong?' he muttered to himself.

'Cut!' Charles said to Ricky. Ricky cut. Davey looked up. 'Right, now come back over here,' said Charles beckoning, 'and fill our goblets, then sit down at the side of the couch in front of Phoebe. Okay, Action!'

Davey stepped over and round a few more bodies and made his way to the reclining pair, who were being cooled from behind by long ostrich feather fans waved by the two Julies.

Easy this actin lark! thought Davey as he filled the goblets and hunkered down at Phoebe's side.

As the action hotted up Davey watched with a reasonably cool detachment. A detachment, however that did waver when he experienced a worrying little throbbing down below as a result of paying a little too much attention to little tableau's of threesomes that emerged from the general tangle of arms legs and bosoms.

Look somewhere else, he thought, *or else yer gunna get a right stiffy on!* As he thought it, a sound at his elbow caught his attention. He swivelled round slowly and saw Phoebe lapping at an almost empty dish of water.

'Nice kitty,' he muttered, risking a light pat on her head. She looked up and a tongue like a rasp flicked out from between a very efficient looking set of fangs and licked his hand. He flinched then relaxed. She was a leopard not a dog, so she was okay.

'I wunt mind tekkin you 'ome wiv me,' he said quietly. 'All them dogs round our way would shit themselves big time if they saw you out warkin wiv me.' Phoebe appeared to nod in agreement, before returning to lap up the last drops in the dish. Davey licked his lips. He was thirsty too.

'Yeah, it's bloody 'ot in 'ere wiv all them people an them lights. Could do wiv a likkul drink meself,' he said to his new feline friend. Why not, he thought, as he eyed the wine jug at his side. He was about to sneak a gargle when a slender arm snaked out and a red-nailed hand tapped him on the head.

'More wine slave,' slurred Candy. Davey struggled to his feet. *Bloody 'ell, I fort my Zelda could put it away* he thought, as he filled up her goblet from the almost empty jug. He was just about to place the jug back on the floor when the same slender arm reached out and slid up his toga.

'Eh!' said Davey in alarm. 'Ooh!' said Candy as her hand made intimate contact, and her eyebrows suddenly shot up. Davey tried to back off but her grip tightened. Unfortunately this resulted in the usual physical reaction.

'Ooooh!' moaned Davey, as his face drained of colour, his knees trembled and his legs went decidedly wobbly. Charles, his attention diverted from the orgy in progress, turned and yelled 'Cut!' as Davey toppled over.

'Not my fault!' said Candy defensively and shrugging her elegant shoulders. 'All I did was grab his pecker.'

'Must be the heat,' said Charles. 'Better get him a drink of water.' With the camera stopped, Zelda strode through into the room.

''Ee'l be all right, 'ee just needs a bit of fresh air,' she said, easing the little figure back to his feet. Charles, looking sternly at Candy, said: 'Right, take five. We need to refill the wine jugs anyway.'

Out in the hall Davey was feeling better.

'I kunt 'elp it, she slipped 'er and up me kilt an grabbed me todger,' he said. Zelda looked him squarely in the eyes.

'Yeah, well ogling all those others 'avin it off probably didn't 'elp did it?'

'No, suppose not . . .'

'Well if it starts to come on agen you better fink of somefin else to tek yer mind off it.'

'Right.'

Five minutes later back on set and with the wine jars replenished, the action, which in truth hadn't wound down with the short filming break, was in full swing.

Davey studiously kept his eyes away from any of the more gymnastic action as he flitted about stepping over writhing bodies and refilling mugs.

After a complete circuit he made his way back to the chaise longue and was about to plonk himself down when Charles said: 'See that pair at the end of the room, her bending over giving that fat chap a blow job?' Reluctantly, Davey looked.

'Yeah.'

'Right, make your way over and flick her dress up and give her a bang.'

'Er, I don't fink so.'

'What do you mean, you don't think so?'

'Er, I'm just a waiter . . .'

'Ah, I see, you want extra payment do you to add to your waiting money?'

'Extra payment?' said Davey, struggling with the dilemma induced by negative thoughts relating to a probable upcoming physical problem – versus positive thoughts relating to a definite incoming cash boost.

'An extra twenty okay?' Mammon won.

'Okay, but I don't fink I can do it proper like.'

'What do you mean?'

'I don't fink I can get a stiffy on, not in public like . . . wiv all these people.'

'Right, just pretend then. Off you go.' Charles signalled to Ricky to follow the little man as he slowly made his way over to the other end of the room. Once there, Davey looked down at the shapely buttocks straining against the linen dress. He swallowed hard and placed a hand on the hem of the dress and slowly raised it up onto the slave girl's back.

'Oh shit!' he moaned softly, as under the bright light of the camera the ripe mounds sprang free. 'Oh shit!' he moaned again, as he lifted his toga, moved in close and turned his gaze back towards a distant Charles, who made a rapid slap slap motion with the back of his right hand into his left palm. Davey banged.

Then, as he felt a warning twitch, he bent his head back away from the action and said (with immense feeling) 'Fink about somefin else! Fink about somefin else!' Then it came to him. Yeah, he thought, when United slipped eight up Arsenal a while back! So as he banged he shouted: 'Yeah! Stick it up 'em! Make 'em 'ave it all the way! Go on my sons! Nice one! Four, five six, seven eight, give 'em bleedin stick!' Yeah! Yeah! Yeah!'

'Doesn't seem to be having much trouble,' said Candy to Charles, as from the other end of the room they watched the animated performance.

After a minute or two – by which time Davey had re-run all six goals three times through his mind's eye – the camera light moved on to another piece of action, and Davey was able to "dismount" and make his way back.

'Well done', said Charles. 'Nice unusual bit of action that; should add a nice debauched touch.' Davey wasn't sure what debauched meant but he was glad he hadn't made an arse of himself again.

Over the next twenty minutes or so Davey made three more rounds with a wine jug. On the first of these, he had been pulled up by a well-lubricated and bloated-faced Eddie, who had just returned from a comfort break.

'Ere Stumpy,' he had beckoned, 'bring that bleedin jug over.' Davey had done as ordered and was about to top up Eddie's goblet when the thin man had said: 'No, give it 'ere, I'll do it meself.' Davey had shrugged his shoulders and passed the jug over.

He didn't notice Eddie open his hand and tip a quantity of white powder into the dark liquid after he poured himself a top up.

'Should liven fings up a bit more,' muttered a grinning Eddie as he handed the jug back.

After the third excursion, Davey made his way back to the *chaise longue* and plonked himself down next to a slowly panting Phoebe, who was squatted on her hind legs watching the goings-on with a casual *sang-froid* detachment.

'Firsty girl?' he asked, reaching for her water bowl. It was empty.

'Oh well,' he muttered after checking to see

that no-one was watching, 'don't suppose a likkul drop of wine will do you any 'arm, eh girl?' he said as he poured some of the liquid into the bowl and pushed it in front of her.

Phoebe climbed stiffly to her feet, leaned forward and sniffed. She wasn't too sure . . . but she was very thirsty. After a couple more sniffs thirst won out over caution. Her tongue snaked out and she took two quick laps. A second later she sprang back a foot, thin black-lined lips drew back over ivory white fangs and a sound like two sheets of very rough sandpaper being rubbed together rasped from her mouth.

Davey grimaced and took a quick dekko around to see if anyone had noticed. Fortunately, the Two Julies, with bored looks on their dark faces were staring ahead into space and Candy and Charles on the *chaise longue* were busy playing hide the sausage.

Phoebe stared into the bowl, then inched closer, sniffed again . . . then embarked on a serious bout of lapping.

'That's it girl, put 'airs on yer chest that will!' said Davey, as he watched the liquid disappear.

When the bowl was empty Phoebe nosed it around the floor for a few seconds before her eyes slowly crossed and her legs gave way under her.

'Whoops,' said Davey, 'maybe what weren't such a good idea after all.'

Phoebe dreamed. And in her dream she was

running free, bunched muscles rippling along her yellow and black dappled body as she ate up the ground under her bounding stride.

The quarry was twenty yards ahead. The odour of fear and panic fanned back in waves against her face and her heart hammered against her ribcage with the beautiful exertion, and the joy of the chase.

Five yards, three, two . . . and she leapt. In her sleep the claws on her front paws unsheathed and a low growl of triumph rose from her chest. The quarry was down. She darted in and her fangs closed around its throat in the final suffocating grip.

The scene wavered like a heat mirage then shattered. She awoke. And distantly remembered smells, azure blue sky, burnished orange sun and sprawling green savannah were replaced by a mad swirl of pulsing colour and eye-stabbingly bright spears of white light.

She tried to focus her eyes on a writhing movement in front of her; on a huge creature with many limbs and heads, from the mouths of which moans, groans and barked laughter battered her suddenly ultra sensitive ears.

She bared her fangs at the beast as its chokingly thick, hot rank odour, seeped into her flared nostrils and triggered alarm in her drug-fogged brain. Fight or Flight? She turned her head slowly. She was trapped. There was nowhere to run.

She climbed groggily to her feet and extended her head forward focussing on the beast. The swirling movement slowed and she saw that it was not a single huge beast, but many smaller one or two-headed ones. Ancestral memory kicked in. It wasn't something to fight – it was something to eat. Pick the weakest. She turned her head slowly and there it was. At the end of a narrow deep purple flattened strip of grass a single creature, head bowed – unaware.

Eddie had drank, snorted and shagged himself to a standstill. Now he just wanted to get his head down for half an hour or so before the bell for round ten rang.

'Be all right in a bit,' he mumbled into the sticky wine-matted hairs on his exposed chest. 'Yus need a likkul bit of a kip.' It was not to be.

Eyes fixed ahead, ears pinned flat back Phoebe clambered groggily up onto the table and tottered (but in her mind, flowed) towards her prey. Three yards . . . two . . . one. What now? She swayed from side to side her vision swimming in and out of focus. A foot in front of her Eddie stirred as hot fetid breath fanned his face.

'What?' he slurred. 'Fukoffouterit I'm knackered.' The breath did not take itself away.

He raised his lead heavy head and struggled to focus his eyes on the blurred features. The blurred features did the same. Phoebe's face swam into view.

'Fuk off you mangy twat,' mumbled Eddie. The mangy twat ignored him — so Eddie did a very silly thing, he sent a looping, lumbering, roundhouse right clumping into Phoebe's mouth. The big cat jumped back and snarled, then, as a trickle of blood ran onto her tongue — instantly bringing back the memory of her recent dream kill — she pounced.

'Aaaggghh, you fukin baassttarddd!' Yelled Eddie, as Phoebe's gaping jaws closed on the top of his head and the awful sound of bone grating on bone filled his ears.

As the Lexus crunched over the gravel in the drive and the photoelectric cell activated the iron gates, Davey turned to Zelda.

'That was somefin else that weren't it?' Zelda nodded.

'You can say that again.'

'Good job one of them men was a doctor, eh?'

'Yeah.'

'Shudda took 'im to 'ospital though, don't yuh fink? Zelda glanced across and thought: *What a bloody innocent.* She shook her head.

'What, an say "can you take a look at this bloke 'oo just 'ad is 'ead munched by a leopard at a Roman orgy that was attended by a load of big wig businessmen?"'

'Right. I suppose that could be a likkul bit awkward . . .' Zelda nodded.

'Yeah, just a bit. Anyway, 'ee should be okay after the sedation wears off an 'ee's 'ad a good night's rest. Oh by the way,' she said through a secret little smile aimed at the back of the fat cannonball of a head behind the wheel, 'by the way Tommy, when you come back to pick 'im up tommerer be sure to give 'im our regards an tell 'im we 'ope is 'ead gets better real soon.'

'What,' said Davey, 'you fink all them 'oles in is crust will 'eal up all right?' Zelda shrugged then allowed herself a genuine little smile.

'Probably, but that pretty scar 'ee come in with 'as now got plenty of company. 'Ee'l be left with an 'ead like a bleedin old chewed boot that's for sure.'

24

'An then this leopard jumped on 'im an chewed is shed big time!' said Davey to Fred, who was in the seat behind. Fred turned his eyes heavenwards and made a tutting sound.

'Yeah, yeah,' said Fred, 'and then I suppose this pink elephant jumped out of the wall and smashed the leopard with a cricket bat . . .' Davey frowned.

'Don't be daft . . .'

'Everyone on board?' Billy Senior shouted, as he turned in the driver's seat and looked back along the coach.

'Yeah Da,' said Billy Junior. 'Let's 'it the road!' In the seat behind Billy Senior, balaclava clad Ernie bounced up and down in excitement, causing Davey sitting next to him to levitate six inches in the air for a second.

'Whoa!' Calm down Ernie!' said Fred, leaning forward and placing a hand on the big man's shoulder. Ernie grinned hugely.

'I n-never b-bin on a sh-sharrer before. It's g-good I-int it!' he said to Davey.

'Oh yeah, it's a real big deal,' was the intentionally *blasé* reply.

The Beswick Reds and their intrepid band of 12 supporters from the *Derby Arms* were on their way to a meeting with destiny, and Davey's internal spring, in spite of his attempt at appearing cool, was winding up nicely. As the coach turned into Peter Street he thought *I need ter be as nippy as a mad moggy onna 'ot tin roof.* He nodded firmly and muttered 'Yeah, like a mad moggy onna 'ot tin roof.'

'W-what?' said Ernie.

'Nuffin. Jus windin meself up a likkul bit.'

'Oh. Do y-you w-want a b-b-butty?' Davey,

distracted from repeating his new mental mantra, turned to the big man.

'A butty? Yer mam put you up some butties fer a ten minute bus ride?' Ernie nodded.

'What's on 'em then?' Ernie un-wrapped the newspaper parcel that he had taken from his overcoat pocket and opened one of the six double-decker doorstops.

'Sardines an st-strawberry j-jam.' Davey's eyes battened onto the appalling sight.

'Eeu! Sardines an bleedin strawberry jam! Yer mam bin swiggin 'er tonic this mornin as she?'

'Y-yeah, 'ow d-did you know?'

'Just a wild guess.' Ernie was impressed.

'Y-yer r-real cl-clever. You w-want one?'

'Fanks, but I fink I'll pass,' muttered Davey as the bus rolled to a stop outside the *G-Mex Centre*.

'Hey!' said Curtley as they stood up to disembark, 'this is just like gettin off the team coach outside Wembley Stadium fer the Cup Final!' Davey felt a little thrill of excitement tickle his spine.

'It's just a five-a-side final,' he said coolly. Curtley grinned.

''Oo you fink yer kiddin me main man! Yer up fer it big time!'

'Yeah, well, okay then . . . LET'S KICK SOME ARSE!' The whole coach cheered as Davey, followed by Ernie, led the troops off the battle bus. As they all pooled together at the coach door Billy Senior shouted down to junior.

'I'll pick you up at six o'clock on the dot.'

'Right Da,' said a grinning Junior. 'An you'll 'ave an extra passenger – a big beautiful tin pot fer the *Derby* trophy cabinet!'

Billy Senior crunched the coach into gear, and took off as his passengers danced up the approach steps and made their way through the glass doors to a kiosk in the entrance foyer. Fred, as befitted his status as team captain, pushed through to the front.

'The Beswick Reds,' he proclaimed. When this statement met with a blank stare from the green-jacketed occupant of the kiosk, he added: 'Northern Five-a-Side Final.' The man sniffed and glanced at a clipboard on the desk then shook his head.

'No,' he said firmly without looking up. 'No mention of any, what was it, Beswick Reds?' Fred frowned.

'Must be,' he said firmly. 'We're in the final.' The man shook his head.

'Problem?' Berserker Billy pushed his way through from the back of the little knot of reds. Fred shrugged.

'He says we're not on the list.' Billy gently took hold of Ernie's sleeve and led him to the front of the little queue.

'Problem?' he asked softly. The jobsworth sniffed again.

'Not on the list,' he said snootily. Billy turned to Ernie and said quietly: 'Ernie, smile fer the man.'

Ernie, as ordered grinned – and it was not a pretty sight.

'Now,' said Billy, as the man stared up into a mouthful of teeth that resembled two rows of broken gravestones, 'I suggest you 'ave a real good look at that clipboard of yours; coz if you don't find us on it, my friend 'ere;' he indicated Ernie with a jabbing thumb over his shoulder, 'will tek that fukin board an ram it where the sun don't shine.' The man blanched and quickly flipped over to a second page.

'Oh, yes,' he muttered, 'there it is, Beswick Reds. Right no problem, just through the double doors and turn left.'

'Thank you,' said Billy graciously.

Inside the Exhibition Centre proper, the playing area was split into two curtained-off halves, each of which were at the moment displaying two teams of youngsters going at it hammer and tongs, as what sounded like a thousand kids and proud mums and dads in the temporary stands cheered and shouted their support.

'Bloody hell!' said Captain Fred as he led the Reds and their followers over to another kiosk that sat beneath a large registration sign. 'It's like the Stretford End!'

'Yes, can I help you?' Tommy turned to the young green-jacketed fair-haired woman in the kiosk.

'Yeth,' he replied. 'We're the Bethwick

Redths.'

'Pardon? Fred made his way to the front of the little knot of players and supporters and gently moved Tommy to one side.

'The Beswick Reds. We're in the Northern Final against the *Pig and Ferret* from Poynton.

'Ahh, yes, if you would like to register your players here,' she said placing an A4 form on the worktop in front of the kiosk.

'Okay lads,' Fred beckoned, 'come on then and sign your lives away for the pretty lady.' She smiled shyly as one by one the team stepped forward and penned their signatures. As Davey stepped up last her smile faded into a look of mild embarrassment.

'It's only the players that need to sign,' she said, as she looked down at the little figure.

'Yeah, I know,' said Davey brightly, as he picked up the pen and slowly, as he wrote his name, said out aloud: 'David Ignatius Montgomery Parker.' The young woman picked up the form and looked down at the writer, then looked back at the form.

'My word,' she said flustered, 'that's certainly a very big name for a . . . yes . . . very big . . .'

'Yeah; an 'ee's got a very big . . . talent . . . ter go wiv it anall', said Billy. Her cheeks a fetching shade of red, she murmured: 'Right then, er there are another eight junior matches before you are due to go on, so it should be about an hour and a half wait for you.' Billy nodded.

'No probs, where's the bar?'

Back at Fort Beswick, Zelda was feeling a little bit guilty. *I should've gone with 'im*, she thought. *It might only be a silly game of football, but then it's a big day for 'im an ee doesn't get many of them poor likkel sod.*

She was constantly surprising herself these days. Not so long ago if someone had said that she and Davey would end up getting along with each other almost like two normal people, she would have laughed in their face; but there it was, they were getting on pretty well at the moment, what with the extra cash and the Club and all.

'Yer a selfish bitch,' she chided. 'You should take an interest, even if it is only a poxy game.' As she spoke she accepted the fact that the long-held icy grip on her emotions that she had cultivated so single-mindedly for years was slowly melting away.

'I'm goin soft,' she muttered. *So, not before time you pinch faced cow*, said a little voice in her head. She nodded in agreement. *Yeah, right*, she thought. *It's about time I counted me blessings. I've got a great job with a good future. I've got enough money comin in to buy a pair of shoes when I feel like. And Davey. . . yeah, 'ee's okay really when I think about some of the shits that've crapped on me over the years.*

'Yeah,' she said with a firm nod, 'I'm goin to treat 'im better from now on.' And just to prove it she made her way to the bedroom, opened the doors on her double wardrobe and after a quick admiring downward glance at the long rows of assorted shoes, she reached up and took her nurse's uniform off the hanger.

She draped it over one shoulder as she strode over to a chest of drawers on her side of the bed, opened the top drawer and removed a length of orange coloured rubber tubing with a ball attached, and marched purposely through to the kitchen, where she dumped them both into the pedal bin.

As the pedal bin lid clanged shut on an already fading little chapter of her life she nodded.

'There'll be no more need for that,' she said firmly. 'An no more need for mister Smiff.'

'Right then, two pints only,' warned Captain Fred, as with their entourage they settled themselves in the bar. 'I don't want you losing your edge,' he added, to nods of approval from the Reds for his wise words.

'No probs *mon capitan*, we'll be up fer it all right . . . RIGHT?' Billy challenged the other Reds.

'Yo!' yelled Curtley.

'Yeth! shouted Tommy.

'Kick arse!' boomed Davey.

'Yeah, but not just yet. Wait till we get in the changing room,' said Fred taking a long pull on his pint of lager.

Two pints down the line, and in the temporary changing rooms, Billy, as he slapped a knobbly fist repeatedly into the palm of his other hand, put the evil eye on his target, a short, wiry "Scholesey" look-alike.

'What's he looking at?' muttered the ginger nut in a posh South Manchester delivery to one of his team-mates as they slipped into their kit.

'Don't know,' said the other, in an *I'm not really interested* voice often employed by those who were safely ensconced well behind the line of fire. 'Why don't you ask him?' The ginger nut looked across at a scowling Billy – and decided it would probably be prudent not to take up the invitation.

'Looks can't hurt me,' he muttered not too confidently, as a knock on the door announced zero hour.

'Are we ready?' yelled Fred.

'YO!

'Yeth!'

'Grrrr!'

'Kick arse! An gimme a igh five!'

As the two teams spilled out onto the pitch, Gerry Roper stuffed the last inch of the hot dog into his mouth, wiped his hands on his pants legs, hoisted his camera to his shoulder and trained it on the playing area. *Might as well get focused ready for the main event later*, he thought. In seats next to him a couple who had just been cheering on their little darling in a junior match also focused on the pitch.

'Aw, look!' said the woman pointing, 'they've got a little dwarf mascot! And aw, bless, look, he's only got one arm!' Gerry zoomed in on Davey as the small figure made his way to one of the nets, adjusted a large floppy cap and bounced up and down.

'No, don't be silly,' muttered Gerry. Then: 'Bloody 'ell!' as Fred fired one in and Davey launched himself into the air and the ball cannoned off his chest.

'This I've got to see!' said the cameraman as the referee called the captains together before the kick-off, and in goal, Davey gave each of his posts a quick rap with his right foot.

The ref adjusted his watch, nodded to both teams and blew his whistle. Ten seconds into the game Billy's pebbly elbow met only empty air as Ginger waltzed around him and passed the ball to a team- mate.

'Cocky bastard!' mouthed Billy to the retreating back. 'Next time arseole.' Two minutes later he tried a knee – with the same result. Only this time Ginger slipped past Curtley and let fly. Davey launched himself to his left and the ball cannoned off his head, straight to the feet of another attacker, who casually side-footed it into the net. On the halfway line Billy boiled.

For the rest of the first half the game ebbed

and flowed. Davey distinguished himself with two brilliant full-face stops and Fred rattled a post, before, with seconds left, Curtley netted. Half time one-all.

As the teams retreated to their ends of the pitch for a tactical review, Gerry took out his mobile and dialled his boss at Granada.

'Boss. It's Gerry. Have I got a story for you!'

'I don't know, have you?' came the laconic reply.

'I'm at *G-Mex* for the old pro's five-a-side . . . '

'What? Has one of the old buggers gone and joshed it on the pitch?'

'No. They don't kick off for, oh, another hour or so. '

'So, what is it then?' Gerry smiled.

'Okay. What would you say was the most bizarre goalie you could think of?'

'I don't know. Stevie Wonder? Julian Clarey?'

'Not even close boss. How about a one-armed dwarf!'

'Yeah right, you've been on the sauce again haven't you; I've warned you about that.'

'No. No shit boss. I've just shot him in action and 'ee's the dog's bollocks!'

Back on the Sports Desk in Granada Studios the super cool Senior Sports Editor raised an eyebrow – which was pretty much equivalent to a normal person doing cartwheels. He was always on the lookout for the more bizarre items as fillers to spice up the run of the mill schedules, and this had the smell of something good.

'Right Roper. Get him on camera. Then when his match is finished, collar him and get his contact details. I'll see you in the morning and we'll take a look at the footage you've got.'

'Right boss,' said the cameraman, as the ref blew for the two teams to line up for the re-start.

As the second half kicked off Ginger found that he had acquired another shadow; only this one kept closer to him than the original.

'Yer mine bitch', whispered Billy in a tone that would have done justice to a Strangeways hard man greeting a new and pretty young blond inmate.

Ginger edged closer to the referee and each time the ball came his way he got rid of it post haste. Unfortunately this sudden decision to melt into the background didn't save him from the inevitable. As another pass came his way and he ballooned it forward, his shadow took on extremely hard substance. With everyone's attention on the ball, berserker Billy slipped a roundhouse knobbly knee smack into an unsuspecting thigh to produce a state-of-the-art dead leg.

'Aarrrgghh!' yelped Ginger as he collapsed to the deck grasping his thigh in agony.

'Sorry pal,' said a contrite Billy as the referee ran over.

'What happened?' asked the man in black. Billy, the picture of innocence, pulled a concerned face.

'Collision ref, I couldn't stop in time. 'Ere mate,' he added solicitously, holding out a helping hand, 'let me 'elp you up.'

'Aarrgghh geroff!' moaned the victim, as he staggered to his feet and hopped about on his good leg, while gripping his injured thigh.

'He did it on purpose ref. He's a nutter!' The referee frowned and turned to Billy, who shrugged.

'Like I said ref I couldn't stop in time. I'm nowhere near as nippy as 'im.'

'I'll be keeping an eye on you mate,' said the official after Ginger limped off to be replaced by a sub and the match restarted.

The sub, it soon became obvious, was pretty sub-standard, so Billy considered himself free to concentrate on the finer points, like tackling (fairly) and passing. One such incisive through ball found Tommy on the edge of the 'D' and he of the gangly legs unintentionally bamboozled the keeper into an early dive, leaving an open net for him to slip one into the corner.

As the clock ran down the *Pig and Ferret* laid siege to the Red's goal. Shots rained in from all angles as Davey bounced about whispering his new mantra, 'Mad moggy onna 'ot tin roof … Mad moggy onna 'ot tin roof.'

He saved with his legs, he saved with his body; but mostly he saved with his face, until: 'Phweeett'. Game over.

The little knot of Reds fans whistled and cheered as a bloodied but grinning Davey was carried off for the trophy presentation on the shoulders of Billy and Fred.

'Here's to you big man!' said Fred in the bar as soon as they had got changed. He held the pint pot up to his mouth in salute and the rest of the reds followed suit.

'Aw it was nuffin really,' said a bashful Davey, wiping away a little trickle of blood from his left nostril. 'It's what goalies does.'

A brilliant day was only slightly clouded, when an hour later, United old pro's crashed out of the competition early to Everton.

Six o'clock sharp, and their coach pulled up. Then, just as they were streaming towards the exit doors in front of the Hall, they were halted by an urgent voice.

'Hold on lads!' Fred turned to see a man lugging what appeared to be a TV camera bearing down on them. 'Hold on!' he repeated breathlessly, 'I've been looking for you everywhere.'

'Shudda looked in the bar,' said Curtley.

'Oh, right. Anyway, I need a word with your goalie.' Davey turned and frowned.

'What for?' He was always suspicious of people who collared him for "a word".

'I watched your match. I've never seen anything like it!' Davey shrugged.

'It wasn't that good. We've 'ad a lot better

288

games than that.' The man shook his head vigorously.

'No I'm not talking about the game. You. You were great!' Davey blushed.

'Hey!' crowed Billy, 'ee'l be askin fer your autograph next!' The man smiled.

'No,' he said, 'but I do want your phone number for my boss at Granada.'

'What, Granada television?' Davey's eyes widened.

'Yeah. There's a chance we might be able to use some of the footage of your match on our footie programme ...'

'On't telly!'

'Maybe, like I said, it depends on my boss.'

'Bleedin 'ell!'

A slightly bemused Davey had just given Gerry his phone number, when there was the toot of a horn from an impatient Billy Senior.

'Right,' said Gerry to Davey as the Reds entourage made for the doors, 'we'll probably be in touch in a day or two.'

Back at the *Derby Arms* and with the cup proudly displayed on the bar, the party was in full swing when the front door opened and Zelda walked in.

'Ayup Davey!' warned Billy. 'Are you in lumber or summut?'

'What you on about?'

'Your Zelda, she just walked in, an she's comin

over, an she looks . . . funny, she's . . . she's smilin!'
Davey turned, and yes, she was smiling.

'She's doin it a lot nowadays,' he said matter-of-factly.

'Bloody 'ell!'

'Yeah, amazin int it.'

'I see you won then,' Zelda said, nodding towards the cup on the bar. Billy grinned at her.

'Yeah, fanks to the big man, 'ee was brill.' Davey shrugged.

'It was nuffin really.' Zelda placed a hand lightly on his shoulder.

'Yeah? Well, well done anyway. What you 'avin?' Billy gawked. He had never seen Zelda smile before. He'd never seen her lay a hand gently on Davey before, and he sure as hell had never heard her speak to him in anything other than a "talking down" tone of voice. She was being positively pleasant!

'I'll 'ave a pint of Boddies.'

'Yeah an I'll 'ave the same,' said a still shocked Billy. Zelda's grin faded.

'I wasn't torkin to you knob'ead!' she said icily.

Ah, thought Billy, *that's more like the Zelda we all know an love*.

'Sorry, no probs,' he apologised. Then, to change the conversation he said: 'Hey, guess what, we might be on't telly soon!' Zelda frowned.

'What you on about, on the telly?'

'Bloke from Granada said. 'Ee was filmin over at *G-Mex* an 'ee said he was goin to talk to is boss about maybe puttin us on.'

'Oh yeah, right, Granada's gonna show a poxy five-a-side game!'

'Well,' Billy admitted, 'ee was there fer the senior's competition really; an then 'ee took some shots of us – but it wasn't really the team 'ee was interested in; it was yer man 'ere!' he grinned poking a finger into Davey's chest. ''Ee took yer phone number din't 'ee Davey, an said 'ee would get back in a coupla days.' Davey nodded and Zelda looked quickly from Fred to the little man.

'That right?'

'Well, yeah,' said Davey shrugging, 'but nuffin will proberly come of it.'

'Well if 'ee does ring up, you let me talk to 'im, right.' Davey shrugged. He didn't really expect to hear anything more.

'Yeah, no sweat; where's me drink then?'

Two days later and the Sports Editor at Granada rang up.

''Ee's not 'ere,' she said. 'I'm 'is . . . partner.' Davey stood up quickly, she motioned him down again.

'Why?' she asked bluntly into the mouthpiece. On the other end of the line the editor echoed her 'Why?'

'Yeah, why do you want to put a poxy likkul five-a-side match on the telly?' At her elbow Davey

291

bridled just a little bit.

'Well, to be honest,' the editor said, 'it's more us wanting to put on, er, sorry, what's his name again?'

'Davey.' she said coldly, ''Is name is Davey.'

'Sorry. Yes, Davey. Well we are really taken with Davey's remarkable goalkeeping abilities.'

'You mean remarkable cause 'ee's a one-armed dwarf?' Davey shifted uncomfortably on his chair.

'Well yes, in part; but we also feel that it represents a remarkable story of triumph over adversity . . .'

''Ow much?'

'How much?'

'Yeah 'ow much is the fee for us lettin you display this remarkable story of triumph over adversity?'

'A hundred and fifty pounds?'

'Two 'undred.'

'Right. Two hundred.' Zelda nodded firmly and winked at Davey.

'What?' he mouthed. She made a shushing sound.

'Right, I'll 'ave a word wiv 'im when 'ee comes in and see if 'ee'l do it. Get someone to give me a call back in a couple of 'ours.' After she hung up she repeated the details of the conversation. He was over the proverbial moon.

'Two 'undred quid, bleedin 'ell!' he crowed.

'Are you sure you want to do it?'

'What you on about? Two 'undred quid!

'You know they want to put it on cause of 'oo you are.'

'So; fer two 'undred quid I'll show me arse at the altar at Saint Brigid's in the miggul of a bleedin Requiem!'

At the back of her mind a little voice nagged away. She knew why they wanted to put it on. *Triumph over adversity my arse*, she thought. But then, he was happy with it. She had told him what she thought, but the imminent arrival of two hundred quid – an amount he had never had in his life before and the fact that he had never had anything like approaching the fifteen minutes of fame everyone was supposed to be due – won the day.

'You can 'ave arf,' he had offered. She refused graciously.

'No, it's your money. You can do what you like wiv it.'

'Wow! No shit?'

'Yeah, no shit.'

'I'll buy you a new pair of shoes outer it then.' She smiled again.

25

The Reds and their supporters, along with a few of the other regulars of the *Derby Arms* were crowded into the Games Room. They were, to a man and woman, watching the high level television in one corner that was showing the closing stages of the day's football preview programme.

'When y-yuh c-comin on't telly D-Davey? Ernie had never been in the company of a television star before and he was excited.

'I tole yuh, in a minit, when they stop chunnerin on about rotten Arsenal.' As Davey spoke the screen faded back to the studio and to the middle-aged, grey-haired presenter, who was sat at a desk opposite two younger men on a sofa.

'Well,' he said, smiling into the camera, 'that's just about all on the football front from me and from Mark Sorenson and Alan Janson. But before we take you over to the one-thirty at Doncaster, we'd like to share with you a remarkable story of triumph over adversity.' Zelda pulled a sour face as the announcer continued.

'A few days ago we screened a short piece from Manchester on an ex-pro's five-a-side competition, which I'm sure you all enjoyed. I know I did. What we didn't show you however, was that there were a number of other matches at the venue between a wide cross section of fun footballers.

No flash cars or mega-bucks salaries here folks – just pure enthusiasm for the people's game played by kids of all ages.

One game in particular, the final of a Manchester pub cup competition stood out as an example of what the sport can offer to those who society sometimes struggles to accommodate. Just watch this.'

The camera faded to a long shot of the playing area at *G-Mex*, then zoomed in on two teams of players as they ran out onto the pitch.

'L-look it's D-Davey!' Ernie shouted, as the camera dwelt on a tiny figure dressed in an iridescent goalkeeper's jersey and wearing a large floppy flat cap. The camera stayed with him as the little man jogged over to one set of goals, adjusted his cap and bounced up and down. Seconds later one of his team -mates hammered in a shot, and the goalie took off and made a flying save.

For the next two minutes the camera recorded a succession of attacks which apart from one, resulted in a remarkable series of saves utilising head, chest, groin, legs, arm and in three particular instances, the face. This was followed by the referee whistling for the end of the match and a close-up shot of jubilant red-shirted team-mates chairing a grinning and bloodied little goalie off the pitch in triumph.

The picture faded and re-focused back in the studio on the urbane grey-haired presenter, who winked at the camera.

'Said it was a bit special didn't I. Sign him up for Brighton I say. What do you make of that Mark?' he added turning to the two men on the sofa.

'Well Les, I must say that was very very interesting. He was certainly very very agile, wasn't he? And very very brave too, I might add.'

'And probably very dedicated too, Alan?' said the presenter to his other guest.

'Aye pro'ly. He pro'ly perfected that remarkable goalkeeping technique over many months or years, pro'ly. And like you said earlier, he pro'ly did it all for the love of the game.'

'I'm sure that's no lie,' said the presenter with a little sideways tilt of the head and a wink into the camera, as the picture shifted to a racetrack scene.

The atmosphere back in the *Derby Arms* was buzzing. Zelda looked around the room and cringed lightly as her ears were battered by whistles and cheers of approval as Davey took a series of slightly bashful bows.

Well that's it, she thought. *Ee's 'ad is likkul bit of glory an once 'ee gets over the bangin 'ead 'eel 'ave in the mornin, we'll be able to get on with life in the real world*. So she thought . . . but before very long she was going to be proved wrong.

26

In a smart high-rise apartment at the end of Deansgate, a high-powered television executive picked up the phone and dialled the number of the station's senior sports editor.

Two hours later Zelda took the call while a comatose Davey stewed in his pit. She listened for a few seconds then her eyes widened in surprise.

'The Dick and Trudy Show!' she said. 'When?' She nodded dumbly into the handset. 'Well, I'll 'ave to discuss it wiv 'im first.' Then as the habit of a lifetime kicked in, she added: 'what sort of fee are we talkin?' Her eyes widened a little more.

For the next hour or so she wrestled with her conscience. She knew, no matter how it was wrapped up in noble rhetoric, that the real reason they wanted him was for the freak factor that his appearance would cause.

They didn't give a toss really; all they cared about was their bloody ratings and the chance to get one over on their rivals by screening something that would get wider exposure through a voyeuristic public.

"Did you see the Dick and Trudy show yesterday?" she imagined them saying. "You've never seen anything like it. It was crazy, they had this little one-armed dwarf on and you'll never guess what . . . he was a goalie in a football team!"

Okay so what if they did say that? It would hardly be anything that hadn't been said before about him was it, so why not take their money and stick two fingers up to them?

'Why am I beatin meself up about this?' she muttered. But even as she said it she knew why. She felt sorry for him and she felt, what, protective? Yes, sorry and protective.

She had spent years railing at life's kicks in the teeth, always blaming something or someone else – when all along she had had choices. He had never been given that luxury.

Now for the first time for as long as she could remember, her life was gliding along smoothly; but that didn't lull her into a false sense of security. There had been too many times in the past when a casual step to the left or right or backwards had led to major upheaval. It was always as though something was lurking around the corner ready to leap out and smack her between the eyes.

No, she decided, the club was working out brilliantly and he was in his element dressing up as a cowboy and strutting his stuff. Why should they take a diversion into the unknown just when they were doing so nicely?

Her life's experiences told her that one didn't tempt a gently snoozing Fate by delivering a hefty dig in its ribs, before donning a blindfold and embarking on a stroll across the M6 during rush hour.

But then, being practical, there was the money. A thousand quid for a few minutes slot on the Dick and Trudy Show wasn't to be sniffed at was it?

'Shite', she muttered, 'I've got to tell 'im about it and let 'im make is own mind up.'

An hour later when he dragged himself out of bed and wandered bleary-eyed into the kitchen she was ready for him.

'We 'ad a phone call when you were kippin,' she said casually, as he plonked himself down at the kitchen table, stretched and yawned.

'Yeah, so?'

'It was from some big wig on the Dick and Trudy show.' He frowned, trying to make a connection.

'The Dick an Trudy show? What, that programme on daytime telly?'

'Yeah.' She took a slow breath. 'They want you to go on it – but I don't fink you should do it,' she added quickly.

'Bloody 'ell!' Then: 'Why not?' She pulled a face.

'I've told you before why not.'

'Did they mention money?' he asked, ignoring the 'why not'. Zelda sighed lightly.

'Yeah, they did.'

''Ow much.'

'A grand.' He slid down from the chair and did a little jig of delight.

'A fousand! Blee-din 'ell!'

'So you're going to do it then,' she said quietly.

For the next couple of days he was like a dog with two wotsits.

While he pranced around, Zelda firmed up on the arrangements with the studio. They were to travel down to London by train (she had insisted on first class) where a car was to pick them up at Euston and whisk them to the set. Once there Davey was scheduled to meet with Dick and Trudy to discuss the interview format (she insisted that she had to sit in on the meeting). She had also argued (unsuccessfully) that she should sit in on the actual interview. She had no desire to see herself on telly she said, she just wanted, figuratively speaking, to hold his hand, because he wasn't used to dealing with such situations.

'We appreciate your concern,' they had said, 'but Dick and Trudy will look after him, trust us'.

Zelda laid the white shirt and grey slacks on the bed, bent down, picked up the little black slip-on shoes and placed them next to the slacks. She leaned over and picked a tiny loose thread of cotton from the shirt collar then ran her hands over the slacks to smooth them out.

'I've put yer gear on the bed,' she said through the open bedroom door. Davey, who was sitting in the living room watching Play School on their new second hand telly – bought on the strength of money coming in, turned his head.

'What gear?' he said.

'For the trip, I've picked out yer best shirt an slacks an, them black slip-on shoes.'

'I'm goin down in me kit,' he replied casually.

'Whoa, whoa, whoa!' she called out as she made her way round the bed and out to face him. 'No way!'

'Why not? They said I was ter wear me kit on the show.' Zelda had reluctantly agreed when they had told her that they wanted him to appear in his full kit. 'It will set the scene for the interview,' they had assured her. She didn't believe that for one minute. They wanted him in his kit for the bizarre impact it would cause; but then it was, she said to herself, a case of pipers and tunes.

'The show's one thing,' she conceded. 'But we're travelin down first class with loads of businessmen an wimmin. So there's no way I'm gonna be sittin next to you wearin yer kit an that daft floppy flat cap.'

'That's me trademark that is, me flat cap!'

'Yeah, well it goes in yer United bag with the rest of yer gear, right.' He gave in.

'Yeah, right.'

He was about to turn back to his programme,

when a thought struck him.

'Are yuh goin ter put up some butties an brew a flask?'

'Butties an a flask?'

'Yeah, fer the train.' Zelda sighed.

'I told you, we're travellin down first class. That means we'll be 'avin a full silver service breakfast.'

'What wiv bacon an eggs?'

'Of course, an with mushrooms, sausages, fried bread, toast an marmalade, an tea out of a silver pot.'

'Wow!' Zelda in spite of herself, smiled. She was catching herself doing that quite a bit lately.

'Yeah wow,' she said, her smile turning into a full-blown grin.

The trip down to London was unremarkable, other than for the fact that Davey behaved like a ten-year old kid on his way to Disneyland. He babbled on about never having been to London on a train before. He bounced up and down on his seat. He read out the names of every station they stopped at, and as they pulled out of each, he asked 'Are we nearly there yet?'

Zelda heaved a little sigh of relief as they pulled into Euston and they stepped down onto the platform.

'This way up to the concourse,' she said. 'There should be a bloke in a chauffeur's 'at waitin under the clock wiv a card wiv Mister Parker wrote

302

on it.'

'Mister Parker?'

'Yeah.' Davey grinned at the thought and clutching his Man.U. bag to his chest, he trailed along in her wake. 'MISTER Parker, eh,' he repeated. 'Wicked!'

They spilled out onto the crowded concourse area where Zelda spotted the chauffeur and shepherded Davey over in his direction. As they pulled up at the uniformed man's side Davey looked up.

'It's me mate, MISTER Parker,' he said nonchalantly. Zelda looked squarely into the man's face as he replied.

'Welcome to London Mister Parker, Madam. If you'll be so good as to follow me . . .' Zelda was impressed, the flunky didn't do a double take or anything when Davey had introduced himself. Maybe this wasn't really going to be as bad as she had feared after all.

'Is it a real Bentley?' Davey asked as the smiling chauffeur held the rear nearside door open.

'Yes sir, it certainly is.'

'It's a real Bentley,' Davey said softly as they sank into the plush upholstery. 'Eh an look it's got a likkul drinks cabinet!' he chirped, stretching out a hand.

'Gerroff an be'ave yerself!' she warned, rapping his fingers. 'I don't want you arseoles before you even get anywhere near the camera.'

Suitably chastised, he blew on his fingers and settled back to enjoy the ride.

Once inside the building, Zelda, in spite of her determination to remain on the icy side of cool, was impressed again. Like the vast majority of the population she had never been inside a television studio complex before, and the reality of the unreal world, where fact and fantasy, drama and documentary, comedy and tragedy, were formed, nurtured and rolled out for the consumption of the masses, excited her.

'Look!' she whispered as they reclined on a two-seater sofa in the large plush hospitality suite. 'Int that that doctor wotsit woman off *Casualty*?' Davey followed her gaze.

'Don't know,' he replied casually.

'An over there, in the corner is that . . . yeah it is, it's 'im with the orange face off that Antiques programme 'oo's always sayin "Cheap as chips"!' Davey nodded then yawned.

'Yeah, looks like 'im.' She frowned lightly. He'd been jumping up and down earlier in the day, but now he looked so laid back he could drop off to sleep.

'Aren't you nervous?'

'No.'

'What, not even a likkul bit?'

'Not really.'

Zelda shook her head slowly. She'd never really taken the time or indeed, had the inclination, to study his character before. He could get all wound up about taking a train ride, yet the prospect of sitting in front of a camera with who knows how many zillions of people watching didn't seem to faze him at all. She shook her head again.

'What you shakin yer 'ead for?'

'Nuffin really,' she said, 'except sometimes you surprise me a bit.' Before he could ask why, she suddenly sat forward in her chair and looked fixedly over his head towards the door of the suite.

'It's them!' she said. 'It's Dick an Trudy!' Davey turned around in his chair to see an early middle-aged couple, led by the young woman who had greeted them earlier in reception, come striding over.

'Hello, I'm Dick,' said the slim, tallish man.

'And I'm Trudy,' said the older, well-upholstered woman, extending a manicured hand. Zelda rose quickly to her feet, wiped a suddenly sweaty palm on her skirt, and with a sudden stab of embarrassment at the state of her own nails, shook hands quickly.

'Zelda, Zelda O'Flerhity,' she managed.

'And this must be David,' said the smiling woman, looking down at the small figure in the chair.

'No me name's Davey.' Trudy's smile never wavered as Zelda's foot made sharp contact with his ankle, and she made a sharp get up gesture with her head. Davey got up.

'Pleased to meet you Davey,' said Trudy.

'Likewise,' he muttered rubbing an instep against a suddenly sore ankle.

The young woman who ushered them in turned and left and Dick made a gesture towards a nearby table that had four chairs arranged around it

'Shall we?' he motioned.

As the others took their seats Dick leaned over towards Zelda.

'What would you like?' he said smoothly. Zelda's cheeks coloured.

'Pardon?'

'To drink; what would you like?'

'Oh. Er a gee an tee would be very nice, thank you.' Dick smiled charmingly.

'And you, Davey, what's your tipple?'

'A pint of bitter an a Gold Label . . . please,' he added as Zelda shot him a look.

'Bitter and a Gold Label? That's barley wine isn't it? Quite strong I believe,' said Dick to Davey.

'Knock you on yer arse before you know it,' replied the other.

As a grinning Dick made his way over to the bar Trudy said: 'We've already had a chat with the others who are on the show. We've got a young mother, and I mean young, from Liverpool, a chap from Wolverhampton, and an ex punk rocker from London on today. You've come down from Manchester haven't you?' she added. Zelda nodded. 'We're from there too originally. Do you know Wilmslow at all?' Zelda shook her head.

'Er, no not really, we live more towards the, er, City centre.'

'Oh, right. I believe there are some really lovely apartments there now.'

'Not in Fort Beswick,' said Davey to another look from Zelda.

'Oh,' said Trudy, as Dick returned carrying a tray of drinks containing two gin and tonics, two pints of bitter and two bottles of Gold Label barley wine.

'Thought I'd try one myself,' he chirped, as Trudy raised an eyebrow and said in an aside to Zelda:

'He always does that, calls it his ice breaker.'

'Good old northern drink is it?' Dick asked Davey.

'Sort of.'

'We're from Manchester too you know,' Dick said to Zelda, who nodded.

'Yes. Trudy was saying.' Davey took a good pull of his beer and then topped the pot up from the bottle of barley wine.

'Oh. It's not a chaser then,' Dick mouthed, following suit.

'You wouldn't want to drink it that way,' replied Davey in his booze buff voice. Dick took a good swig, then, following Davey's example, he topped up his pot with the barley wine, took a good mouthful and then held the pot up to the light.

'Hmmm sparkles quite nicely, quite a distinctive taste too. Not unpleasant though. No, not at all in fact.'

For the next ten minutes or so while Dick paid full attention to his drink, Trudy outlined the show format and went over some of the questions that they would be asking Davey during his brief show opening slot in an hour's time.

It all seemed pretty innocent and innocuous and Zelda was quietly assured by Trudy that Davey's disability would be treated with appropriate sensitivity. Davey, for his part, was quite content to sit outside the main conversation loop and concentrate on his drink. Pretty soon he was staring into an empty pot.

'Same again?' Dick chirped, as he drained the dregs in his own glass.

'Ace!' said Davey, while Trudy and Zelda, with their glasses still half full, both declined.

'I must say, it really is quite more-ish,' Dick admitted a couple of minutes later, as he held his pint pot up to the light again and studied the sparking amber liquid. Davey licked the foam off his lips and nodded.

'Put airs on yer chest that will mate.' Dick grinned.

'Wow!' he said after another deep swig. 'You're not wrong there my old son. It's got an interesting kick to it.'

'Believe it,' muttered Davey.

'Aye,' said Dick, slipping into the northern vernacular, 'this Gold Label kicks that southern crap into life big time!' Trudy looked across sharply.

'Yes, well better make sure that one's your last,' she said slowly. 'I'm off down to make up, so don't be long.' She drained her glass, smiled at Zelda and Davey and got to her feet.

'Dick will bring you down to make-up Davey . . . when he's finished his drink,' she added pointedly. 'Oh, and Zelda, Alice will be up for you in a few minutes.' Zelda looked a little non-plussed. 'She's the girl who was here with us a few minutes ago,' Trudy filled in. 'She'll take you through to the audience hospitality suite and from there you'll all go through to the studio.' As she left Davey frowned.

'What she mean I've got ter go down ter make-up. I'm not a turkul! Dick looked slightly confused.

'Turkul?' he said, 'What's a turkul?' Zelda sighed.

'He means tur-tle.'

'Oh. What's a turtle got to do with it then?'

'It's another word for a puffter . . . I mean a gay pers—'

'Yeah,' Davey butted in, 'I'm no poncey Lundun pansy!' Zelda sighed.

'It's the lights, everyone on the telly 'as to 'ave make up,' she said patiently.

'Do you 'ave it anall?' Davey asked Dick.

'Certainly, everyone does.' Davey thought about it for a couple of seconds.

'All right then,' he accepted. If getting made up was okay for his new drinking mate, then it was okay for him.

'Right then, I'll see you after the show,' said Zelda, after Alice came over a couple of minutes later and led her across the room. As she reached the door she turned briefly and mouthed: 'be'ave yerself', to him.

'Women eh!' said Dick. 'They think we can't be trusted for five minutes.'

'Yeah, well they may be right there mate . . . are you gettin 'em in agen then or what?'

'I'm gettin 'em in agen then!' replied Dick with a little giggle as he climbed somewhat unsteadily to his feet.

'This way little buddy,' slurred Dick twenty minutes later, as he pushed open the make-up room door. 'We better hurry or it will be slapped wrist time for me off the little woman.'

'You're cutting it fine. Trudy's been in twice looking for you,' said Susan, the show's make-up woman.

'Uh-oh slapped wrist time!' giggled Dick as he collapsed heavily into one of the chairs and motioned Davey into the seat next to him.

'It will have to be a rush job,' Susan chided, as, under Davey's wary eye, she reached for a large fluffy powder puff.

At the same time as Dick and Davey were receiving the attention of Susan, and Davey then changed into his kit, backstage, Trudy was slowly burning, while in the audience, Zelda chuckled along with the rest as a warm-up man told a few topical jokes.

'This way little buddy,' Dick slurred as he approached a po-faced Trudy.

'*Dick*!' she snarled, making the word sound like the male dangly bit.

'Don't fuss me dear!' Dick said with a double-handed calm down motion. Trudy pursed her lips and bit her tongue. Now was not the right time to prolong the discussion.

'But just wait', she muttered under her breath. Any other mutterings were cut off as Alice appeared backstage and placed a hand on Davey's shoulder.

'You wait here with me,' she said, 'then when I give you the signal you just walk on and sit down on the sofa, okay?'

'Right, no probs,' said a fully kitted-out Davey from under his flat cap.

The front of stage announcer went through his introduction, and Trudy with a fixed smile and a slightly floppy Dick in tow made an entrance to whistles and wild applause.

As soon as they were seated they were given the countdown and the on-air sign lit up.

'Welcome,' said a smiling Trudy. 'We have a

really interesting show for you today.'

'Yes,' said Dick, squinting at the autocue, 'er you can say that again Trudy . . .' Trudy, ever the old pro, stepped in quickly.

'Yes *Dick* (dangly bit) we have a man from Wolverhampton who is going for a world record at sticking plastic clothes pegs on his face; we have a pregnant thirteen-year-old single mum of two from Liverpool, who says she wants to offer her baby for sale on the Internet; and we have a chat with Phil Phlegm, ex lead singer with punk group, Cupid Stunts.'

'Glad you announced that one Trudy, couldda been a can-candidate for Spoonerism of the year that could if I'd have had to say it!' Dick chipped in with a leery look and a wink at the audience.

'Yes, thank you *Dick* (dangly bit). Phil Phlegm will be chatting about, among other things, his new-found passion for needlepoint embroidery. But before that, we have something very different . . .'

'You could even say bizarre!' slurred Dick, suppressing a burp. 'Just take a dekko at this . . .' Dick and Trudy were then faded out, and replaced by a two-minute tape of the Beswick Reds' recent triumph.

While the tape was running a grim-faced Trudy ordered Dick out of his chair, and motioned a couple of stagehands to move their sofa a little closer to the autocue.

'Tha's better,' he said squinting, 'I can almos

see it now.'

'Shit!' she muttered, as the Reds' tape faded out, the on air sign winked back on, and the camera focused briefly on a grinning audience.

'Well!' Trudy smiled into the returning camera. 'That was certainly a bit special. So let's meet that remarkable goalkeeper now. Ladies and gentlemen let's hear it for David Ignatius Montgomery Parker!' Offstage, Alice gave Davey a smile and then a gentle nudge in the back.

'Just walk over to the spare sofa and sit down,' she whispered.

Davey, blinking slightly under the bright lights, strolled out to loud applause, a few nervous giggles and one or two loud guffaws.

'Welcome David,' said Trudy as Davey hitched himself up onto the sofa.

'His name's Davey dear,' said Dick. Trudy flashed her partner a twenty-watt smile.

'Sorry, welcome to the show . . . Davey.' Davey nodded.

'S'alright.'

'Well Davey that clip was really something special. You seem to have a quite remarkable goalkeeping style (laughter from the audience) how did it develop?'

'I suppose,' interrupted Dick, 'that being a one-armed dwarf had a lot to do with it?'

'Well, yeah, I suppose,' Davey conceded.

'Actually, *Dick* (dangly bit) the technical term

313

for Davey's condition is Achondroplasia, it affects almost one in forty thousand children and it is caused, I believe, by a chemical change in a single gene.'

'What was that term again Trudy?'

'Achondroplasia.'

'Wow. I'd never be able to get my tongue round that one; mind you,' he added winking at the audience, 'there's a lot of things I can't get my ton-tongue round!'

While the rest of the audience broke out into gales of laughter, Zelda's face took on the aspect of a wet weekend in Hartlepool.

'So, Davey, obviously, as *Dick* (dangly bit) says, your condition must have had a bearing on the way you play the game; but tell me, have you always wanted to be a goalkeeper?'

'Yeah ever since I was a likkul kid. Even before this mad Alsatian dog bit me arm off.'

'Heavens! That must've been truly awful for you!' said Trudy sympathetically.

'Yeah, it was. It really put the mockers on me playin fer Man. United' As laughter in the dark from the audience rang out, Davey turned towards them and grinned.

'So,' Dick said, 'that was an ambition of yours was it Davey, to play in goals for Manchester United?'

'Yeah, it was . . . an they could do wiv me now!' he added as a Boom! Boom! for the benefit of the audience, most of whom broke up with laughter.

'Well,' said Trudy admiringly, 'you don't seem to let your disability get you down at all do you!' Davey grinned then put on his serious face.

'Well Trude, I'd be a liar if I said I dint get pissed off sometimes (audience laughter) but then yuh got to play the 'and you got ant yuh? An I only 'ave the one!' (Boom! Boom!). One or two in the audience pulled out handkerchiefs to wipe the tears of laughter from their eyes. Zelda sucked on a metaphorical lemon.

'So,' said Trudy, 'coming back to the present, your team, the Beswick Reds?'

'Yeah?'

'As we've seen from the video clip, they won that competition in Manchester. Where do you go from there?'

'Back to our local fer a good piss up.' (Gales of laughter – plus one bright red face).

'No Davey, said Dick, 'I think Trudy means what's next for your team .'

'Thank you *Dick*.' (dangly bit). 'Yes, what are the team's plans now?'

'Oh. Well, nuffin much really. We 'ave regular kickabouts an if the same competition's on next year we'll be back to defend our title.' Trudy smiled and nodded. Dick grinned wickedly and chimed in:

'So, would we be right in sayin' that you would be open to off-offers then, if any big teams out there are lookin' to tighten up their de-defence?'

'Yeah, course.' (Audience laughter). With a slightly manic fixed smile Trudy stepped in and brought the slot to a premature end with: 'Ladies and gentlemen . . . Davey Parker! Thank you Davey !'

Back on the train, Davey – who obviously had been operating on a different level to everyone else during the preceding events – was well chuffed.

'That was good eh?' he said turning towards his slightly po-faced companion.

'If you say so.'

'You get the cheque?' Zelda patted her handbag.

The journey back to Manchester proved uneventful . . . and quiet; as unlike on the trip down, Davey sat for most of the time with a smug little look on his face. The only bit of conversation of any length revolved around Dick's antics.

"Ee made a bit of a pratt of 'imself, din't 'ee?' said Davey.

'Yeah 'ee did an 'oo's fault were that then?'

'What you lookin at me for? I din't make 'im neck four pints an four Gold Labels, did I?'

'Well, no,' she conceded, 'but you should've warned 'im not to get carried away.'

'I did, din't I. I told 'im it would knock 'im on 'is

arse. Not my fault if 'ee's a pratt.' Zelda had to concede again.

'That Trudy was spittin fevvers big time eh?' Davey added.

'Yeah she was, but still, it was a bit out of order, lampin 'im one int snot box like that, in front of all them backstage lot.' Davey nodded.

'Yeah, an that Producer woman she was well pissed off anall weren't she?'

'You can say that again! If looks could kill 'ee would be wearin a wooden overcoat an pushin up bleedin daisies.'

'Yeah.'

'Pratt.'

'Yeah...'

27

Back in Beswick, Davey revelled in his new found fame. For the first time in his life that he could remember, there were people who actually smiled in the street when they saw him; some even stopped and entered into conversation!

'You'll be givin out autographs next,' Zelda said tartly when his constant smirkiness finally hit a raw nerve.

'Well,' he replied coolly, 'I am a bit of a telly star yer know.'

After a couple of days of his preening Zelda decided that enough was enough. A bit of bubble popping was called for. Okay, the little sod didn't have much to crow about in his life before now, but he needed to be put straight for his own good.

'Look,' she said not unkindly, 'you've 'ad yer fifteen minutes of fame – but it's gone now.' Davey frowned.

''Ave you been on't telly?'

'No, course not, but–'

'Well then.'

'Yeah, well, look . . . I don't want to piss on yer likkul parade but . . .' Davey frowned again. It looked like the heavens were about to open big time.

'But what?' She took a slow deep breath. This was going to be surprisingly hard. *Not long* ago she thought *I would've got a big kick out of puttin im down . . . but now . . . somehow I'm worried about 'urtin 'is feelings*. She steeled herself to tell him straight.

'People look at you like you're . . . like that . . . John Merrick bloke,' she said flatly.

''Oo's ee when 'ee's at 'ome?'

'You know, that bloke they called the Elephant Man.'

'What, like in that film on't telly?' Zelda nodded slowly. Davey bridled.

318

"Ee was a ugly bastard! I'm not a ugly bastard!'

'No, no, course not. I'm not sayin you are. What I mean is 'ee was a . . . curiosity. Yeah okay, 'ee was famous, but 'ee was only famous cause 'ee was so different from . . . normal people.' Davey shook his head.

'I was the one 'oo won us the match. I was the one they asked ter go on't telly an talk about me goalkeeping.'

'I know,' murmured Zelda, 'but there's thousands of goalkeepers and football teams, what do you fink it was that made them pick you out? It was only a poxy likkul five-a-side contest after all.' Davey considered her words.

'I dont know,' he muttered. 'Maybe they fought it were a good story or sumfin . . .'

'Yeah, they did, but only good fer a giggle. Din't you 'ere em laffin, them people in the audience?'

'Yeah, so?'

'They were laffin AT YOU,' she said firmly. 'They were laffin at 'ow ridiculous it is to 'ave a four foot one-armed goalie.' There, she had said it . . . in spades.

Davey opened his mouth to reply; then he shut it again as the slow realisation seeped into his brain. He fought it.

'But what about all them people round 'ere 'oo stop an talk to me now int street?'

'Some people,' she muttered, 'would stop an talk to a chimp if it 'ad bin on the telly.' Davey's shoulders slowly slumped. She was right. Wrapped up in the warm afterglow of victory and sudden centre stage attention, he had allowed himself to dream that he really was somebody at last – not just a little berk that everyone took the piss out of.

'I'm a freak,' he said softly.

Zelda felt a little stab of guilt for doing what she had said she didn't want to do – piss on his likkul parade.

'You're not a freak, you're just . . . just . . . different,' she said with a sad little smile on her thin lips.

'Yeah, well,' he muttered, 'I'm goin out fer a walk.'

'Okay,' she replied with forced brightness to his retreating back, 'but don't be long; I'm doin a sausage casserole fer tea.' He didn't bother to answer as he went through the door.

Down on the street, hand in pocket, he began a sad little conversation with himself.

'I'm not Billy No Mates me. I got plenty of mates,' he muttered. 'There's the lads, an all them people in the club. They don't laff at me. They don't fink I'm a likkul freak.'

"Ow do you know? argued a little voice in his head. *"Ow do you know they don't piss their selves when you're not there?"*

'Curtley an Tommy an the lads, grew up

togevver we did,' he argued back doggedly as his aimless stroll drew him towards the precinct.

'Bin frew a lot we 'ave over the years. That Alsatian, our kid buggerin off ter Canerda, me mam dyin. They was all there fer me then, the lads, right from bein likkul kids we was allus mates.

'An I was there fer them anall; when Curtley's bruvver got killed in the crash in that car 'ee nicked; an when Tommy's dad topped 'isself when the dust from Bradford pit choked is lungs an 'ee kunt put up wiv it no more; an when Billy got nicked fer GBH, no-one went ter see 'im more in Strangeways than me.

'Yeah, an Fred; when 'ee first moved in a lot of the lads fought 'ee was a bit of a toffee nosed bastard coz 'ee'd bin to university an all that, but I could see 'ee was all right. It was me what got 'im into the Reds.

'Yeah, okay they was there fer me – but I was allus there fer them anall.'

"Yeah you was," said the little voice, *"but yer still a likkul freak to the rest of the world."* He turned this over in his head for a few seconds then nodded slowly in quiet acceptance, before pushing back his shoulders and setting his face.

'Yeah, okay, if that's the way it is, then the rest of the world can go fuk itself wiv the wide end of a Ragman's trumpit,' he muttered, as he found himself standing outside the Bookies.

Casually, he fingered the loose change in his

pocket.   'Not even a quid,' he said quietly and was about to turn around and wander off somewhere else, when the frosted door opened and a large and worryingly familiar figure almost collided with him.

'You!' the big man snarled.

'Oh shit!' Davey mouthed.

'I'll give you shit you likkul bastard, c'mere!' The big man reached down and thumped a ham fist onto Davey's shoulder.

'Oh Shit!' Davey yelped, as he twisted away from beneath the hand, engaged fourth gear, and with a lumbering pursuer on his heels, legged it back the way he had come.

As he sprinted up Grey Mare Lane he was chased by a breathless, shouted: 'I'll 'ave you, you likkul gett just you wait an see!'

28

Davey squeezed through a gap between a fencepost and the concrete buttress of the bridge that spanned Ashton New Road.

Once safely through he made his skittering way down the steep embankment that led to the canal bank. There, he turned and looked back the way he had come. There was no sign of pursuit.

'Fink yer big eh . . . chasin a likkul cripple,' he muttered in the direction of the fence.

'Well just come on down!' he shouted (as his pursuer did not appear).

'We'll see just 'ow tough yer are! Come on! Kick you one up the arse I will, just you see!'

''Oo yuh t-torkin to D-Davey?' Davey jumped in alarm and whirled round to face a tall, bulky, balaclava-clad figure that emerged from the gloom beneath the bridge.

'Oh it's you is it,' he said with relief. Ernie smiled his tombstone smile.

'Yeah it's me. 'Oo y-yuh talkin to eh?' Davey made a tough face.

'Just 'ad ter smack a bloke fer bein cheeky . . . sorted 'im out good an proper I did . . . fink twice before 'ee comes messin wiv me agen!' he said, turning briefly to shake a small fist in the direction of the fence.

'W-wow!' said Ernie in admiration. 'W-wud yuh really kick 'im one up the a-arse, eh Davey!'

'Yeah, course, I'm a bugger me when I gets goin.' He pulled a face and looked mean. 'Anyway,' he said, 'what you doin down 'ere? I fought yer mam said you kunt come down ont cut?' Ernie frowned.

'Aw, d-don't tell er w-will yuh D-Davey; she-she-she'll make me s-stay in i-if she knows!' Davey returned the frown.

'Might not. Anyway, what you doin down 'ere?' he repeated.

'I w-was 'avin a l-look fer a n-new fish, my likkul goldfish w-went an d-died,' he said sadly. Davey nodded lightly.

'Oh right, I 'ad a goldfish once,' he reminisced. 'Bloody clever fish it were; it could tap dance.'

'W-wow!' Wh-what's tap dance D-Davey?'

'It's what this likkul fish usedta do when I emptied the water outer is bowl, an waited fer a minute before I turned the tap on full on topper it.' Davey laughed.

'Oh.'

'Yeah. Clever fish that was!' said Davey, grinning at his turn of wit.

'W-what 'ap-'appened to it D-Davey?'

'Daft fing went an died anall,' the little man answered matter-of-factly.

'Oh.'

'Anyway. There aint 'ardly any fish in 'ere,' said Davey, looking around at the weed clogged, brackish, and in parts rainbow-hued oil slicked water that glistened like the iridescent surface of a black pearl.

'Is,' Ernie said emphatically. 'L-look. I f-found one!' he pointed over the edge.

Davey peered into the dark brackish water and saw, close to the side, a small silver fish. Like a tiny sliver of new moon that had fallen from the sky, its body lay in a curved rictus of death, tiny black eyes staring blindly, mouth gaping as if for air.

'Oh yeah. Proberly killed by all the oil an stuff in there,' he said, nodding in the general direction of the water.

'Aw, sh-shame that I-Int it Davey?' Davey nodded again.

'Yeah suppose so, it dunt tek much ter kill a likkul fish like that. Sharks though,' he said casually, 'they wunt die from the oil an stuff. They can live in anyfin sharks can.' Ernie shivered theatrically and shook his great balaclava covered head.

'Sh sharks! I d-don't l-like th-them! Th-they e-e-eat people!' Davey smiled.

'Yeah' they do . . . an yuh know what?'

'W-what? Davey's head slipped back into slow – you can take this as gospel – nodding mode.

'There's some sharks in 'ere right now,' he said casually. The big man's lantern jaw dropped.

'N-n- no!'

'There is,' said Davey quietly. 'LOOK THERE'S ONE NOW!' Ernie screamed, and stumbled back to fall in a tangle of legs and whirling arms.

Davey edged towards the water and made a show of peering into the murky shallows.

'N-no, c-cum back D-Davey! It-it'll gob-gobble you up! Davey, with his back turned to the big man, smiled.

'Naw. It's okay, it's gone now,' he said. 'Forty foot long it was, if it were an inch. Yep that muvver cud eat an 'orse wiv one bite 'ee cud.' He turned towards the fallen Ernie, and snapped his teeth together loudly. Ernie scrambled to his feet, his face a stricken mask of fright.

'Wh-where's it g-gone Davey?'

'Proberly gone 'untin for some ducks or sumfin.'

Ernie regained a little courage and edged slowly over to Davey's side.

'D-don't l-like sh-sharks me,' he muttered. 'They gob-gobbles people up fer their dinner.'

'Yeah, yer right there,' Davey agreed. 'Specially daft people.' Ernie didn't answer. He was still peering cautiously into the water, when Davey said casually:

'Shark it were that bit me arm off.' Ernie, with a puzzled look on his face, turned slowly towards his companion.

'I f-fought it w-was a d-dog . . .'

'Naw . . . dog shark it were. They is the most deadly. Yeah dog shark . . . killed 'im though I did . . .stabbed 'im wiv a knife.' Ernie's eyes opened wide.

'Wiv a-a real knife!' Davey sighed.

'Course a real knife, dummy. Yuh can't kill a forty-foot shark wiv a rubber knife can yuh!'

'Wow! Where's i-it n-now, eh D-Davey?' Davey shrugged.

'Don't know. They proberly cut it up and made a load of cat food or summat. You must a

326

seen it . . . it were in all the papers.' Ernie bowed his head slightly and embarrassed said:

'Aw, y-yuh know I c-can't read very g-good.' Then brightly: 'N-no n-not the sh-shark . . . the knife!'

'Oh. Well . . . the coppers took it off me. Yeah . . . they said I wuz too 'andy wiv it, like . . . like them mafia villuns.' Ernie's loud off-key whistle of admiration bounced off the bridge wall.

'Wow!' he said, before adding sadly: 'I aint n-never 'ad a knife m-me.'

'Yeah, well that figures. You as ter be proper grown up.' Ernie nodded agreement, but then carried on regardless.

'If I d-did though I b-bet I cud b-be one of them mafias v-villuns eh D-Davey!' The little man pursed his lips and shook his head slowly.

'Don't fink so. It's best if you is likkul like me then you can sneak up on 'em uvver villuns an stab 'em wivout 'em seein yuh.' Ernie was well impressed.

'Aw, wow I wish I w-wuz lik-likkul like you Da-Davey; then I c-cud be a mafias villun anall.'

'Yeah, maybe,' said Davey, lowering himself onto the towpath and dangling his legs over the water. Ernie, thanks to a very short memory span, didn't hesitate to hunker down beside him.

'Eh Davey!'

'What?'

'What's i-it l-like only 'avin one a-arm?'

'What yuh mean, what's it like?'

'Is it l-like only 'avin one l-leg?' His small companion glanced across at him with a look of disdain.

'Don't know do I. Got two bloody legs me ant I? Daft bloody question that!' he said tutting loudly.

'Oh, y-yeah.' They sat in silence for a few seconds until:

'D-Davey?'

'What now . . .'

'If y-you only 'ad one leg y-yuh would fall o-over, wunt yuh?' Davey sighed heavily.

'Yeah course yuh would . . . fall flat on yer bloody arse wunt yuh! Daft bloody question that.' Ernie accepted the rebuke without question.

'Yeah. An i-if you ad n-no l-legs,' he continued brightly, 'yuh w-wunt be able to get u-up agen w-wud yuh!'

'Course not . . . But then if yuh 'ad no legs yuh wunt be out bloody walkin in the first bloody place would yuh!' The I'm a clever dick look faded from Ernie's face.

'Oh yeah . . .' They sat in silence for a few seconds more, then: 'I s-saw a film ont telly once b-bout this m-man 'oo 'ad tin l-legs.'

'Oh yeah, I saw that one,' said Davey casually. 'It were called *The Wizard of Oz*.'

'W-was it?' said Ernie.

'Yeah, it was all about this girl that fell asleep an dreams she guz to this queer place wiv witches an lions an tin men an fings . . . an there is some likkul people in it, like me . . . only they all as two arms.'

Ernie's heavy eyebrows met in puzzled concentration.

'Was it?'

'Yeah, an it was a bit scary in some bits . . . but it all come right in the end.'

'D-did it?'

'Yeah . . . you saw it dint yuh?'

'Yeah, but . . .' Ernie's face took on a look of intense concentration.

'Yeah but what?'

'What about the Ger-Germans an the machine g-guns an the p-planes?'

'What Germans, wot machine guns, what bloody planes?'

'They was sh-shootin at each uv-uvver. DER! DER! DER!' said Ernie, making like a machine gunner. Davey took a turn at looking puzzled.

'Was they?'

'Yeah a-an the Ger-Germans they cat-catched this m-man an took 'is t-tin legs off so 'ee kunt r-run away an put 'im i-in a prison c-camp!'

'No they dint!'

'Did!' said an adamant Ernie.

'Did they? said a puzzled Davey.

'Yeah.'

Davey ran the memory of the film though his mind and could find no Germans, machine guns, or planes.

'No they dint! This tin man got all wet an is legs went all stiff an rusty . . . an this girl put some oil on em . . . an 'ee was okay.'

'Oh . . .'

They sat in silence for a while staring into the murky water – then a heavy penny thudded.

'That weren't *The Wizard of Oz*! That was a war film that was!'

'W-was it?'

'Yeah. Bloody daft you Ernie!' The big man pursed his lips in an obstinate pout.

'N-ot!'

'Are! Bloody dool alley you!'

'N-not!'

Davey craned his head back and looked up into Ernie's frowning face. Normally he would not have put himself in such a position with a big person; knowing that if he did, he would probably end up with a fik ear. But Ernie was different. Ernie was another unfortunate.

To Davey, Ernie, here and now, presented a rare opportunity to lord it and – due to the mood he was in after his recent deflation at Zelda's hands and another rotten chasing – he wasn't about to let the chance slip by. Today the Good Book's instruction to Do Unto Uvvers was a definite no-no. His eyes narrowed.

'Alluz was daft you, daft . . . an mucky.'

'What y-yuh m-mean mucky?' Ernie was

sidetracked.

'You know MUCKY!' Ernie looked puzzled.

'N-not. All-alluz as a wash e-evry day me . . .'

'Not torkin bout dirty 'ands an face,' said Davey knowingly.

'What then?' said a confused Ernie.

'YOU KNOW!' said Davey.

They sat in silence for a while and Davey hummed softly to himself, while Ernie's face gradually contorted and reddened as his slow brain laid a thickened forefinger on the meaning of Davey's words.

'Th-that weren't my fault,' he said quietly. Davey snorted.

'Oh yeah, not your fault. Attacked you did they, them two likkul girls!' Ernie moaned.

'N-n-not m-my f-fault!'

'Oh yeah? 'Oo's fault were it then?' Ernie's mouth worked but no sound came out.

They sat in silence. Davey whistling softly — Ernie wrestling with a jumble of thoughts and a tumble of emotions.

'They w-was cheeky g-girls they was. Th-they kep a-askin me tuh sh-show 'em me w-willy . . .'

'Oh yeah. Yeah that's right,' said Davey, feigning sudden returning memory. 'I remember now. My Zelda said the police shudda cut yer plonker off . . . LIKE THAT!' He made a savage slashing motion with his hand.

'N-n-no!'

'Dirty ole man my Zelda said . . . pervert, she said.' The big man wrung his huge hands in an agitated fervour of feeling and a strangled sob was forced from his mouth.

'Arrggh! N-no, w-weren't my f-fault. Th-they kep laff-laffin at me and say-sayin rude fings . . . an I w-went all 'ot an funny an k-kunt breeve . . . kunt 'elp it!'

'What yuh do then, when yuh went all 'ot?' Ernie looked down into the little man's face.

'What?'

'What yuh do then; to them likkul girls?' Ernie's wildly twitching facial muscles slowed slightly as he tried to apply memory.

'Don't know, he muttered softly. 'I can't m-member.' Davey snorted.

'My Zelda said you wiggled yer waggler at them likkul girls.'

'Weren't my f-fault,' the big man said quietly to himself. 'The d-doctors s-sed i-it weren't my fault.'

Davey, unconvinced, 'hmmmed'.

'What they do to yuh, them doctors then?' Ernie shook his great balaclava-clad head in an effort to dislodge a series of unwelcome thoughts.

'They g-give me a op-operation . . . an n-now I'm all-all right. An, an, me m-man gives me some likk-likkul yellow p-pills ev-every day an I don't get all 'ot an f-funny no more . . .'

Davey had known of Ernie's troubles. There

332

had been a bit of a stink at the time, but Davey knew that he had not really done anything to harm the little girls.

In his childlike way he had thought of it as a game, and when the girls had teased him and asked him to show them his willy, the big man had giggled and obliged.

Anyway, Ernie didn't get all hot any more and he didn't come over all funny, so it was all history.

Mind you, Davey thought to himself, *there's a lot of 'funny' people around nowadays.*

'My Zelda, she duz funny fings sometimes,' he said to the dark water. 'Wiv emena fings . . . don't like it me . . . but she's big, an she looks after me . . . sometimes.'

Ernie had calmed down now and his big knotty hands lay like two lump hammers at rest in his lap.

'W-what's an em-emena fing Davey?' he asked quietly.

'Not a emena fing, dummy . . . a emena,' Davey muttered, still looking into the murky water. 'It's... it's a rubber tube fing wiv a big rubber ball, an, an, it's too 'ard fer dummies to understand.'

'Oh.'

'Yeah all the world is bloody funny if yuh ask me. . . What wiv emenas an wet bloody winder levvers, an uvver bloody fings!' Ernie was impressed.

'Wow I w-wish I w-was clever like you D-

Davey!' The little man looked up from the water and peered into the animated face.

'Tough,' he muttered. Ernie didn't appear to notice the knock back.

'I 'ad a b-budgie once th-that were clever like you D-Davey! It c-cud say 'oo's a p-pritty b-boy then.' Davey snorted.

'I don't fink that's clever . . . bloody budgie that stutters!'

'N-no,' said Ernie, 'that w-weren't the bud-budgie, that were m-me!'

'Oh. Anyway, what 'appened to it then?' A sudden sad expression clouded the big man's heavy features.

'It d-died. Cat b-bit its 'ead off.'

'Oh yeah.' That'd do it I suppose. Mind you budgies is mard likkul fings . . . say boo to a budgie an it craps itself an falls down dead. Cats though,' Davey said with authority, 'is buggers. But,' he added with an edge of hardness creeping into his voice, 'they's not as bad as dogs – they is vicious!' Ernie grinned

'I like d-dogs me! They l-licks my f-face 'an 'ands an 'as t-tails that go all w-waggly!' Davey glared up into Ernie's smiling face.

'Listen to me,' he said firmly, 'DOGS IS VICIOUS!' Ernie was not having any.

'Aw y-you is j-just sayin that c-cos a dog b-bit yer a-arm off.'

'I tole yuh, it weren't a dog it were a DOG

334

SHARK!'

While Davey muttered darkly to himself, Ernie, feeling a little miffed at the little man's tone, climbed to his feet, retreated a few feet along the towpath, plonked himself down again, and dangled his heavy boots over the edge.

Davey glanced along the path and smiled thinly.

'Oh, an torkin bout sharks,' he said conversationally; 'LOOK OUT IT'S CUM BACK!' Ernie screamed and scrambled to his feet as Davey's laughter skittered across the brackish water and bounced back off the grimy bridge wall.

'Y-you sh-shunt make f-fun of me Davey P-Parker!' Ernie's face was blood gorged with alarm and the first blossoming signs of anger.

'Well you shunt be so bloody daft then,' Davey said calmly.

'N-not daft! Anyway;' Ernie said mockingly, 'you is f-feared of d-dogs . . . so there!' Davey's face clouded over and his voice took on a sharp edge.

'Go on, 'op it daft Ernie!' he snarled. 'Before I kick yuh one up the arse!'

Ernie, with an angry backward glance, shuffled ten yards further along the path.

As Davey watched with a sour prune expression on his face, the big man muttered something to himself, peered carefully into the weed-choked water to make sure there were no sharks lurking, and squatting down, dangled his size thirteen's carefully over the side.

Davey watched as Ernie, with another little bout of muttering picked up a stone and turning to face the canal, moodily tried to flip it along the water. It plunked straight to the bottom.

He turned and after some more muttering, selected another piece of stone and repeated the exercise. Plunk. Annoyed, he glanced back at Davey, who it seemed, was taking nothing more than a casual interest. Ernie tried again. Plunk and again Plunk.

Davey began to whistle a little tune. Ernie turned to look back in the little man's direction, saw him nonchalantly lean over and select a small piece of slate from the path, and flip it onto the oily surface. It skipped three times before clattering into the side of a half submerged shopping trolley.

'Fifteen . . . not bad . . . did twenty seven once.'

Ernie glowered, his cheeks glowed and his lips pursed in determination. He picked up another stone and hurled it into the water, where it dived straight to the murky bottom.

'Awww b-bum! he yelled. Davey cackled.

'Awww t-t-titties!'

'Ay-up; I fought you dint fink of fings like that now,' said Davey. Ernie jumped to his feet and hopped up and down.

'B-bum b-bum, t-titties!'

'Oo you naughty boy. Torkin bout titties an

bums. I fink I'll 'ave ter tell yer ole mam, then she'll give yuh a clout round the bleedin earole!'

Ernie's agitated hopping stopped, and the angry look on his face melted and was replaced by one of concern.

'N-no d-d-don't tell me m-mam Davey. She'll t-tek me tut d-doctors an they'll do f-fings to me!' Davey shrugged.

'No problem,' he said lightly. 'They'll just get a big knife an cut yer plonker off . . .'

'N-N-Nooo!' pleaded Ernie.

'It won't 'urt, they'll 'it you ont 'ead wiv a big 'ammer first . . .'

'N-N-Noooo!'

'Don't know what yer mitherin bout; you only uses it ter pee wiv . . .' Ernie was beside himself.

'I-I-I'm feared of d-doctors. They m-might l-let me go dead when they 'it m-me ont 'ead! Davey made as if to consider Ernie's fears.

'Naw, I don't fink so . . . eh tell yuh what though . . .'

'What?' said Ernie with a hint of hope creeping into his voice.

'Maybe when they knocks you out they could cut one of yer arms off, and chop yer legs off here,' he made a slashing motion below his knees, 'then yuh cud be jus like me . . . 'ow bout that then?'

'Arrrgghhh!'

'No, dint fink so,' Davey muttered sourly.

Ernie looked pleadingly at the little figure.

337

'Aw y-yuh won't t-tell me mam, w-will yuh Davey?' I w-won't say them n-naughty words agen.'

'What words is that then?'

'T-titties an b-bum!' Ernie said eagerly, sensing a chink in Davey's resolve.

'Aww yuh sed 'em agen!' Ernie looked stricken.

'N-no! You tole me t-to s-say em!' Davey sighed.

'Do yuh allus do what people tell yuh?' Ernie considered the question carefully.

'Y-Yeah, I as to coz I c-can't f-fink very g-good.'

'Makes yer 'ead 'urt does it, finkin?' Ernie nodded several times quickly.

'Yeah an, an sumtimes m-me n-nose bleeds anall.'

'Does it?'

'Yeah an w-when I tries 'ar-'ard ter fink, sumtimes m-me 'ead guz all d-dizzy . . .'

Davey nodded slowly and made a little moue with his mouth.

'Well yuh better not try an fink too 'ard, or yer 'ead might jus go BANG! an explode like a fat balloon!'

'Eh?'

'Yeah, I saw this bloke ont telly once. 'Is 'ead exploded. Right mess it were; blood an snot everywhere. Yeah an brains all over the place.'

'I-It d-dint d-did it!'

'Yeah. It were on some old repeats on channel

338

five, Kenny Ebberitt show it were called. Yeah blood an snot an brains everywhere. Course,' he added casually, 'if yer 'ead exploded it would only be blood an snot . . .'

'What 'a-'appened to 'im th-then?'

'What yuh mean 'what 'appened to 'im? He was dead weren't 'ee! No bloody 'ead. Can't wark around wiv no bloody 'ead can yuh? No 'ead yuh can't eat can yuh, so yud starve ter bloody def.'

'Oh y-yeah . . .' Davey sniggered at his own wit. Ernie frowned and his eyebrows knitted together in serious thought. Davey noticed.

'Ayup!' he said in mock alarm, 'I fink it might just blow now!' Ernie shook his head.

'No it w-won't. That d-dint 'urt.'

'Pity'.

'Our budgie,' said the big man slowly, 'when the c-cat bit its 'ead o-off . . . it d-dint st-starve ter def. It j-jus fell d-down . . .'

'Yeah, well, like I said before, budgies is soft as shit.'

'Oh.'

'Anyway, you was sayin naughty words you was,' said Davey, climbing to his feet and dusting off the back of his trousers. Ernie wrung his hands.

'Aw y-you won't t-tell me m-mam will yuh D-Davey?'

'Don't know, might not if–' suddenly his words were cut off by a loud bark from behind. Panicked, he whirled round to see the frighteningly

339

familiar figure of the large dog that had almost attacked him weeks earlier in the precinct, bounding towards him, mouth slobbering, fangs bared.

'Arrrgghh!' he screamed - then whirled round and cannoned straight into Ernie. The big man's arms windmilled in an attempt to steady himself as he teetered on the edge of the canal bank, before with a 'Noooo!' he toppled backward to land with a mighty splash in the greasy water.

Davey spun round to see that the beast was almost upon him. It was the devil or the not so blue sea! The not so blue sea won out.

He whirled round again and with a shouted 'Oh shiiittt!' launched himself towards the floundering Ernie who was a good ten feet from the bank. He hit the water, sank, rose and spitting out a mouthful of oily water wrapped his arm around the only little island of sanctuary in sight... Ernie's head.

'Arrrgghh!' yelled Ernie as Davey's weight threatened to force him under. 'G-G-Gerroff, I can't sw-swim!'

'Neever can I!' Davey yelled as Ernie's feet frantically scrabbled under the murky water against a sunken object that offered some support. The object shifted, tilted then thankfully seemed to become stable again allowing Ernie to keep his head and the little limpet wrapped around it, above water.

On the canal bank the dog's claws scrabbled

over the cinder track as it skittered back and forth in response to the frantic splashing and the loud voices. Voices that got louder still as they began to shout for help. Ears pricked up, the dog joined in and within a minute the mad cacophony of sound brought a response.

'What the bleedin 'ell is that!' the elderly man said to his wife as they passed across the road bridge above the canal.

'Dunno,' she answered.

'Sounds like someone in bovver.'

'Yeah it does. Sounds like someone in bovver all right Arfur...'

'Better take a gander,' Arfur said.

'Yeah you take a gander Arfur...' He placed both hands on the stone wall and tried to hitch himself up far enough to look over.

'Give us a bunk up Martha; can't get 'igh enough...' Martha, who was much meatier than her husband, obliged by wrapping her not inconsiderable arms around his knees and heaving.

'Whooaa!' the man yelled as he almost shot over the wall. 'Bleedin 'ell Martha you silly cow! Nearly 'ad me over an in the bleedin cut!'

'Sorry Arfur...Well what do you see?' The man snorted then looked down into the water.

'Bleedin 'ell Martha there's someone in't cut...no not someone...two someone's. An I fink one of 'em is tryin to drown the uvver one!'

'Tryin to drown 'im?'

'Yeah 'ee's got an arm wrapped round the uvver one's 'ead an is tryin to climb on top of 'im to push 'im under!

'Oh my God Arfur what we goin to do!'

'Well I aint jumpin in there that's for sure!'

'Allo, Allo' What's goin on 'ere then?' Martha turned her head quickly at the sound of the voice.

'Oh thank God officer!' It's two blokes in the cut an one of 'em is tryin to drown the uvver one!'

The officer hitched himself up alongside Arfur.

'Bloody 'ell!' he yelled, adding his voice to the frantic shouts and mad dog barking from below.

Within ten seconds - and in accordance with a Universal law which stated that any dramatic scenario that involved other people would quickly attract an interested audience - a curious little knot of rubberneckers had magically materialised out of thin air.

'What's goin on?' said a woman.

'Murder by the look of it!' said Martha.

'Fukin 'ell! slurred a hooded alky with a half drunk plastic litre bottle of cider in his hand. 'Nowt ter do wiv me..' he muttered as he staggered on his merry way.

The officer scrambled down from the wall dragging Arfur with him. 'C'mon man!' he shouted.

'We need ter get down there toot sweet!'

Together, they raced to the end of the bridge (That is to say, the officer raced...and Arfur limped along after him because he had scraped his boney shins on the rough stone wall).

'Follow me!' the constable ordered as he skidded around the corner and down the grassy bank that led to the canal. There he pulled up sharply at the water's edge and shouted: 'You there I'm an officer of the law an I've got yer number...get off that poor sods 'ead NOW!

''Elp!' Davey shouted. ''Elp I can't swim!'

'Me nee-neever!' Ernie pleaded in a muffled voice because Davey's arm was wrapped around his mouth. The constable's brain did a quick re-assessment. *Doesn't look like a murder* it decided with a distinct hint of disappointment. *Looks like a simple case of two silly sods playin silly buggers an then fell in... So what do I do now...looks bloody cold in there and there don't seem to be any need for heroics...*

''Old on!' He ordered. 'We'll get a rope.'

It took a good five minutes for one of the now considerable little party of bystanders to commandeer a washing line from a nearby garden.

'Okay, grab 'old," the constable ordered as he slung the line out to Davey.

'I can't let go!' Davey moaned as the line plopped into the water a yard from his head. 'I've only got one arm!'

'Bollocks!' the constable muttered under his breath. 'Okay you, big fella,' you grab it when I throw again.'

Ernie's arm appeared from under the water

and after the line had slipped through his frozen fingers twice he managed to get hold of it.

'Right hold on tight,' the officer said an I'll pull you out.' He pulled... and nothing happened. 'What the fuk! What's the matter why aren't you commin?'

'Me l-l-leg's stuck!' Ernie moaned.

They tried again. No luck. 'Oh bollocks!' the constable said under his breath. 'Looks like I'll 'ave to go in after all!'

He had stripped off his tunic jacket and threw his helmet onto the canal bank, when the clang clang of a fire engine bell announced a welcome arrival.

'Thank fuk fer that!' the constable muttered as two firemen carrying a long aluminium ladder came to the rescue. 'In there lad's; the big guy 'as got 'is foot stuck. I was just about to dive in!'

The firemen ran the ladder out until it was level with Ernie's head and the lighter of the two inched his way along it after the heavier one and the constable sat on the other end.

'Right little fella grab old of my 'and...' Davey slowly unwound his arm from around Ernie's face and with a quick lunge reached out and grabbed on. Seconds later he had been heaved up out of the water and was sitting on the ladder. 'Okay now follow me', the fireman said as he began to inch his way backward. Another minute and they were both safely back on the canal bank.

'What's wiv the big fella?' the constable said.

'Don't know,' Davey replied. 'I fink 'ee's got 'is foot caught in a sunk shoppin trolley or sumfin that's stuck in the mud...'

'Someone will 'ave to go in then an release is foot...' said one of the firemen.

'Don't look at me then,' the constable said firmly. 'That's fire brigade business that is...'

It took another fifteen minutes to free Ernie and he got a good round of applause from the crowd as he placed his sopping wet size thirteen's onto dry land.

'Can you tell me what happened sir?' said a middle aged man with an open notebook in one hand and a ballpoint pen in the other. Ernie shivered and shrugged his huge shoulders.

'I f-f-fell in the water,' he said.

'And what about you sir, fell in too did you?' Davey shook his head

'No I jumped in...'

'You jumped in!'

'Yeah.'

'My word! You just jumped in! A one-armed disabled non-swimmer... and you *just jumped in!*

'Well, yeah...'

'Wow, what a story!'

As the man's words registered, the twenty watt bulb in Davey's head began to glow brighter. *Ernie said 'ee fell in't water dint 'ee... an 'ee did... an I jus said I jumped in dint I...an I did. So, no porkie pies there then. So as long as I keep pretty shtum, Bob's yer aunt Fanny an I'm a big 'ero...'*

'What's your name then sir,' the man said as he licked the end of his ballpoint pen.

'David Ignatious Montgomery Parker.'

'My word... And you sir,' he addressed Ernie, 'what's your name?' Ernie shook his head.

'Not tellin, me mam will k-k-kill me if she knows I've b-b-b-in int cut!' The man shrugged. Okay he thought as he mentally composed the headline: ***Disabled Hero Saves Mystery Man From Drowning!***

As the man smiled and nodded slowly, he was suddenly dragged back to the here and now, when the sky; which had been steadily darkening, gave birth to a huge obsidian cloud that, shot with the silver of lightning flashes, rolled overhead like a tumbling black marble headstone.

Seconds later to the accompaniment of a portentous clap of thunder the bruised heavens opened and a lancing downpour of rain... pennies that became saucers... that became dinner plates... pummeled the dark water, turning it into churning brown froth.

Drama obviously over, the rubberneckers performed a scrambling exit, leaving the stage to the main players who with shoulders hunched against the stinging drops braved the downpour...that almost as suddenly as it began...stopped.

Ernie wiped the back of a hand across his face and with no-one else apart from Davey close enough to hear him said: 'Yuh won't tell me m-m-am I've b-bin int cut will yuh D-D-Davey?'

'Well okay,' Davey said, 'As long as you promise not to say anyfin to anyone eever...'

'Cross m-me 'eart!' Ernie said with feeling.

29

In the tiny untidy kitchen of a second floor flat in *Fort Beswick,* a thin woman with over bleached dead dandelion hair smiled lightly and hummed a little tune as she busied herself with the preparations for a meal.

She opened a drawer, took two knives and forks out and carried them through to a drop leaf table in the next room. She laid them out at the sides of two well-worn place mats, then turned and made her way back to the kitchen. There, she reached up, opened a cupboard door and took out two glass half-pint pots. She held them up to the light, frowned at finger marks, took them over to the sink and gave them a good rinsing.

Satisfied, she put them down on the drainer and then carefully, with two hands, she picked up a heavy tan and dark brown earthenware dish that contained the makings of a sausage casserole, stooped and placed it in the oven.

As she shut the oven door and straightened up, her attention was taken by a sudden deep gloom that had crept without any warning into the room.

She turned towards an open window, shivered lightly, reached up and with a firm tug closed and locked it against what promised to be the mother and father of a gathering storm.

An hour later after a bout of thunder and lightning and a heavy downpour, the front door opened and a bedraggled little figure squelched into the front room.

'Bloody 'ell, you got caught in it then. Better get out of them soppin clothes before you catch your death!' she said with a definite edge of concern to her voice.

'*Bloody 'ell is right,*' he thought. '*This new Zelda is tekkin some gettin used to...*'

She came into the bedroom with a fluffy bath towel and rubbed him down vigorously before he put on the dry clothes. 'I've done a sausage casserole for tea,' she said. 'That'll warm you up a treat.' He shook his head in wonder.

Late the next day she called in at Choudrey's newsagents for a bottle of vodka and was then greeted by a smiling owner. 'You must be most proud!' he said as he took her money.

'Must I?'

'Oh yes! Most proud! He is a hero!'

'Who is?'

'Your Mr Davey...Oh yes a big hero...' he said pointing to a copy of the local paper on the counter where a bold headline proclaimed: ***Disabled Hero Saves Mystery Man From Drowning!***

Zelda frowned lightly and picking up the paper, read the lead story.

'Why didn't you tell me about this!' she said waving the paper in front of him. He shrugged.

'It was no big deal...'

'No big deal!' she crowed. 'Bloody 'ell you, 'oo only 'as one arm an can't swim, jump in the cut to save a drownin man - an you say it's no big deal! He shrugged.

'Jus did what anyone would...' She shook her head in wonder.

'You know what you are?' she said softly.

'No, what?'

'You're a bleedin 'ero that's what you are! So come on tell me all about it. Who was the mystery man?'

'It was Ernie, but 'ee asked me not to say anyfin in case 'is mam got to know an gev 'im a beltin...'

'Well she'll get to know now when she reads

the paper!'

'Don't fink so, she's usually too pissed to see straight enough ter read...

'Yeah, well anyway tell me what 'appened...'

He shook his head slowly and when he answered in a soft, reluctant hero kind of voice, her blossoming admiration for him went into overdrive.

'I don't really want ter talk about it...' he said.

Made in the USA
Charleston, SC
17 April 2015